DON'T CRY FOR ME

RACHEL LACEY

COPYRIGHT

ISBN: 978-1-7321519-7-0

Cover Design © Perfect Pear Creations

❀ Created with Vellum

1

Eve Marlow's heels clicked confidently against the polished floor as she strode down the hall toward her producer's office. She paused outside the door, running her fingers over the front of her dress to smooth any wrinkles before lifting her hand to knock.

"Come in," Greta called from inside.

Eve grasped the handle and pulled the door open. Greta sat behind her desk, glasses perched on her nose as she looked up from her computer screen. But she wasn't alone. Bruce Koslowski, *Life & Leisure*'s director of advertising, stood beside her. "Greta," Eve said with a polite smile. "Bruce, this is a surprise."

"Hello, Eve," Bruce said with an equally polite nod.

"Have a seat." Greta gestured vaguely to the guest chairs in front of her desk.

Eve sat, placing her laptop on the edge of the desk.

"I'm afraid I have some bad news," Bruce said.

Eve nodded. "Greta told me this morning that the ratings for our season two premiere weren't as high as we'd hoped, but I've put together several proposed adjustments to *Do Over*'s advertising plan that I think should—"

"Actually, that's not why I'm here," Bruce interrupted. "You can discuss advertising with Greta later."

More bad news? Eve straightened in her seat, clasping her hands loosely in front of herself. "All right."

"We have to pull episode eight," Bruce said.

"The ice cream shop?" Eve said, incensed. "That's one of our strongest episodes. Why on earth would we scrap it?"

His lips drew into a frown. "The owner has been charged in a sexual assault."

Fuck. Eve felt a heavy sensation in her stomach, as if the remnants of her lunch had hardened into concrete. "That's...not good."

"I know," Greta agreed. "It's a publicity nightmare. There's no way we can air it."

"Is there time to shoot a replacement?" As the CEO of Marlow Marketing, Eve had built an empire helping underperforming small businesses reach their potential. Two years ago, the *Life & Leisure* channel had offered her a television show—*Do Over*—that followed her as she worked. Each episode featured a different business, offering viewers the chance to become invested in their success as she helped them rebuild. Season one had been a runaway success. So far, season two was off to a lackluster start, and without this episode, she might be in real trouble.

"It's possible," Greta said. "But the timing would be extremely tight."

Bruce's frown deepened. "I'm afraid there's no room in the production budget to reshoot, even if you were able to fit it into the schedule."

"I'll make room in the budget," Eve said automatically. This was what she did for a living, after all. She saved failing businesses, and now she would save her television show, because if she didn't get her ratings up, *Do Over* would never get renewed for a third season. "I'll draw up a revised advertising plan."

"If you're able to make room in the budget, I'll think about it, but I'm not making any promises," Bruce told her. "Have it on my desk by the end of the day."

She nodded. "Consider it done."

Bruce left, and Eve slumped in her chair. "How much time do I have to find a new client and shoot a replacement episode?"

"Not much," Greta told her apologetically. "You'd need to bring me the client's name by Friday, with filming to begin next week."

Eve pressed her knuckles against the edge of the desk in front of her, letting the cold wood bite into her skin, providing an outlet for her frustration. "Friday, as in the day after tomorrow?"

"Yes. And first, you've got to make room in the budget and have Bruce sign off on it," Greta reminded her.

"I'll do that right now." Eve stood, picking up her laptop.

Greta nodded, waving a hand in Eve's direction. "Go work your magic. You'll pull this off. I have full confidence in you."

"I will," Eve confirmed. She left Greta's office and strode down the hall toward her own. They had hundreds of leftover applications from their season two casting call. The trick would be finding someone who could bring her the ratings she needed, when she'd already chosen what she'd believed to be the ten strongest applicants from the bunch. Hopefully, she'd overlooked a potential breakout star.

First things first. She closed the door to her office and spent the next two hours reallocating funds from *Do Over*'s already stretched advertising budget to allow her to shoot the replacement episode. As much as she needed those advertising dollars, she needed a full season more. She emailed the revised budget to Bruce and settled in to sift through previously rejected season two applications.

But as the sun slid behind the Manhattan skyline outside her window, she was no closer to finding a replacement client and her stomach had begun to growl obnoxiously. Stifling a growl of her own, she packed up to head home. She'd find something to eat, change into her pajamas, and keep working.

Preferably with a glass of wine.

Since it was going to be a late night, she stopped in the break room to fix herself a coffee for the ride home. She spent her thirty-minute subway ride making notes on her phone, outlining ways to maximize what remained of her advertising budget. While Marlow Marketing wasn't in any trouble, *Do Over* was dangerously close to cancellation. She enjoyed filming the show. It had become an important part of her brand, and perhaps most importantly, it had tripled her income. She wasn't going to lose it, not when she knew it could be saved.

Her cell phone rang as she exited the subway, and Greta's name showed on the screen. Eve connected the call. "Please tell me you're calling with good news."

"I am, actually," Greta told her. "They've signed off on your revised production budget. All you have to do now is bring us a new client in time to get the replacement episode filmed."

"Excellent." Eve exhaled in relief as she dodged a bike messenger, stepping aside to let him pass. "I'll let you know as soon as I have a name."

"Friday," Greta reminded her.

"Got it." Eve tossed her empty coffee cup into a nearby trash can. A tiny, muffled cry echoed from somewhere, and she paused. "Did you hear that?"

"Hear what?" Greta asked.

"Nothing. Listen, I'll check in with an update tomorrow morning, okay?" She strode down the street toward her building, intent on getting upstairs, out of these heels, and warming up something for dinner. Where had that cry come from? Had it been something on Greta's end of the line? It hadn't sounded human, more like an animal. Probably someone nearby on the street was watching a video on their phone or carrying some kind of exotic pet. This was New York City, after all. She'd once seen a man carrying a tiny pig in a backpack.

But an uneasy feeling deep in her gut worried that the sound had come from inside the trash can, and it only grew stronger with each step she took. Holding in a sigh, she turned and walked back to the bin. It was filled almost to the top with garbage. Eve couldn't believe she was even contemplating poking around in a public trash can. God knew what was inside, but it was sure to be disgusting.

She grimaced as she stood there, listening. Other than the steady hum and honk of traffic, laughter from a couple passing by, and the distant roar of a jet overhead, she couldn't hear a thing. She was being ridiculous. Hours of work awaited her in her apartment, so she had no idea why she was standing here, staring at a trash can. To satisfy her conscience, she turned on the flashlight on her cell phone and shined it inside.

There was her coffee cup, laying on a plastic grocery bag at the top of the garbage pile. No animals. Nothing but gross, smelly trash. She wrinkled her nose, shining the light quickly over the rest of the bin, but...did that bag just twitch?

Oh, hell.

It twitched again. A sick feeling washed over her, all thoughts of ratings and clients wiped from her mind. With her free hand, she reached cautiously into the bin, nudging aside her coffee cup to uncover the bag beneath it. She hesitated before touching it. What if the movement was caused by a rat, rooting through the rubbish? Or something even less friendly?

But that stubbornly uneasy feeling in her gut made her grasp the knot where the bag had been tied shut and lift it out of the bin. Something inside squealed, and Eve's heart slammed into her ribs. Her skin prickled. Oh God, there was really a live animal trapped inside this bag. What kind of sick joke...

She knelt and placed the bag on the ground. Cautiously, she tore a hole in the plastic, keeping her fingers well away from the opening in case whatever was inside tried to bite her. She'd just free the rat and be on her way. But the tiny creatures inside weren't rats. The bag was full of some kind of baby animals that looked like...were those kittens? Tiny newborn kittens, eyes closed and barely moving.

Eve exhaled harshly, as if the wind had been knocked out of her. She ripped the bag all the way open and reached inside. Her fingers brushed soft black fur, and the kitten mewled softly, rooting its head toward her hand. It was cool to the touch.

"Jesus," she murmured, scanning the rest of the animals. She counted six total, a mixture of black, gray, and one solid white kitten. Not all of them were moving. Oh *fuck*. Were they even alive?

She stripped out of her blazer and laid it on the ground.

Carefully, she lifted the kittens out of the bag one by one and placed them inside her jacket, trying not to notice how cold and stiff they felt beneath her fingers. The temperature hadn't quite reached seventy today, average for mid-April in Manhattan. She needed to get them inside and warm, and then...what?

She'd call the animal shelter. Yes, that was the logical next step. She eyed the bag they'd been inside of. Should she take it with her? Was it evidence? Was it a crime to throw a litter of kittens in the trash? She sure as hell hoped so. And so she balled up the empty grocery bag and tucked it inside her blazer, which would be going straight into the wash—if not the trash—once she got home. She scooped the edges of the fabric together, forming a makeshift sack for the kittens, and hurried toward her apartment building.

A cool breeze whipped through the thin material of her blouse, and she shivered. Several people gave her strange looks as she cradled her blazer in front of herself. She resisted the urge to tell them off, reasoning that in their position, she'd give herself an odd look too.

Eve Marlow, up-and-coming reality television star, behaving bizarrely among rumors that Do Over's *second season is off to a disappointing start.*

This day could really just stop now. She'd had enough. Walking briskly, she rounded the corner and approached her building. She'd take the kittens inside, call the shelter, and get them on their way to help and veterinary care. Then she could get back to work.

Morris, the doorman, held the door open for her. "Good evening, Ms. Marlow."

"Evening, Morris. Thank you." She offered him a brief but grateful smile on her way to the elevator. There hadn't been a peep out of the kittens since she'd put them in her blazer. No wriggling. God help her if she was carrying a jacket full of dead kittens up to her apartment right now. What if they were covered in fleas? Or had rabies? Was she endangering herself by bringing them inside?

She punched the button with her elbow and waited, toe tapping impatiently, until the elevator arrived. It carried her swiftly to the eighth floor, and she let herself into her apartment. There, she stood for a moment, unsure what to do next and halfway terrified to look inside her blazer.

But her discomfort was no excuse for further endangering their lives. She lay her blazer on the kitchen table, spreading it flat. A few of the kittens stirred, mewling as they scrambled toward each other for warmth.

Several of them didn't move at all.

She shuddered. They were so cold. Thinking fast, she went into the bedroom, rummaging through her closet until she found the heating pad she used when her back started acting up. She carried it to the kitchen table and plugged it in before laying the jacket full of kittens on top of it. "Now to find someone to take you."

She washed her hands—just in case—then sat at the table and pulled out her phone. She looked up the nearest animal shelter, only to receive an automated recording that it was closed for the night. Same story at the next shelter. And the next. It was only seven o'clock. Wasn't there any place to take abandoned animals after hours? These kittens wouldn't make it until morning. Not to mention, she didn't have time to deal with this, not in general and especially not tonight.

Eve stared at the furry pile of kittens. What the hell was she going to do with them? She'd never had a pet, never cared for an animal in her life. She had no idea how to care for these, but they were obviously too small for solid food.

They probably needed milk. Maybe she could warm up some of the half-and-half she kept in the fridge for her morning coffee, but what would they drink it out of?

They were so small, so helpless.

Irritation warred with concern inside her as she typed "what to do if you find abandoned kittens" into the search bar on her phone. The top result was a YouTube video with the thumbnail of a woman with lavender hair holding a kitten about the size of the ones Eve had found. For lack of a better option, she pressed Play.

"Hi, everyone. It's your favorite kitten rescuer, Josie Swanson, here to tell you what to do if you find an abandoned kitten or litter of kittens," the woman in the video said.

Eve leaned back in her seat as the knot in her stomach loosened. This video might be exactly what she needed. Josie was pretty, with warm eyes and an endless smile. Eve had never been a fan of unnatural hair colors, but the lavender seemed to work for Josie, accentuating her bubbly personality.

Unfortunately for Eve, the video mostly covered how to care for newborn kittens rather than where to take them. But, worst-case scenario, it might help her keep them alive through the night until she could drop them at the shelter in the morning.

"The important thing to remember is to never bring a litter of orphaned kittens to an animal shelter," Josie said, staring earnestly into the camera. "Most shelters aren't staffed to care for bottle-fed babies and will have to euthanize them. The best thing to do is to reach out to local animal rescues and ask for their help. I've included a list of resources in the description below."

Well, this wasn't good news, but that seemed to be the

theme of Eve's day. Then again, maybe she could find an animal rescue that would take the kittens tonight. She scrolled through the links below the video until she found a kitten rescue in New York City. According to the contact information, Josie herself ran it. Maybe Eve's luck had turned. She'd give the kittens to Josie and be done. Josie would know exactly how to care for them. She had over a million subscribers and countless videos detailing all the kittens she'd saved.

Eve clicked on the contact button and composed a quick message detailing her situation, adding URGENT to the subject line, because she wasn't sure these kittens would survive another hour without intervention, let alone overnight. And as much as she needed to get to work and find a client for her replacement episode, she did *not* want a pile of dead kittens in her kitchen...or on her conscience.

Not knowing what else to do, she rewatched Josie's video while she waited. They'd need kitten formula, which she could apparently get at most pet stores. So much for the half-and-half in her fridge. She had just pulled up a list of local pet stores when her phone rang with an unknown Manhattan exchange.

Eve connected the call. "Hello."

"Hi," came the vivacious voice from the video. "This is Josie Swanson. You've found a litter of abandoned kittens?"

"Yes," Eve told her gratefully. "Someone dumped them in a trash can."

"It happens all the time, unfortunately," Josie said. "About how old are they, if you had to guess?"

"Newborn, maybe," Eve said. "Their eyes are still shut, and I think their umbilical cords are still attached. Can I bring them to you tonight? I'm honestly not sure how long they're going to survive otherwise."

"I'm so sorry, but I can't take them. I'd be happy to meet you, show you how to care for them, and give you some supplies, though."

Eve's stomach clenched in a combination of disappointment and frustration. She'd been so sure Josie was going to help her. She was tired and hungry, her feet ached, and she needed these kittens out of her apartment so she could get back to the mountain of work awaiting her. "I don't understand. You run a kitten rescue. Why can't you take them?"

"I really wish I could, but I own a bar in Brooklyn, and we're short-staffed at the moment. I'm tending bar twelve hours a day, and these guys will need round-the-clock care."

Eve bristled at the implication. "I work full-time too. I can't keep them."

"Look, you're in Manhattan, right?" Josie asked.

"Yes."

"Tell you what. Bring them here. I'll make some calls while you're on your way and see if I can find someone to take them for you. If not, I can give you some formula and show you how to care for them, at least temporarily."

"Bring them to your bar?"

"Yes," Josie confirmed. "Sorry, but I'm working all night."

Eve's entire body tensed, and her pulse quickened. She couldn't handle walking into a bar, especially not tonight. Her gaze fell on the kittens. What choice did she have? But if she brought them to Josie's bar, she was going to convince her to keep them, because there was no way Eve was bringing them back home with her. "I'll be there in half an hour."

2

Josie Swanson carried a frothy lager in each hand, plunking them on the bar in front of the two men seated across from her. "Haven't seen you guys all week. I was starting to think you'd found a new bar." She pressed a hand against her chest. "Don't break my heart like that."

Dougie laughed heartily, reaching for his glass. "Wouldn't dream of it, Jo."

"Been working late, is all," Sal added.

"Well, I missed your handsome faces," she told them affectionately. Dougie and Sal had been coming to Swanson's every evening for a beer after work since Josie was a little girl, doing her homework in the back room at her dad's desk while he tended bar. As her list of regulars dwindled, she'd come to depend on their business as well as their company.

"And we missed you," Dougie told her.

"Glad to hear it," she said as she slid down the bar to check on the loner a few stools over who'd been drowning his sorrows in whiskey for the last hour. "Another?" she asked.

He nodded.

She poured his drink, and he took it with muttered thanks, his gaze dropping to the glass in front of him. "Bad day?" she asked, offering a sympathetic ear. Bartending 101, her dad had called it.

"Lost my job," he told her before taking a gulp of whiskey. "Budget cuts."

"That's terrible," Josie said. "I'm so sorry to hear it. Next one's on me, and after that, you need to slow down, okay? Drink some water."

"Yeah, yeah, thanks." He drained his glass, eyeing Josie. "What time do you get off?"

"I don't," she told him with a smile, taking that as her cue to move down the bar to where her best friends Kaia and Adam sat in their usual seats, deep in conversation. "More beer?"

"Yes, please." Kaia nudged her empty glass in Josie's direction. "Did that guy just ask you out?"

"He sure did." Josie took both of their empty glasses, bending to load them into the dishwasher below the counter.

"Wish he'd ask me out," Adam commented, glancing down the bar. "He's hot, in a nine-to-five kind of way."

"I don't think you have a shot with him," Josie told him, "but didn't you have a date last night anyway?" She grabbed two clean glasses and began to fill them from the tap.

"I did, but..." Adam made a face.

"That bad, huh?" Kaia asked, smoothing back a black curl that had escaped the knot on top of her head. Her brown skin was flawlessly smooth, a byproduct of her current job selling all-natural cosmetics at a little shop in Chelsea Market.

The three of them had been friends for years, and consequently, Kaia and Adam were regulars at Swanson's, showing up almost as frequently as Dougie and Sal.

"Not terrible, just...blah," Adam told Kaia.

"Blah could define every recent date of mine," Josie said as she set fresh beers on the bar in front of her friends. "I'm not sure I even remember what sparks feel like at this point."

"I've had plenty of sparks," Kaia said, taking a thoughtful sip of her pilsner. "But my relationships all seem to go up in flames."

The front door opened, and Josie glanced up to see a brunette wearing a gray pencil skirt and a white blouse step into the bar. She carried a large blue bag, held delicately in front of her as if it might contain a litter of tiny kittens. This had to be Eve. Except... "Oh my God."

Kaia followed her gaze, sitting up straighter on her barstool. "No kidding. Now *she* is hot. I bet she could give you sparks, Josie."

"Do you know who that is?" Josie asked, eyes still locked on the brunette in the doorway.

"Should we?" Adam swiveled on his barstool to stare at Eve.

"Do you have a hot date you didn't tell us about?" Kaia asked, raising her eyebrows.

"Don't be ridiculous," Josie told her. "I'm working. No, she found a litter of kittens in a trash can, and she's brought them here for my help, but she only gave me her first name over the phone. That's Eve Marlow. You know, from *Do Over*? That business makeover show on the *Life & Leisure* channel?"

"I did," Josie confirmed, her gaze falling to the bundle on the table between them. "I haven't found anyone yet who's able to help, but I'll keep calling."

"I can't keep them," Eve repeated, not letting herself look at the kittens. She focused instead on the woman before her. Josie was even prettier in person than she had been in the video Eve had watched. Her hair, which had been long and lavender on YouTube, barely brushed her shoulders now, blonde streaked with turquoise.

There was something intoxicatingly...vibrant about her. Her hazel eyes gleamed with affection as she watched the kittens, something so warm and pure there. Eve could get lost in those eyes if she let herself. Which she definitely could not. She needed to convince Josie to take the kittens, and then she needed to get the fuck out of here.

She hadn't stepped into a bar since...

She blinked away the memory before it had even formed. She couldn't be here. And she couldn't let herself get emotionally attached to these kittens. She couldn't do any of it, least of all let herself feel anything but annoyance for the woman sitting across the table from her.

"I'm working twelve-hour shifts downstairs this week," Josie said. "These kittens need to be fed and cared for every two hours. I can't do it, Eve. I had to leave a friend of mine behind the bar just to come up here with you. I mean, who knows what kind of mayhem he's caused by now." She laughed, but it wasn't the same effervescent laugh that had captivated Eve when they first met. Now, she sounded somewhat panicked, eyes darting from Eve to the bundle of kittens.

"I guess we have a problem, then," Eve said quietly.

"I'm working until we close at two," Josie said. "These

next twelve hours are critical for them. Please keep them tonight, and I'll make more calls tomorrow."

Eve's skin flushed hot as Josie met her eyes. *No. Absolutely fucking not.* "I've never cared for an animal in my life, not a full grown, healthy one, and certainly not a half-dead newborn one that requires round-the-clock care."

"They aren't half-dead anymore," Josie countered. "And you've done a great job with them so far."

"All I did is bring them to you, because I don't have the first clue what to do for them."

"Which was exactly the right thing to do," Josie said, eyes snapping the way they did when she got passionate about something. "You saved their lives when you pulled them out of the trash, and then you searched until you found someone to help you revive them. You wouldn't take them to the shelter to be euthanized."

Eve lifted her chin. "I would, if you leave me no other choice."

Josie grinned as she called Eve's bluff, revealing dimples that might be Eve's undoing if Josie hadn't apparently already undone her. "No, you wouldn't."

"Tonight," Eve heard herself saying. "Just for tonight."

Josie's smile grew to encompass her whole face, glowing as brightly as the neon dye in her hair. "Tonight's a start. We're going to save these guys, Eve, you and me."

"You are," Eve corrected her. "You're going to save them."

"With your help." Josie bent her head and kissed the white kitten on top of the pile. "I'll even let you name them."

Eve huffed in annoyance. She was exhausted and starving, had been ready for the quiet comfort of her apartment hours ago, and yet here she was, still in her heels and covered in cat pee. "I don't want to name them. I don't want anything to do with them."

"I'll name them, then," Josie said with a shrug. "And I'll put together a box of supplies for you. Call me anytime with any questions. I've bottle-fed hundreds of kittens, even smaller than these."

"All the more reason you should be doing it, not me."

"I would if I could," Josie said. "It kills me that I can't take them, but I need to get back to the bar before Adam messes up too many orders and has everyone drinking on the house."

"Fine." Eve tugged at her blouse, wincing as she felt the urine-soaked fabric stick to her skin. Ugh. It smelled awful. And it looked worse.

"Do you want a clean shirt to wear home?" Josie asked.

Eve opened her mouth to decline, but the thought of wearing this shirt for the thirty-minute ride back to her apartment... "Actually, that would be great."

"You bet." Josie went through the open door to their left, entering what Eve presumed was her bedroom. She returned a minute later with several shirts. "Whichever you like. Bathroom's in there."

"Thank you." Eve took the garments and went through the door Josie had indicated, finding herself in a small bathroom painted a sunny yellow. A large orange cat rose from where it had been asleep on the bathmat, glared at her, and stalked out of the room.

Eve closed the door. She unbuttoned her blouse and slid out of it, taking a moment to rinse the cat pee off herself at the sink before she grabbed a fitted black tee off the top of the pile and pulled it over her head. It was such a relief to have on something clean and dry, she wouldn't have cared if the shirt was as iridescent as Josie's hair.

She balled up her soiled blouse and walked back to the kitchen, where Josie was busily putting supplies in a box.

She grinned. "I had a bet with myself that you'd pick that one."

"It was on top," Eve snapped, then sighed, reminding herself none of this was Josie's fault. "Thank you for lending it to me. And for the supplies."

"No problem. And please, call me at any hour if you're worried about them or have any questions. I'm working until two, so chances are, I'll be up anyway."

Eve nodded. *Just tonight.*

"Okay, I've packed you a day's worth of formula, towels, warmers, a stuffed cat for them to snuggle against as a replacement for their mother..." Josie kept going, rummaging through the box as she spoke, going over feeding schedules and formula preparation. "I know it's a lot to remember, but I've got YouTube videos detailing all of it. If you just search my channel, you'll find them."

"I'll do that."

"And they'll need to see a vet tomorrow," Josie told her.

"I don't have time—" Eve cut herself off at the hurt look on Josie's face. Maybe she could send one of the interns to the vet with them while she worked. "Fine."

"I'll email you the name of a vet I've worked with in Manhattan who'll put their bill on the tab for my rescue."

"I can pay for it," Eve said reflexively. She could afford it, and she had the impression that most small charities like Josie's struggled in that area.

"Okay," Josie said evenly, not putting up the fight Eve had expected. "I really appreciate that. If you send me a copy of the bill, I'll give you a receipt from the rescue so you can write it off as a charitable donation on your taxes."

"Perfect."

"I'll help you carry this stuff out, on my way back to the bar," Josie said. "Did you come here in a cab?"

"I did. It didn't seem wise to take a sack of barely alive kittens on the subway."

"Probably not." Josie paused, eyes locking on Eve's. "Before you go..."

"Yes?"

"You probably guessed that I watch your show, and..." She looked away, seemingly flustered for the first time since they met.

Was she trying to ask for an autograph? Sometimes people did, and it still caught Eve off guard. She used her marketing skills on television, fixing real businesses for real people. Yes, some of it was staged, but she didn't consider herself a celebrity, or even a public figure. She was a businesswoman at heart, and she always would be. "I did assume that, yes."

Josie sucked in a breath, meeting her eyes. "I don't know how to say this other than to just...say it. Swanson's is in trouble. It's...it's on its last leg, to be frank. I can't pay the bills, and I'm working almost every shift because I can't afford to hire a staff. I actually put in an application to *Do Over*, but it was rejected."

Eve straightened as she realized what Josie was asking. Not an autograph request after all. And this was worse.

"I know you probably have someone screen the applications for you, but now you're here, and it feels like kismet, so I have to ask." Josie's hazel eyes bored into Eve's, steady and intense, dripping with emotion. "To beg, really. Have Swanson's on your show. Do your thing, work your magic, save my bar. Please."

Eve took a step backward, jaw clenching. "I don't do bars. I'm sorry."

~

"Don't think of it as a bar. Think of it as my home. Please, Eve. I grew up here. It's all I have left of my parents." Josie felt a hot flush spread over her skin and the prick of tears behind her eyes. "Please."

"I can't." Eve's voice seemed to have shrunk, no longer edged in steel but something else, something Josie couldn't place. "I'm sorry."

"I'm doing everything I can to help you with these kittens. Please at least consider helping me in return." She knew immediately it was the wrong thing to say, and truly, she had given her help to Eve without expecting anything in return. Her plea to save the bar was something completely separate.

Eve's nostrils flared, her iron-clad armor back in place. "Season two has already been filmed, and we aren't accepting applications yet for season three. Even if I wanted to, I couldn't help you."

"Fine," Josie acquiesced, for tonight anyway. But surely fate had brought Eve Marlow to Swanson's tonight for a reason. Right now, Eve felt like her last hope, and Josie could be as persistent as a cat trying to catch the red dot from a laser pointer when she wanted something.

But first, she needed to get back to the bar, and Eve needed to get the kittens home. She settled the bundle of kittens inside a box she often used to transport kittens to and from vet appointments. Then she lifted the box of supplies while Eve picked up the box of kittens, and together they walked downstairs. Eve called an Uber, and it arrived almost as soon as they made it outside. She opened the back door, speaking briefly with the driver before tucking the box of kittens inside.

Once the supplies were stowed, Eve turned to her. "You'll

be in touch tomorrow after you've spoken to the rest of your contacts?"

"I will."

They stared at each other for a beat of silence before Eve said, "Thank you for your help."

"You're welcome." She watched as Eve slid into the backseat of the car, somehow managing to make even Josie's black T-shirt look stylish. She was everything and nothing Josie would have expected her to be—cool and businesslike, at times downright intimidating, but beneath it, there was a softness to her that Josie hadn't anticipated.

She hadn't expected this attraction either, and it was inconvenient, to say the least. She didn't want to like anything about Eve, not her reluctance to keep the kittens, not her refusal to even consider helping Swanson's, and certainly not those piercing brown eyes that seemed to see right into Josie's soul.

The animal rescuer in her felt intensely uncomfortable sending those vulnerable kittens off with someone who had threatened to have them euthanized, someone with absolutely no experience in caring for them. But she didn't exactly have a choice, and deep down, her gut said Eve would never harm them. If nothing else, Josie had always trusted her gut impression of people.

Turning, she walked back inside, where she found Adam deep in conversation with the man who'd hit on her earlier, and from the look of things, Adam might have a chance with him after all. Kaia sat on her usual stool, texting on her phone, the only other customer in the bar.

Josie's stomach dropped. A few years ago, this place would have been packed. Something had changed since her father died. She suspected the influx of newer, trendier bars in the neighborhood had played a part, but surely her inexperience was a factor too. Maybe her customers could sense that Swanson's wasn't her true passion the way it had been for her father. Maybe she was singlehandedly ruining everything her family had worked so hard for.

"How did it go?" Kaia asked, interrupting Josie from her spiraling thoughts.

"Okay, I guess." Josie made her way behind the bar, tapping Adam's shoulder to let him know she was back but not wanting to interrupt whatever he had going on with the sad businessman...who had a fresh tumbler of whiskey in his hands. Josie filled a glass of water and plunked it on the bar in front of him. "Drink this next," she told him with a gentle smile.

He returned it with one of his own, giving her a mock salute. "Yes, ma'am."

"Oh, Jesus Christ," she muttered as she made her way down to Kaia. "Please tell me I'm not old enough to be called ma'am."

"Thirty-two?" Kaia looked her up and down, lips pursed. "I hate to say it, babe, but I think you've entered ma'am territory."

"Shut up. You're only a year younger than me."

Kaia's lips twitched with amusement as she sipped her beer. "Tell me more about Miss Television Star with the rescue kittens. Did you get her number or what?"

"I already had her number, actually. She's...I don't know, all business, I guess. She really doesn't want to keep those kittens."

"Can't blame her there." Kaia's nose wrinkled. "You know I love you, Jo, but I can't imagine doing what you do for those kittens, being up with them all night? Wiping their butts? It's a lot to take on."

"I guess." She blew out a breath, checking to see that the

sad businessman was indeed drinking his water. "On her show, she goes into struggling businesses and gives them a makeover. She fixes them up and gives them a fresh start." Josie paused, scraping her thumbnail against a rough spot on the bar top. "I asked her to save Swanson's."

"Save Swanson's?" Kaia's eyebrows rose. "What are you talking about?"

"Look around, Kai." Josie hadn't told her friends how dire things had gotten, but they had eyes. It was no secret Swanson's was struggling.

"Are you in trouble?" Kaia leaned forward, dark eyes locked on Josie's. "Honey, why didn't you tell me? Shit, and you've been letting me run this tab forever."

"I don't want your money. It's not about that. I love having you guys here. I just need customers. I don't know where they've all gone, really, but they're not here anymore."

Kaia swiveled in her seat, scanning the bar as if she'd never truly seen it before. "I had no idea. I just thought...I don't know what I thought."

"It's not your job to think anything about it. It's mine. And I've been trying, but I don't know what I'm doing wrong. So I asked Eve to help me, begged her, really."

"And?"

"She turned me down flat."

"Damn, that's cold," Kaia said, whistling softly under her breath. "Did she say why?"

"She doesn't do bars, whatever that means."

"Maybe she's a recovering alcoholic," Kaia suggested.

"Hmm." Josie thought of Eve's odd reaction to her request, that brief moment when she'd seemed to retreat inside herself. "Yeah, maybe. I didn't think of that."

"Ask her out, and maybe she'll tell you."

Josie gave her a frustrated look. "I'm not going to ask her

out. I don't even know if she dates women. And anyway, I'm not finished pleading my case. I promised to call her tomorrow about the kittens, so I'm going to do some research in the meantime and come up with an irresistible argument to convince her to have me on her show."

"That's the spirit." Kaia raised her beer in Josie's direction.

"Yeah, well, just cross your fingers for me that it works." Because one way or another, she was determined to land herself a spot on *Do Over*.

4

Eve sat cross-legged in bed, box of kittens in front of her and her laptop beside it. Somehow, feeding them had been astronomically easier with Josie there to guide her. Eve had fumbled through her first solo feeding two hours ago, but now, everything was falling apart. She'd spilled formula all over herself while she was feeding the black kitten, and she couldn't even wake the white one up, let alone make it eat. It was one in the morning, and Eve had only managed an hour of sleep. Annoyance buzzed in her veins as she laid the white kitten across her thigh while she held the syringe to its lips.

No luck. The kitten rolled over, snuggling into a crease in her pajama pants. She took a paper towel and helped it pee, hoping that might wake it up, but the kitten was still lost in dreamland. Leaving it in her lap, she pressed Play on a video about syringe-feeding newborn kittens, unnerved to hear Josie's voice in her otherwise silent bedroom. The kittens really didn't make much noise, except when she lifted them out of their box.

"You want to make sure to keep them upright while

you're feeding them," Josie told her from the screen, hot pink hair in a high ponytail on her head. This video was a few years old, and Josie looked younger, impossibly bubbly and energetic...adorable, in a word.

Eve sighed. Exhaustion pressed over her, weighing her down. Caretaking didn't come naturally to her. She wanted to pour some food in a bowl and leave the kittens to it. Syringe-feeding newborns was foreign and tiresome and stressful. She eyed the white kitten, currently nestled against her hipbone and still fast asleep.

Frustrated, she lifted the gray one out of the box and successfully got it to eat a small amount of formula. She had similar success with the gray-and-white kitten. The video ended, so she clicked on Josie's avatar to bring up a list of all her videos, hoping she might find one that would help her deal with the sleepy kitten in her lap.

Until about two years ago, Josie had uploaded videos regularly, many of them with hundreds of thousands of views. There were instructional videos, educational videos about animal rescue, videos chronicling the stories of various kittens she'd cared for, and a series of livestream Q&A sessions.

By all appearances, Josie had been doing well for herself with her channel and her rescue. What had changed? She'd mentioned that she took over the bar after her father died. It would make sense that she'd had less time for kitten rescue after that. And now, despite her personal sacrifice, she was on the verge of losing Swanson's too.

Eve felt for her. She really did. But she couldn't work in a bar. She just couldn't. Reflexively, she rested a hand against the ache in her lower back. She looked down at the white kitten, its tiny face pressed against Eve's belly.

"We'll take turns with the two a.m. feedings."

"I'll believe that when I see it," Lisa said, nudging her playfully. "You're a beast when you don't get your beauty sleep."

"I'm serious," Eve told her, meaning the words from the bottom of her soul. "I want to share it all with you."

Lisa laced their fingers together. "You will."

Eve's breath hitched, her fingers clenched into fists, anger burning past the emptiness that usually occupied the place in her chest where she'd once loved so fiercely. Why wouldn't the damn kitten eat? Why couldn't Josie just take them? Why had some pathetic excuse for a human being thrown them out like trash in the first place?

In that moment, she hated him, whoever he was, hated Josie for asking Eve to save her bar, hated herself for not having the patience to feed the damn kitten. She hated *everything*.

This fucking day...

She leaned back, fists braced against the mattress behind her, breathing past the pain, blinking furiously through the moisture in her eyes. Sometimes it snuck up on her like this, in the dark hours of the night, how much she missed them. Her fingers twisted in the blanket beneath her, clinging to it until the moment had passed.

Sitting up, she lifted the white kitten. It lay limply in her hands, letting out a tiny whimper, utterly helpless. It was the smallest of the surviving four and by far the weakest. Would it live? Was she fighting a losing battle trying to save it?

"Come on," she muttered, holding the syringe against the kitten's mouth. It turned away, mouth stubbornly closed. Eve was at her wit's end. She needed the kitten to eat so she could try to sleep for a few hours before she had to do this all again. She had to go to work in the morning, and she was going to be a zombie. Already, she'd lost hours of time that should have been spent looking for a new client to shoot the replacement episode. "You've got to help me out here," she told the kitten, receiving a whimper in response.

This was exactly why the kittens should have stayed with Josie tonight. She'd know what to do. No doubt, she would have had them all fed and cleaned and been back in bed ten minutes ago.

Eve yawned, eyes watering with fatigue as she glanced at her phone. It felt ridiculous to consider calling Josie in the middle of the night, but she'd told Eve to call with questions at any hour, and in fact, she was probably still at work. She'd said she would be tending bar until two. After the way they'd left things earlier, Eve didn't want to talk to her again so soon, or at all, really. But if she wanted to get any sleep tonight, she'd better just get it over with.

Decision made, she picked up her phone, scrolled to Josie's name, and dialed. It rang twice before Josie answered, sounding somewhat muffled. "Eve?"

"Yes. Do you have a minute?" Her voice sounded way too loud in the otherwise quiet bedroom.

"Yeah. I was just closing up. Everything okay?"

"I thought you worked until two," Eve said.

"Well, no one's here, so I decided to close early."

Eve decided to ignore that rather than get into another conversation about the future of the bar. "I can't get the white one to eat."

"Did she eat earlier?" Josie asked, shifting neatly into the role of kitten rescuer.

"A little bit, but not as much as the other three."

"How is she acting otherwise?"

"Sleepy, lethargic." Eve looked down at the kitten in her lap.

"Is she warm?"

Eve rubbed a hand over the kitten. "Not as warm now as she was when I took her out of the box with the others."

"Okay, the first thing we need to do is warm her up. Why don't you put her back in the box and make sure she's on the heating pad. Put the other kittens right up against her to get her nice and snuggly."

Eve did as Josie said, trying not to notice how cold and empty her lap felt after she'd put the kitten back with her siblings. "Now what?"

"Give her a minute," Josie said gently. "How's everything going otherwise?"

"I'm tired." Eve sounded irritable even to her own ears.

"Do you believe in karma?" Josie asked.

"No."

"Well, you're doing a good deed," Josie said. "And I like to think we reap what we sow."

"You know as well as I do that's not always true."

Josie let out a little sound of disbelief. "Wow, you really are a cynical one, aren't you?"

"I have every reason to be." Eve couldn't believe they were even having this conversation. Briefly, she wished she hadn't heard that cry in the trash can earlier. She never would have known these kittens existed. She could have gone about her evening as planned without four tiny lives weighing on her conscience.

"Is she perking up at all yet?" Josie asked, shifting them back on topic.

Eve looked into the box, where the white kitten was nuzzling at the stuffed cat Josie had given them. "A little, yes."

"Look in the box of supplies I sent over. You should find a toothbrush in there."

"A toothbrush?" Eve slid out of bed and peered into box of supplies. Did kittens this small even have teeth?

"Yes," Josie confirmed. "You can groom her with it. It feels like her mom licking her. That might help wake her up and get her ready to feed."

"Oh." That actually made sense. Eve rummaged through the box until she found the toothbrush. She crawled back into bed, reaching in to rub the white kitten with its bristles. In response, the kitten began rooting around on the stuffed animal like she was trying to nurse. "I think it's working."

"Great. You can feed her right there in the box if you want. Just make sure she's in the right position, belly down, head up."

"Okay." Eve pressed the phone between her cheek and her shoulder as she took the kitten's head in her left hand, positioning her for feeding. She brought the syringe to her mouth, and the kitten began to suckle. "She's eating."

"Yay," Josie said softly. "You can rest one finger gently against her throat to make sure she's swallowing. Just keep pressing the syringe really slowly to make sure you don't overwhelm her with milk."

They fell quiet as Eve fed the kitten, successfully getting about two milliliters of formula into her. She wiped off the kitten's face and set the box on the floor. Suddenly, Eve was alone in her bedroom in the middle of the night, on the phone with a woman she was uncomfortably attracted to. "I should go," she said.

"Call me tomorrow to let me know how they're doing," Josie said. "And get them in to see the vet." She paused. "And don't forget to weigh them. You need to make sure they're gaining weight, preferably about ten grams a day."

"Okay." Eve rubbed her brow, exhausted at the very thought. She'd have to bring the box of kittens with her to the office tomorrow, and *that* ought to go over well. "Thank you for your help."

"You're welcome. Good night, Eve."

"Good night." She set an alarm for two hours from now, shut off the light, and crawled under the covers. Lying in the dark, emptiness yawned inside her the way it always did, like she was slowly sinking into an endless void. Years of practice had taught her how to breathe past it, how to clear her mind to sleep, passing these lonely nighttime hours as quickly as possible.

Josie woke to the sun streaming through her window and a warm, heavy presence on her chest. "Morning, Nigel," she murmured, lifting a hand to rub the orange cat sprawled on top of her. In response, he started to purr, claws pricking at her shoulders as he expressed his pleasure.

Her thoughts drifted to Eve, wondering how the rest of her night had gone and if she'd gotten any sleep. Josie had cared for so many kittens, sometimes she forgot how overwhelming it could be for someone without experience, especially someone like Eve, who'd never cared for an animal before.

Actually, Josie wasn't sure what a night with newborn kittens would be like for someone in Eve's position. No wonder she'd balked at keeping them. Josie felt a wash of guilt for not being more sympathetic last night, but then again, she hadn't really had a choice. She couldn't give them the care they needed while she was working at Swanson's, but maybe she'd be able to find another rescuer to take them today.

To that end, she got up and got ready for her day, then

called all her contacts in the rescue community, hoping someone had room for them. Nigel sprawled on the couch beside her, belly up, tail twitching as he vied for her attention. She reached over to rub him as she placed her last call, leaving a voicemail for a friend of hers who worked primarily in dog rescue but might be willing to take a litter of kittens, just this once.

Then she dialed Eve.

"Have you found someone to take them?" she said in lieu of hello.

"Good morning to you too," Josie said, fighting a smile. A sigh carried over the line, reminding her who she was talking to. "Not yet, but I've left a lot of voicemails, so something may still pan out."

Dead silence.

"Eve," Josie said, amusement fading fast. "I'm doing the best I can."

"Try harder," Eve hissed. "There's a box of kittens behind my desk right now. It's unprofessional."

"Hey, I'm doing you a favor." She tugged at a turquoise strand of hair, twirling it between her fingers. "You could at least pretend to be grateful for it."

"The way I see it, I'm doing *you* a favor, and my sense of philanthropy has dried up."

Josie opened her mouth and closed it again, feeling an uncharacteristic urge to smack something...or someone. "Wow. That's cold, even for you."

More silence from Eve.

Josie shouldn't get her feelings hurt about this. After all, Eve had a reputation for being exactly like this. But for a few minutes yesterday in her kitchen, and again last night over the phone, Josie thought she'd glimpsed a softer, gentler version of television's favorite ice queen. "Do you have any idea how animal rescue works?"

"You know perfectly well I don't," Eve snapped, and Josie tried to remind herself that Eve was tired. She probably hadn't gotten much sleep last night and was working a full day at the office today, kittens in tow. Still...

"Well, here's a quick rundown for you. Animal rescues are volunteer run. I don't get paid for any of this. The donations I receive go straight to care and supplies for the kittens, and it usually isn't enough to cover what I've already spent. I take in orphaned kittens because it's something I feel passionate about, and it brings me joy when I'm able to save a tiny life. But here's another uncomfortable truth...I can't save them all. Do you have any idea how many phone calls I get from people like you?" She didn't pause to wait for an answer.

"It's kitten season, Eve. There are more orphaned and abandoned kittens than we know what do to with this time of year, and if I could care for them all myself, I would, but I have to pay my bills too. I have a bar to run, and right now, I'm the only full-time bartender. I can't even call out sick, because I'm the boss too. And yet, when you called, I invited you into my home, I showed you how to care for them, I gave you a box full of supplies, and I called everyone I know in animal rescue to try to find someone to take them for you."

Josie sucked in a breath. "Maybe it's unprofessional to have a box of kittens behind your desk. It's unfair that you're stuck caring for them, but it's also unfair for you to expect anything more from me than what I've already given you."

"Are you finished?" Eve asked.

"Yes," Josie said, cringing in anticipation of whatever

verbal lashing she was about to receive in response to her lecture.

"I'm sorry," Eve said. "I guess I just thought of it as your job to take them, but that was wrong, and I apologize."

Josie blinked in surprise. "Oh."

"Are you absolutely certain I can't take them to the animal shelter?"

"Unfortunately, yes," Josie told her. "I know for a fact we don't have a shelter in the Manhattan area that's equipped for bottle babies at the moment. Well, if you brought them in, they'd call me. I take as many as I can."

"But you can't save them all," Eve said quietly. "Got it."

"How are they today?"

"Well, they're still alive."

Josie smiled. "And how's the little white one?"

"Still the weakling of the group. I don't know how to tell if she's okay or not."

"They should see the vet today," Josie reminded her, earning herself another weary sigh from Eve. "Tell you what. I have a few hours before the bar opens. What if I come get them and take them to the vet for you?"

"I would appreciate that."

"Okay. Text me the address, and I'll be there in a little while." She ended the call and dialed her vet to make an appointment, then grabbed her laptop, because she didn't intend to arrive at Eve's office empty-handed.

Thirty minutes later, she printed out a piece of paper she hoped might change her future. Eve had been willing to listen to a commonsense argument about animal rescue. Josie could only hope she was willing to open her mind one more time.

She grabbed her bag and headed out, mapping the address Eve had sent her to see which subway line she should take to get there. What did Eve do in her office anyway? Josie had never been sure how much of reality shows like *Do Over* was real and how much was staged for TV, but she certainly wouldn't have pictured its star working in an office when she wasn't filming.

Josie rode the A train into Manhattan and walked two blocks to a sleek gray building that certainly looked like it would house the offices for a television network. She gave her name at the front desk and was issued a visitor's tag and told to take the elevator to the fourth floor.

"Fancy," she muttered under her breath as the sleekly polished elevator door slid shut behind her. This building was a world away from Swanson's, which had admittedly seen better days. The doors slid open on the fourth floor, revealing a blindingly white reception area. White marble floors gleamed beneath white leather furniture. A glossy reception desk stood along the far wall, with the *Life & Leisure* logo hanging behind it. Determined not to feel out of place in her ripped jeans and aqua-tipped hair, Josie walked to the desk and gave her name.

"Third door on the right," the young receptionist told her without batting an eye. "She's expecting you."

"Thank you." Josie set off down the hall, locating Eve's office easily. And...no wonder she hadn't been thrilled about bringing the kittens with her to work. Josie paused in the doorway, taking in Eve's workspace, which was as sleek—and white—as the rest of the building. Eve sat at her desk in a black sheath dress, hair pulled back from her face, fingers clattering over the keyboard of her laptop.

Josie had never gone for the businesswoman type before, but *damn*, that dress was really working for her. Eve looked up, and Josie felt a ping in the pit of her stomach as their gazes locked. "Hi."

"Thank you for coming," Eve said diplomatically, apparently having taken their earlier conversation to heart. "And I meant what I said last night. I'll pay for it. You can have them call me with the bill."

"Well, since it's a donation to the rescue, I won't turn you down, and I really appreciate it." Donations were practically nonexistent these days, apart from the small income that her YouTube channel still generated.

Eve nodded toward the box on the floor behind her. "They're so quiet, I keep thinking they're dead."

"At their age, they mostly sleep between feedings." Josie walked around the desk to crouch by the box. She reached in and stroked the gray kitten on top of the pile. "Are you sure you don't want to name them?"

"Positive." Eve swiveled her chair to face Josie.

Consequently, as she looked up, she was faced with a most distracting view of Eve's legs, bare from the knee to her black heels. An infinity symbol was tattooed on her left ankle. "I usually let viewers on my channel name them for me, in exchange for a donation to the rescue."

"Then do that," Eve said, crossing one tanned leg over the other.

To keep herself from staring, Josie dropped her gaze to the box of kittens. Their little bellies were rounded from a recent feeding. And, *oh my God*, was that...? Josie lifted a piece of paper taped to the side of the box, on which Eve had documented their schedule and weight after each of their feedings.

She cares.

Josie couldn't let it go to her head, because she still had an ulterior motive in coming here today, and it was probably going to involve pissing Eve off again. "You're doing a great job with them."

"Despite what you may think, I don't want them to die."

"I never thought you did," Jose told her with a smile. "Or you would have taken them to the shelter and been done with it."

"I called the police this morning. They sent someone over to take my statement, although I didn't get the feeling anything would come of it."

"Probably nothing will," Josie agreed. "But it's good that you got it on record. I meant to suggest it last night." She stood, lifting the box, and set it on the corner of Eve's desk. Now, she was standing close enough that Eve's shoe bumped her jeans as she swiveled in her chair. Close enough to see the redness in her eyes and the shadows beneath them. "Did you get any sleep last night?"

"Not much," Eve admitted.

"Well, I'll get them out of your hair for a few hours, anyway."

"Thank God."

Josie laughed, nudging Eve's shoulder as she picked up the box of kittens. "Oh, please. Don't even pretend you aren't going to miss us."

5

Eve's knee bounced restlessly beneath her desk. She blinked past the grittiness in her eyes, focusing on the application on the screen in front of her, a single mom selling handcrafted jewelry in an online marketplace. She seemed nice enough and had real talent with her jewelry, but unfortunately, there wasn't a lot Eve could do for her, at least not within the context of the show. A big part of the draw for *Do Over*'s audience was the makeover at the end, when she debuted the client's new space and held a splashy reopening event. Having a storefront was essential.

She clicked on the next application, and a familiar face filled her screen. Josie had told her she'd applied to the show, but somehow, Eve hadn't quite believed it until this moment. Why didn't she remember receiving this application? Probably she'd taken one look at Josie's business and moved on. Bars were an automatic "no" every single time.

It's not you, Josie. It's me.

Curious, Eve moved her cursor to the right and clicked on the video Josie had recorded to accompany her application. She sat on the couch in her living room, talking earnestly to the camera as she described how she'd inherited the bar from her father, how it had belonged to his parents before him, and how she was currently on the verge of losing it.

Tears glistened in Josie's eyes as photos appeared beside her on the screen, a slideshow of family pictures showing a middle-aged man with Josie's same infectious smile pouring drinks behind the bar, a little girl with blonde pigtails reading a book on the floor behind it. The next photo showed young Josie gazing adoringly up at her father.

"I grew up here," present-day Josie told her. "This is what the bar used to look like on a Saturday night." Footage showed a packed bar buzzing with the sounds of laughter and conversation. Josie and her father were side by side behind the bar, tirelessly mixing drinks. "And this is what it looks like on a Saturday night now."

She cut to a video showing about a third of the former crowd, empty stools everywhere. "Please help me save my bar. I run a popular YouTube channel and am very comfortable in front of a camera. I'm also a loyal viewer of your show, and I think Swanson's would be a perfect fit for your audience. Thank you for your consideration."

Eve closed the video and rested her forehead against her palms. Yes, Swanson's would be a perfect fit for *Do Over*. The camera loved Josie, and Eve's viewers would too. But the thought of walking back into that bar—of spending every day for the next two weeks there—it was too painful. She'd set certain boundaries for herself years ago, and she had to respect them.

She'd find someone else, someone even better, an overlooked ratings gem lurking somewhere in this pile of discarded season two applications. She'd record a replacement episode so solid, the network would have no choice but to give her a third season.

Do Over had never been part of her career plan, but it had become invaluable to her. Even though some of it was staged and all of it was curated to maximize emotional appeal for the audience, she'd gotten the chance to be a part of something bigger than she'd ever expected. It was exciting. Energizing. It had given her back a part of herself she'd been missing. And she'd tripled her income from Marlow Marketing, which was no small feat.

In short, she wanted a third season. And a fourth. As many as she could get.

She squinted at the next application. Carla from Cupcake Creations was outgoing and funny in the attached video, but her business was already doing reasonably well. There wasn't enough drama here for a *Do Over* segment.

Eve pinched at the dull ache between her eyes. "Dammit."

Someone tapped on her door, and she looked up to see Josie standing there, box of kittens balanced against her hip. She wore ripped skinny jeans with a purple T-shirt that had a picture of a kitten surfing a rainbow on the front. Her hair was loose over her shoulders, gleaming almost fluorescent under the harsh overhead lighting in Eve's office.

Absolutely nothing about Josie's attire should appeal to her, so she had no idea why she had the sudden urge to push Josie against the wall and kiss her. Obviously, it had been too long since she'd had sex, and her hormones were running away with her.

"Clean bill of health," Josie announced, returning the kittens to their spot behind Eve's desk. "And I just fed them too, so they should be ready to sleep for a while."

"Thank you." She leaned back in her chair, glancing

down at the sleeping kittens. "Not to sound like a broken record, but have you found anyone to take them yet?"

"You'll be the first to know as soon as I do. Really."

"Fine." She tried to keep the irritation out of her voice but was fairly sure she didn't succeed. She was just so *tired*. And she had so much to do. The thought of another night spent bottle-feeding kittens made her want to scream.

"If you don't mind my asking, what does someone like you do in an office all day?" Josie asked, glancing around with interest.

"I work." She lifted her eyebrows for emphasis, and at Josie's *no shit* look, she sighed. "I own a marketing company, Marlow Marketing. It's a consulting business. I help my clients streamline their brand and overall presence in the marketplace. It's what I did before *Do Over*, and what I still do when we're not filming."

"So you really are a businesswoman," Josie said.

"Well, I'm certainly not an actress."

"Oh, I don't know. You're doing a pretty good job pretending you don't like those kittens." Josie dropped into the guest chair across from her, apparently intending to stay.

Eve's spine straightened involuntarily. "It's not a matter of liking or disliking them. I don't have the time or capability to care for them."

Josie toyed with a turquoise lock of hair as she met Eve's gaze. "Well, you're doing a great job with them, and when all's said and done, you'll know you saved four little lives. That's worth something, isn't it?"

"I suppose. Was there something else you needed?" She glanced pointedly at her laptop, because she still had dozens of applications to sort through before tomorrow, and apparently she was going to be caring for these kittens again tonight.

"There is, actually." Josie sucked her bottom lip between her teeth as she pulled a folded-up piece of paper out of her bag and flattened it on the desk in front of her. "I did some research this afternoon, because I don't believe in coincidences. There has to be a reason you walked into my bar last night, after I was rejected for the show. This is my second chance, and I can't let it go without knowing I gave it absolutely everything I had."

Eve's left eye twitched. As if turning her down once hadn't been hard enough...

"According to Wikipedia, your strongest ratings are for episodes where you have a human-interest story behind the business you're helping, and there's a further ratings boost when you have a likable business owner." She looked up, meeting Eve's eyes. "And not to sound arrogant, but most people find me pretty damn likable. My dad died right there in Swanson's. Did you know that? He got shot breaking up a bar fight. He literally died for his bar."

"Josie..."

"Your ratings are down so far this season." There was that unflinching stare again, hazel eyes sparking the way they did when she got fired up about something. "You could help me save Swanson's and boost your ratings while you're at it. People love a good sob story, and you have my full permission to sensationalize my dad's death for your show. He would want me to do anything I had to do to save his bar. So...please, Eve, I'm begging you. Save Swanson's. If you won't do it for me, do it for my dad."

If Josie owned a deli or a book store or an art gallery, but... "I can't. I really am sorry, but my answer is still no."

"Because you don't do bars." Josie's chin lifted in a challenge.

"Among other reasons, yes."

"That's bullshit."

Eve forced herself to hold Josie's gaze, keeping her expression carefully neutral. "I don't have to explain myself to you."

"No, you don't." Josie lurched out of her chair, cheeks pink, eyes glossy. "But it wouldn't kill you to show a little compassion from time to time either."

Eve turned away. "You can show yourself out."

"I'll do that. Call me if you need more help with the kittens."

She nodded, keeping her back to Josie, trying not to flinch as the door closed solidly behind her. Even if Josie's business weren't a bar, the attraction Eve felt for her would have forced her to keep her distance. She didn't mix business with pleasure, and she had no intention of engaging in either business *or* pleasure with Josie. She wasn't Eve's type, not these days, anyway. One-night stands when she got lonely, when she craved the touch of another person and the physical pleasure they could provide. But she never formed emotional attachments.

And Josie was bursting with emotion, from the golden depths of her eyes to the heart she wore so proudly on her sleeve.

"Have you lost your mind?"

Eve turned at the sound of her producer's voice. "Not that I'm aware of."

"You turned her down?" Greta stood in the doorway to Eve's office, hands propped on her hips. "That was one of the best pitches I've ever heard."

"It was a good pitch," Eve admitted. "But I'm not interested in fixing her bar."

"Well, you'd better *get* interested, because that girl is your ticket to season three."

"No, she's not." Eve shook her head. "I'll find something better."

"By tomorrow morning?" Greta gave her a skeptical look. "She's adorable. The camera would love her, and so would your audience. Throw in the perfect sob story with her dead father, and you've got yourself a ratings winner."

Eve bristled, not wanting to hear the truth in Greta's words. "Then find me someone else just as camera-ready."

"Well, I was on my way to your office to tell you about a lead, but that girl is a hundred times better. Honestly, I don't understand what your holdup is. What am I missing? You should be jumping all over this."

"I don't like bars." Beneath the desk, her fingernails pressed painfully into her thighs, an outlet for her emotions that allowed her expression to remain impassive.

Greta stared at her like she'd started speaking in tongues. "Since when do you care if you like a client's business?"

"I've always cared," Eve snapped. "I can't remake a business I don't believe in."

"Well, I'm going to run it past Bruce and the rest of the guys upstairs, and if they sign off on it, you'd better find a way to get enthused about this girl and her bar, because you're out of time. The final decision is yours, but if you want a season three, you'll take this job."

~

Josie swept her gaze over the mostly empty bar in front of her, trying to see it with new eyes. The furniture was worn, the paint chipped. Everything in here looked somewhat dated, but it also had that classic vibe that never really went out of style. Now that Eve had rejected her *again*, Josie had decided to save the damn bar herself. If nothing else, these last few days had shaken her out of the fog of denial she'd been living in lately.

If she didn't do something drastic, and soon, she really was going to lose Swanson's, and she wasn't willing to let that happen. She glanced down at the list of ideas she'd typed into the notes app on her phone and added "Fresh paint?"

The problem was, if she had any friggin' clue how to save the bar herself, she'd have done it a long time ago...

"Hey, Jo!"

Josie turned to see her friends Lori and Tamsen heading toward one of the high-topped tables along the back wall. She ducked out from behind the bar and walked over to them. "This is a happy surprise, ladies."

"I got a promotion, so we're here to celebrate," Tamsen told her as she hopped up on a stool.

"That's great," Josie said. "Congratulations."

"You're looking at a senior account manager," Tamsen said with a smile.

"And I thought the moment called for champagne," Lori added, giving her girlfriend's hand a squeeze.

"It does, and you've come to the right place," Josie told her. "I'll be right back."

She went behind the bar and pulled a bottle of Veuve Clicquot out of the fridge. After popping it open, she grabbed two champagne flutes and filled them. She turned around just as the door opened and a slim figure slipped through, backlit by the setting sun behind her, but even so, Josie felt her presence in the pit of her stomach.

What was Eve doing here?

Tossing her a sharp glance, Josie made her way back to Tamsen and Lori with their champagne. She got them settled before turning her attention to the woman still lingering in the doorway, eyes following her every move.

"Where are the kittens?" Josie asked as she ducked behind the bar, placing it as a barrier between them. She hadn't expected to see Eve again so soon, and the sight of her now had Josie's skin flushing with residual hurt feelings. She didn't want to do this, whatever *this* was.

Eve followed her to the bar, glancing over her shoulder at Lori and Tamsen, who had leaned in to seal their toast with a kiss. "One of the interns has fallen in love with the kittens, and she's watching them for me for a bit."

"Lucky you." Josie rested her palms on the bar, waiting for Eve to make the first move.

She stood between two empty barstools, clearly not intending to make herself comfortable. She still wore the black sheath dress she'd had on earlier, and Josie was trying really damn hard not to notice the swell of her breasts beneath it or the hint of cleavage peeking out of the neckline.

For a long moment, they just stared at each other. Josie's heart was racing, her nerves tingling, and seriously, what was the matter with her? It wasn't like her to go all weak-kneed over a woman, certainly not a woman like Eve. Her fingers drummed against the lacquered wood beneath them.

Eve's gaze dropped to Josie's restless hands before returning to her face. "As it turns out, we have some business to discuss after all."

"About the kittens?" Josie asked, because she had no idea what the hell was going on.

"No."

"Eve—"

Eve lifted a hand to interrupt. "Look, due to legal reasons, we can't air one of the episodes we previously filmed for season two, which leaves us with a hole in the schedule that needs filling, and my producer thinks you and Swanson's will be the perfect fit."

"I...don't understand."

Eve gave her a tight smile. "You get your wish. We'll feature Swanson's on the show, and because it's a last-minute reshoot, it'll happen immediately instead of waiting until next year when season three would begin filming."

Josie felt like dropping to her knees and crying with relief, but how had this happened? "I don't know what to say. What changed?"

"Ever heard that you shouldn't look a gift horse in the mouth?" Eve raised her eyebrows.

"In my experience, when things seem too good to be true, they usually are," Josie said. "A few hours ago, you were one hundred percent against having me on your show. I don't think it's unreasonable to want to understand why you've had a change of heart. In fact, I wouldn't be a very good business owner if I just blindly accepted that you suddenly had my and Swanson's best interests at heart, when you so plainly hate bars."

Eve stared at her for another long moment, eyes narrowed, lips parted as if deciding how to respond. "If you must know, it was taken out of my hands. The network executives want you on the show."

"Oh." Josie gripped the bar top. "They do?"

"My producer overheard your little speech earlier, and

she was very impressed." The ghost of a smile touched her lips. "Well done."

"Holy shit." Josie grinned in spite of herself. "Really?"

"Yes."

"And you're...okay with this? You're not secretly going to sabotage me or something?"

Eve's chin lifted, just slightly. "I'm not thrilled about it, but you have my word that I'll do everything I can to help you and Swanson's succeed."

Josie bounced on her toes, wishing Adam or Kaia were here, someone to share her excitement. *You'd be so proud of me right now, Dad.* "Wow. I just...wow." She blinked through her suddenly watery eyes.

"It's important that you understand the terms of the contract," Eve said. "I'll leave a copy of it here with you, and you should go over it with a lawyer, but basically, you're giving me full control. I'll make any decisions I see fit to rebrand Swanson's for the *Do Over* segment. That's how it works."

"Full control?" Josie repeated, her gut tightening. That was a big deal, and despite what she said, Eve didn't like bars. She'd been particularly hellbent on not helping this one. Could Josie really trust her to have Swanson's best interests at heart? Or even to know what was best for a bar if it was outside her usual wheelhouse?

"I have free rein to do or change anything as I see fit," Eve confirmed.

"What if I hate it?"

"Then you can make your own changes after I'm gone." Eve's dark eyes locked on Josie's, laser sharp.

"I don't know, Eve..." She pinched her bottom lip between her teeth. This bar had been her dad's pride and joy. What if Eve turned it into something he would have hated?

"You have to trust my judgment," Eve said. "You watch the show, right?"

"Yes."

"And do you usually approve of my decisions?"

"Except when you make the owners cry." She exhaled on a small laugh, watching as something almost like amusement sparkled in Eve's eyes.

"Only when they're idiots. Or when they're not doing as I ask."

"I'm not that good at following orders," Josie admitted, pressing a hand against her forehead. "If I disagree, I'm going to tell you."

"I would expect you to, and I'll try to take your concerns into account, but ultimately, I get the final say."

"All right. I'll go over the contract this weekend and have a friend of mine who's a lawyer take a look at it, but unofficially, we have a deal." She extended her hand.

Eve took it, her grip warm and firm. "Regardless of what you may think of me, I'll save your bar."

6

Eve stepped through Swanson's front door promptly at noon on Tuesday, box of kittens in her arms and briefcase slung over her shoulder. Her back screamed in insult as she made her way to the bar, gingerly sliding the box onto its sleek surface. It had been five days since she offered Josie the spot on her show, six days since she pulled these kittens out of the trash, and Eve's nerves were frayed beyond repair.

She'd been in the bar all of ten seconds, and already she wanted to scream. Or cry. One of the two. She wouldn't do either.

Josie walked out from the back, dressed in turquoise pants that were a perfect match for her hair and a black T-shirt, a hesitant smile on her face. She approached the bar and peered into the box. "They're doing great, Eve. Look how big they are!"

"The black one is starting to open its eyes." She glanced over at Josie. "I should stop asking, right?"

Josie gave her an apologetic look. "Everyone's got their

hands full right now. It's a busy season for animal rescuers. I promise I'll let you know if anything changes."

She sighed, tamping back her frustration with the situation. She was just so tired.

"You can put them in my apartment while you're here, though," Josie told her. "And I'll help you with them as much as I can."

"I appreciate that." Eve set her briefcase on the bar and slid onto the stool in front of it, wincing at the spasm of pain that slid up her spine.

"You okay?" Josie asked.

"Just a bad back." She pressed a hand against it. "An old injury that I've aggravated by carrying this damn box of kittens all over town."

"I'm sorry," Josie murmured. "Why don't we go upstairs? It can't be comfortable for you to sit on a barstool when your back is bothering you."

She opened her mouth to protest, but sitting for hours on a hard wooden stool did sound tortuous, and Swanson's didn't open until five. "All right. Thank you."

"Of course." Josie scooped up the box of kittens, pausing to lock the front door before she led the way toward the staircase in back. "We can make a video of them while we're at it. I need to introduce them to my viewers so they can start voting on names."

"If you like." She followed Josie up the stairs, settling across from her on the couch with the box of kittens on the table between them. The orange cat Eve had seen the last time she was here walked through the room and hopped up on the couch beside Josie.

She reached over to rub him. "This is Nigel. Don't worry. He won't bother the kittens."

"Is he one of your former foster kittens?"

"Yeah." Josie laughed as Nigel hopped into her lap. "One of my first, and the only one I've kept."

"Lucky cat," Eve commented.

Josie nodded with an affectionate smile at the cat in question. "So, what are we supposed to be doing this afternoon, exactly?"

"We need to go over all the particulars for filming, and then I'll observe you once the bar opens. The film crew will be here around six and will stay for an hour or two, getting some initial footage."

"Tuesdays are my least busy day of the week," Josie said, brow wrinkling.

"That's for the best, then, isn't it?" Eve told her. "No offense, but we want to show the viewers how badly Swanson's is doing so they can appreciate its transformation at the end of the segment."

"Right," Josie said, blinking as if the reality of what she'd signed up for had just fully hit her.

"The photos that you used in your application," Eve said. "The ones of you and your father that show how you grew up in the bar. Where are those?"

Josie's lips quirked. "So you did see my application."

"Last week," Eve told her. *Don't read anything into it.*

"They're in an album," Josie said, gesturing toward a shelf along the far wall.

"We'll want to film those, and I'll ask you about him while the camera crew is here."

Josie blew out a breath, looking down at the cat curled across her lap. "I meant it last week when I told you to sensationalize his death, but..."

"That's not my intention, but we do need to tell your story. It's a big part of the draw for *Do Over*, and as you noted, viewers like a sad story with a feel-good ending."

"And you're still confident we'll get that happy ending?"

"I am."

"Then let's do it," Josie said with a definitive nod.

She put the cat down, and they spent the next hour or so poring over paperwork. Usually, Eve felt a thrill of anticipation as she finalized her plan of attack with a new client. With Josie, though, the thrill she felt had nothing to do with anticipation. It was more of an adrenaline rush, a mixture of discomfort over the idea of spending the next few weeks in a bar and this unrelenting attraction she felt whenever she got within twenty feet of Josie, whenever she so much as *thought* of her.

When the paperwork had been put away, Josie reached for the kittens, lifting the black one into her lap. He mewled softly, paws waving in the air. "It must be about time to feed these guys."

"Yes," Eve confirmed. "And I'm out of formula. I ordered some of the same brand you gave me, but it doesn't arrive until tomorrow. I was hoping you could help me out."

"I can definitely hook you up with more formula." Josie cradled the kitten like a baby, stroking his belly. "Hungry, aren't you?" She stood and walked into her bedroom, taking the kitten with her, returning a minute later with a container of powdered formula.

Eve took it from her and went into the kitchen, familiar by now with the process. She mixed and warmed enough formula for the four kittens and sat on the couch beside Josie to feed them. They each lifted a kitten out of the box.

"It's soothing, isn't it?" Josie said quietly, watching as the black kitten suckled from the syringe.

Eve looked down at the gray kitten in her lap. "I suppose."

"Admit it." Josie nudged her elbow against Eve's. "You've

gotten fond of them."

"I don't hate them, but they're a lot of work."

"You like them," Josie insisted with a grin.

Eve put the gray kitten back in the box and lifted the white one, ignoring Josie as she replaced the black one with his gray-and-white littermate. Once they were all fed and cared for, Josie set up a video camera on a tripod, facing the couch.

"Time to introduce these guys to the world," she said.

"I'll leave you to it, then." Eve stood, crossing the room to get her briefcase.

"Oh, come on. You're a television host. You should be in it with me."

"No, thanks."

"It's good publicity for both of us," Josie insisted. "For someone who touts herself as a marketing expert, you should know this."

"I know all about publicity, thank you. I also know that, after the contract we just signed, it's best for us not to appear in kitten videos together." She had no desire to be in Josie's video, nor did she have the energy for it. Already, it was going to take everything she had to get through the filming later today. "I'll meet you downstairs."

Ignoring the shocked expression on Josie's face, she gathered her things and walked down to the empty bar. She set her briefcase on the bar top, running her fingers over the glossy surface, wood encased beneath a thick lacquered finish. This was a space she needed to get acquainted with, because she'd be spending the majority of her time here for the next two weeks.

Unbidden, a sob rose in her throat. She pressed her palms against the bar, breathing through the pain, blinking Lisa's image from her vision.

"Eve..." Josie's voice filtered in from the direction of the stairs.

"Not now," she bit out, straightening her spine, keeping her back to Josie.

A door shut behind her, and she was alone. She dragged in a ragged breath, wondering at the stinging sensation in her fingertips until she saw the marks she'd made on the bar top, its lacquered coating now embedded under her fingernails. *Fuck.*

Leaving her briefcase behind, she walked out the front door and stood on the sidewalk, sucking in deep breaths of fresh air. She inhaled all the familiar scents of the city, car exhaust mixed with the slightly smoky scent of a nearby restaurant. Italian food, if she had to guess, based on the herbs drifting on the air.

She smoothed her hands over her blouse, adjusting the tuck of the silk fabric into the waistband of her skirt. This was fine. She was fine. The camera crew would arrive shortly, and she'd forget everything else as long as that red light was pointed in her direction. She could bury her discomfort over being in the bar. She was an expert at burying her feelings. There was no reason for this to be any different.

Taking one last breath, she turned around and walked back inside.

Josie had been recording herself for YouTube for years, so there was absolutely no reason for her to panic in front of the *Do Over* cameras. Except...she was panicking. This was all so much bigger and more important than anything she'd ever done before. She was going to be on cable television, for crying out loud.

If her dad could see her now...

She'd stammered through her interview with Eve, and then she'd gotten hopelessly choked up as she took Eve—and the camera crew—through her family photos and showed them the place where her dad had died. Eve assured her afterward that it had gone well, that her emotional response was exactly what they wanted for *Do Over*.

But Josie couldn't help worrying that she was going to look like a total basket case when the segment aired. Thank goodness for Adam and Kaia, who were in their usual seats at the end of the bar, showing their support. Josie had seen Eve interviewing them with the film crew earlier. Kaia had spoken earnestly into the camera while Adam gestured all over the place as he told who-knew-what wildly embellished story about Josie.

Both of them had visited the bar back when her dad still owned it, although they hadn't become regulars until after his death. At first, they'd come to offer moral support to Josie, and over time, it had become their regular hangout, along with lots of their mutual friends.

Josie blinked, resisting the urge to rub her eyes. The *Do Over* team had sent over hair and makeup people to get her camera ready, and the false lashes they'd applied were heavy and itchy, but if they looked half as good on her as they looked on Eve...

Right now, Eve stood near the door, deep in conversation with a member of the film crew. She had on an emerald-green blouse, neatly tucked into a black pencil skirt with sky-high black heels. Her hair was swept into a neat knot on the back of her head, accentuating the graceful curve of her neck.

And Josie was one hundred percent smitten, even if she did want to strangle Eve half the time. She didn't always like her, but she couldn't seem to stop wanting to kiss her. Then there was that moment earlier, when she'd walked in on Eve alone in the bar, looking like she was about to cry. There had been something heartbreakingly raw and vulnerable about her, although it was long gone by the time Josie finished filming her vlog with the kittens.

Whatever it was, Josie hated that being in her bar was so painful for Eve, both emotionally and physically, because she'd noticed Eve rubbing her lower back between takes. Surely, those stilettos weren't helping, but it was hardly Josie's place to judge. Here she was, working herself to the bone for this place that had been her dad's passion, not hers.

Josie had always loved Swanson's. She'd grown up here. It was home. But she'd never wanted to own it. She'd never imagined spending her life behind the bar, serving drinks while her YouTube channel and her animal rescue faded into nonexistence. Someday, Swanson's would be successful enough that she could hire a full staff to run the day-to-day operations so she could get back to doing what she loved.

Someday.

In the meantime, she let herself get lost for a minute watching Eve. A shaft of light fell across her face, illuminating the red sheen of her lips and the chocolate depths of her eyes. She turned to speak to another member of the crew, and Josie's gaze dropped to her ass.

"Someone's got it bad for the pretty television host," Kaia whispered in her ear.

Josie grinned, glancing over at her friend. "No clue what you're talking about."

"No?" Kaia followed her gaze. "Can't say I blame you.

She's hot with a capital 'h.'"

Josie gave her a sharp look.

Kaia lifted her hands with a laugh. "Don't worry. She's all yours. Actually, I had a really hot date the other night, and I'm seeing her again tomorrow."

"Really? Why am I just hearing about this now?" Josie focused on her friend as Kaia told her all about her date. From there, she moved down the bar to pour drinks for a couple who'd just come in. It was unusually busy for a Tuesday night, and everyone was gawking at the cameras. Obviously, word about the taping had gotten out.

Josie tried not to notice them filming her as she worked, but it seemed like every time she looked up, those red lights were aimed in her direction. It was nerve-racking. Around nine, the film crew left, apparently having gotten all the footage they needed.

Eve settled herself at the far end of the bar, typing busily on her phone. She'd been upstairs several times to check on the kittens, reminding Josie of the softness that lurked beneath her steely exterior, although...maybe it was better if she forgot.

Once she'd taken care of her customers, she made her way down to Eve. She looked up from her phone, flawless and poised, and *damn*, her camera-ready makeup was really next level. Her eyes locked on Josie's, a hunger gleaming there that rivaled the one Josie felt burning inside herself. And Eve's brown eyes narrowed, heat recognizing heat.

If Josie had had any questions about Eve's sexuality, they were gone now. She'd already had her suspicions, deepened after she searched Eve online and found not so much as a whisper about her ever having been seen in public with a man. That, and a certain way she looked at Josie sometimes that made her wonder...

Eve's tongue darted out to wet her lips, and a warm flush crept over Josie's skin, spreading heat through her belly. God, how was she supposed to work with her for the next few weeks without kissing her?

"What's a woman have to do to get a beer around here?" Eve said, breaking the loaded silence between them, eyes never leaving Josie's.

"A beer?" she repeated stupidly. Somehow, she'd internalized Kaia's words, assuming Eve was a recovering alcoholic, but was she wrong? Or was Eve so affected by whatever had happened earlier, she was about to fall off the wagon? "I thought...the way you reacted to bars..."

Eve's delicately shaped eyebrows arched as she realized what Josie was trying to say. "My reasons for disliking bars are just that...mine."

"Right." Of course, Eve wouldn't give her an inch, even now. "A beer, then?"

"Whatever you have on tap. Something light, a pilsner or an amber ale."

"Got it." Josie moved down the bar to pour her a pilsner from a local brewery she had on tap. "White Horse pilsner. It's one of my favorites," she said as she set it in front of Eve. "I try to keep as many local breweries on tap as possible."

"That's good to know," Eve said, a thoughtful look on her face that had everything to do with *Do Over* and nothing to do with Josie herself.

"Be right back," Josie told her before moving down the bar to check on her customers. She poured more beer, a couple of shots, and mixed a whiskey sour for one of the women who'd come in earlier to gawk at the camera crew. Kaia and Adam caught her eye and waved, heading for the door.

By the time she made it back to Eve, the beer was half

gone, and Eve was looking a lot more relaxed, elbows on the bar as she looked at something on her phone.

"Are you hungry?" Josie asked. They had been rushing around since the camera crew arrived at six without pausing for dinner, and it was now approaching ten.

"Mm," Eve said, lifting her beer for another sip. "I'll stop for something on the way home." She paused, frowning. "Except I'll have the kittens."

"I was going to order something from the place next door. They have really great hoagies. Pasta too, but I'm partial to the hoagies. I've got their menu." She ducked behind the counter to grab it, scooting it across the bar toward Eve. "They'll send someone over here with the food. We just have to eat in the back so my customers don't get jealous."

Eve stared at the menu, then at Josie, as if trying to think of a reason not to stay. "All right."

"Cool." She headed off to check on her customers again while Eve looked over the menu, but the crowd was thinning fast now that the *Do Over* crew had left. There were two women at the bar and a couple at one of the tables along the back wall, although experience said she'd probably see a few more stragglers before the night was over.

If not, she'd close early again tonight. She was exhausted, more so than usual, probably from the stress and excitement of having the film crew around. It certainly wasn't a good idea to encourage Eve to stay for dinner when Josie was already struggling not to kiss her. But then again, something told her Eve had enough willpower for the both of them.

She would never crack, so really, there was nothing for Josie to worry about.

7

Eve took a bite of her cheesesteak, her gaze sliding to the woman beside her. They were seated side by side in front of the desk in Josie's office, so close their shoulders occasionally bumped as they ate. Not that Eve was complaining. In fact, she might have intentionally let her elbow brush against the soft fabric of Josie's T-shirt as she reached for her beer.

"Long day," Josie commented.

"Yes." She needed to go home, to be in her own space so she could relax. Her shoulders ached from keeping herself so rigid all day, and her back, well...it was not happy with her. She needed sleep, dammit, but that wasn't in the cards no matter how quickly she finished her food and headed out. Mental and physical exhaustion were taking a toll. Spending the day at Swanson's had taken a toll, but at this exact moment, sitting in Josie's office, a little harmless flirting sounded so much more appealing than her empty apartment and the long night ahead.

"I enjoyed seeing you in your element today," Josie said.

"In my element?"

"You know, with the cameras rolling. You're a natural. You make it look easy. I felt like a bumbling idiot every time the cameras were on me." Josie's dimples were entirely too adorable...and distracting.

Eve forced herself to look away. "You did fine."

"So have you started thinking about what you want to change? Should I be scared? Or can you not even talk about it with me when the cameras aren't rolling?"

"Nothing I'm ready to discuss with you yet, no," Eve told her. "I'll spend the rest of the week observing and doing market research."

"And then can you give me a heads-up before we film it?" Josie sat, hands clasped in her lap, expression so earnest, Eve could hardly bear to look at her.

"I'm not supposed to."

"But?" Josie pressed.

"No 'but,'" Eve said, annoyed that Josie had heard her waver. "You signed up to be on a television show, so yes, you have to let us film your reactions. That's how it works."

"Don't make me cry," Josie said with a silly smile in an obvious attempt to lighten the mood between them.

"I never intend to make people cry." Eve crumpled the empty sandwich wrapper in her fist as she stood. "I'll be here the same time tomorrow. If you have any personal suggestions or requests for the relaunch, that would be a good time to let me know."

"Okay."

She paused in the doorway to look back at Josie, wanting to feel that zap in the pit of her stomach again before she left. Their eye contact was electric every single time. "I'll see you tomorrow, then."

She went up the stairs to Josie's apartment to retrieve the box of kittens. It was almost time to feed them, but to sit here in Josie's living room this late at night felt entirely too intimate. They could wait until she got home. She requested an Uber because there was no way her back would tolerate hauling this box across town on the subway.

And speaking of her back, she swapped her heels for the simple black flats she kept in her briefcase. Then she picked up the box and carried it downstairs to the street. Thirty minutes later, she pushed through the door into her apartment. The black kitten meowed, waving its little head around as it sought its next meal.

"Yeah, yeah," she muttered. She set the box on her kitchen counter and put a cup of water in the microwave. The whole process was second nature to her at this point. While the water heated, she went down the hall to change into her pajamas.

Exhaustion came crashing over her now that she was home. All she wanted was to fall face-first into bed, although maybe it was best that she couldn't, because behind the fatigue, something else lurked, something much darker, memories and emotions stirred during the day that waited to haunt her dreams.

She returned to the kitchen and mixed a bottle of formula, setting it in the cup of hot water to warm. The black kitten was still moving around, so she lifted him first. He squinted at her through baby-blue eyes, mewling loudly for his dinner. The sound grated on her nerves, which were already raw from her day at Swanson's. Quickly, she positioned him and offered him the bottle of formula.

And so she went, feeding the gray one, and then the gray-and-white one. She tended to feed the white one last because she was still the most difficult to wake. Maybe because this feeding was a little bit late, the white kitten woke easily and latched right on to the bottle. Her tiny paws kneaded Eve's hand as she drank, suckling hungrily at the formula. Eve stroked her with her free hand, tracing her fingers down the kitten's back. Her fur was impossibly soft and soothing beneath her fingers.

Surely Josie would find someone take them soon. Honestly, Eve couldn't believe she'd managed to care for them even this long. Five days of bottle feeding and wiping butts. Every moment had been a struggle, but sometimes, in these quiet moments late at night, she felt something warm in her chest while she held one of the kittens in her hands.

If only...

She refused to let her mind finish the thought. Instead, she nestled the white kitten in with the rest, set the alarm on her phone, and headed down the hall to get ready for bed. As tired as she was, she wouldn't truly be able to rest until the kittens—and Josie's bar—were safely out of her life.

JOSIE HAD UNDERESTIMATED the amount of work that went into an episode of *Do Over*. Maybe she'd imagined that Eve would show up, give Swanson's a glamorous makeover while the cameras rolled, and voilà...her bar would be successful again.

In reality, Eve was here at lunchtime again on Wednesday, laptop open on the bar, typing furiously as she asked Josie question after question. Today, she had on a gray knit dress that clung to every inch of her body in a way that made it very hard not to stare. But that was probably just Josie's hormones talking.

Since her dad died, she hadn't had much time for dating, which didn't mean she hadn't tried. She'd maintained her Tinder profile and tried to go on at least one date a month.

But only a handful of those had resulted in second dates, and it had been over a year since she'd made it to a third. It was beyond frustrating. She wanted a woman who made her laugh, someone who would sit up with her at night and help her bottle-feed tiny kittens, someone who made her whole body short-circuit the way it did every time she looked at Eve.

Eve, who never cracked a smile and never failed to begin a conversation by asking if Josie had found a foster home for the kittens yet. Eve, with her perfect hair and makeup, her frosty personality, and that body...

"So?" she said, pinning Josie with an impatient look.

"What?" She gave her head a slight shake. "Sorry."

Eve sighed. "Jason is currently your only employee?"

"Yes. He tends bar with me on Friday and Saturday nights." It was embarrassing to admit that she only had one part-time employee, that she was working every single shift. It hadn't been this way when her father was in charge, and not even for Josie until a few months ago. But when her other full-time bartender quit, she hadn't been able to justify hiring someone new. It was only temporary, just until business picked up.

"And what do you do if you're sick?" Eve asked, glancing at her over her laptop.

"I don't know." She shrugged, reaching for a cloth to wipe down the bar. "I'd try to make it down here anyway, I guess. It hasn't happened since I took over full-time."

"It's not sustainable," Eve said. "You realize this."

"I do," she agreed. "It's why I asked for your help. I know I'm in trouble."

"You own the whole building?"

"Yes." Her grandparents had bought it over forty years ago for a fraction of what a building like this would cost today, and thankfully, her dad had been able to pay the mortgage off before his death.

"And you rent out the apartment on the third floor?"

"Yes."

"Any work we do for you as part of the show will be paid for, but you're going to need a plan for success after I'm gone," Eve said, fingers still clacking over the keys. "I'll help you strategize, but you'll probably also need to take out a small business loan or a home equity loan on the building to cover your operating expenses for the first few months while you grow."

"A loan?" Josie swallowed hard. The only reason she'd been able to make it even this far was that she didn't have a mortgage to pay each month.

Eve nodded. "Once I present my business plan to you on Friday, I'll go over my recommendations for keeping the momentum going, areas I think you can improve, and strategies for success."

"That sounds like a lot more than a TV show." And a lot more than she was expecting.

"That's because this is what I do for a living. I want you to be a satisfied client, not just an episode on a television show. And on that note, you're welcome to utilize my services after filming is complete, if you like. I want you to succeed, just like any other client."

"I'm pretty sure I couldn't afford you," Josie said as she began to stack clean glasses from the dishwasher behind the bar.

"Sometimes you have to spend money to make money," Eve said.

"That sounds a lot simpler than it is." And she doubted Eve truly wanted to step foot in this bar again after filming had wrapped, but she appreciated the offer.

"We'll go over all of that once I've got your launch plan ready."

"Okay."

Eve got up from the barstool and began to wander around the space, taking photos with her phone and jotting down notes. She disappeared down the hall that led to Josie's office and the storage room, returning a few minutes later. "What's behind that locked door at the end of the hall?"

"Rooftop access," Josie told her.

"Separate from the stairs that lead to the apartments?" Eve asked.

"Yeah. There used to be a rooftop bar, but I had to shut it down because I couldn't afford another bartender to work up there."

"You had a rooftop bar, and you shut it down?" Eve's eyebrows crawled up her forehead.

"It wasn't as popular as you would think."

"Show me."

"Okay." Josie led the way down the hall, unlocking the door that led to the roof. "Don't get your hopes up, though."

She went up first, with Eve walking behind her, heels clicking against the wooden steps. The stairs doubled back and forth, ending in a black steel door that led onto the rooftop patio. Josie pushed it open and held it for Eve, who walked past her onto the roof.

The space was about half the size of the bar below, divided on the side to hide the HVAC and other mechanical units up here. It had a bare concrete floor, with waist-high walls around the perimeter and a covered bar area against the far wall. Remnants from its former life had been piled everywhere, rusty stools and plastic milk crates filled with trash and covered in bird poop.

Eve walked it end to end, seemingly lost in thought. Josie was embarrassed for even bringing her up here. Once, this space had been nice, but now it was more of an eyesore than a potential source of income.

"It hasn't been used in years," she said apologetically.

"I can see that," Eve responded, walking to the front barrier, where she stood with her arms clasped over her chest, staring out at the city before her. "How would you describe the average clientele before your father passed away?"

"Um, people looking for a drink after work mostly." She thought of Dougie and Sal as she came to stand beside Eve. The view wasn't anything to write home about. They were only three stories up, after all. But the fresh air was nice, and after dark, the city really glowed. Sometimes, she came up here to think. Or she had before she started working so many hours. Now, her only night off was Monday, when the bar was closed.

"Mostly beer drinkers or cocktails?"

"Beer."

"Mm." Eve's response gave no indication if this was what she had expected or wanted to hear. What was she planning for Swanson's? If Josie really let herself think about the absolute power she'd given Eve when she signed the *Do Over* contract, it made her break out in a cold sweat. Deep down, she wanted to believe Eve wouldn't do anything she would hate, but was that really true, or was Josie just being naïve?

The sun beat down on them, drawing out golden highlights in Eve's brown hair. She'd left it down today, sleek and straight over her shoulders. It softened her look...just barely. She turned her head to look at Josie, and she saw the same honeyed tones in the chocolate depths of her eyes and in her tanned skin. Eve Marlow in the sunshine was a golden goddess.

Josie's gaze dipped to her pink lips and then to the pulse pounding in the hollow of her throat. Her own pulse jumped in response, spreading that all too familiar warmth through her as she dragged her gaze back to Eve's, only to find her watching Josie with that laser-like intensity she did so well. She had totally been watching Josie check her out, and she should probably feel embarrassed about that. She definitely should, but she didn't.

Not when Eve's pupils were blown with the same lust currently burning Josie up from head to toe. *Holy shit.*

She grinned, half-drunk off the hormones racing through her body. Sparks were good. Sparks were fun. Sparks were...inconvenient when she felt them for a woman who had the power to make or break her business and almost certainly had no intention on acting on her attraction to Josie, not as long as they had to work together. And maybe not even after, because somehow she imagined she wasn't quite Eve's type, whatever her type might be.

"We should get back downstairs," Eve said, breaking the trance they seemed to have fallen into.

"Right."

"You should be using this space."

"I should?"

"Yes." Eve turned away from the railing, her shoulder bumping Josie's as she led the way back to the stairs, a silky strand of her hair brushing Josie's overheated skin, causing goose bumps to rise in its wake.

Yeah, sparks were fun, all right, even if she never got the chance to let them ignite.

8

"Need a beer?"

Eve looked up from her laptop to find Josie standing in front of her, palms against the bar, friendly smile on her face. Swanson's had opened an hour ago, but thus far, she and Josie were still the only ones in the place. "Sure."

"Same one? The White Horse pilsner?"

"Yeah."

"You got it." Josie turned to grab a glass, drawing Eve's attention to the tattoo on the back of her shoulder. After their trip to the roof, Josie had taken off her jacket, revealing the red tank top she wore beneath it...and her tattoo.

"A dragonfly?" she said, trying to keep her tone even, as if her fingers weren't itching to touch it, as if she had no more than a passing interest in this newly revealed part of Josie's body.

She turned to face Eve as she began to pour her beer. "Dragonflies symbolize transformation or self-realization. I got it after I came out."

"Oh." She'd seen the rainbow pin on Josie's bag, and

more importantly, she'd seen the heat in her eyes when she looked at Eve. But somehow, hearing her say it only intensified the restless urge to kiss her, an urge she absolutely could not allow herself to satisfy. "It's beautiful," she said, meaning the tattoo, but really, the sentiment applied to any part of Josie, if she were being honest.

"Thank you." She slid the beer across the bar to Eve, their fingers brushing in the process, warm skin against cold glass.

Eve lifted it and took a long drink, trying to restore some semblance of sanity in her brain. It was the bar. It was messing with her head. The bar, and the beer. Bad ideas multiplying the longer she sat here.

Had she gotten all the information she needed from Josie today? Maybe she should leave now, get the fuck out of here before she lost any more of herself to this place, or this woman. She'd never shirked her job before, not because of an inconvenient attraction or a personal trigger, and she hated herself for even considering it now.

"Do you have any?" Josie asked.

"What?" Eve set the beer down, staring into its amber depths.

"Tattoos."

"One," she told her, crossing her legs beneath the bar.

"On your ankle, right?" Josie said. "I noticed it before."

"Yes." And she wasn't going to let herself wonder when Josie had been staring at her ankles. Nor was she going to explain it to her, not today or likely ever.

"An infinity symbol?"

She nodded, resisting the urge to reach down and touch it.

"Cool," Josie said after a pause, realizing Eve wasn't going to elaborate. "I like it."

"Thank you." She swirled the glass slightly, watching the golden liquid coat its sides. "It's about time to feed the kittens."

"I can do it if you want," Josie offered. "Just text me if anyone comes in, and I'll come down and serve them."

"All right. Thank you." She wasn't going to complain about skipping a feeding or not having to climb the stairs to Josie's apartment. Her back had been a mess ever since she started lugging around the box of tiny felines.

"No problem." Josie headed for the stairs with a bounce in her step. She truly enjoyed caring for the kittens and was genuinely disappointed she couldn't raise them herself. It was a damn shame Eve wouldn't be able to turn the bar around quickly enough to make it happen.

She stood from the stool to stretch her legs, and since she had the place to herself, she bent forward, stretching her back with an exercise her physical therapist had taught her, loosening the tension in her muscles and alleviating some of the pain. And then, unable to resist the temptation, she ducked behind the bar.

She placed her palms against its smooth lacquered surface the way Josie so often did. It was cool against her skin. Solid. Familiar. Without warning, she heard Lisa's laughter ringing in her ears, saw her twirling a liquor bottle nimbly between her fingers before she began to pour. She heard her own laughter, mixed with Lisa's, felt the warmth of it bubbling up inside her.

And then came the pain, so swift and brutal, it almost knocked the knees out from beneath her. She lowered her head, staring at her hands, waiting for it to pass. She was a different person now, and although Josie's bar stirred memories, it couldn't bring the old Eve back. Nothing could. She'd died in that car along with Lisa and their unborn daughter.

Forcing the memories away, she slipped her professional persona into place as she looked around the room, seeing it the way Josie did every night. It was a nice space, open and inviting, albeit somewhat worn and dated. It would need a facelift, but more than that, Swanson's needed to be fully rebranded to succeed, maybe even take on a new name.

It was no accident that Josie had lost so much business over the last few years. A number of new bars had opened in the neighborhood during that timeframe, fresh and trendy while Swanson's was showing its age. Eve had a few ideas to make Swanson's relevant again, but she needed to do more research and observe Josie in action for the rest of the week before she made any official recommendations.

The front door swung open, and two of Josie's friends walked in, a tall, lanky man with overly styled hair and a pretty black woman with a wild halo of curls. Adam and Kaia. Eve had interviewed them yesterday while the crew was here filming.

"Has she got you tending bar for her now too?" Adam asked jokingly as he slid onto a stool.

"Hardly," she replied, realizing she was still standing behind the bar. "She's upstairs feeding the kittens."

"The ones you found in a trash can?" Kaia asked, sitting beside Adam.

"Yes." She ducked out from behind the bar and sat on the stool in front of her laptop. "She'll be down in a minute if you want something to drink." She wasn't going to text Josie to come down for these two, who she knew never paid for their drinks. Didn't they realize Swanson's was about to go under? How could they take advantage of their friend like that?

"I can do it," Adam said, sliding behind the bar. "I help

Josie out back here all the time. How are things going for the show?"

Eve watched him pour beer as an idea formed in her mind. "It's going well. Actually, there's something I think you could help me with."

"Oh yeah?" Adam said, perking up. "What's that?"

"I have a few questions that you two might be uniquely qualified to answer for me."

An unusual sight greeted Josie when she made it back downstairs after feeding the kittens. Eve, Kaia, and Adam sat together at the end of the bar, deep in conversation. Well, it didn't quite look like they were new best friends. It looked more like Eve was interviewing them without her camera crew—or Josie—around.

"Should my ears be ringing?" she asked as she slid behind the bar, noting the half-empty beers in front of Adam and Kaia.

Kaia's face said "yes," but Eve spoke first. "Your friends were just helping me with a few details in my market research."

"Details?" Josie echoed.

"Yes." Eve rose and walked back to the stool at the other end of the bar where she'd left her laptop, her body language—as usual—indicating she had no intention of elaborating.

And it hit Josie all over again how much trust she'd placed in this woman, how much control she'd given her. Right now, Eve was deciding what she was going to do with Swanson's, without giving Josie even the slightest inkling of what she had in mind. What had she been thinking to get herself into this?

Eve caught her eye, one brow raised ever so slightly, as if she could hear every thought racing through Josie's head. "Is there a problem?"

"No." *Yes.* But it was too late for second thoughts. She'd signed a contract, and there was no backing out now. She had to trust that Eve would do what Josie hadn't been able to—bring in new customers and save the bar. Luckily, a boisterous group of men entered the bar, distracting her from her spiraling thoughts. By the time she'd finished serving their beer, Eve was absorbed in whatever she was doing on her laptop.

Market research.

Josie made her way over to Kaia and Adam. "What did she want with you guys?"

Kaia shrugged. "She was asking about your friends, mostly."

"My friends?" Josie asked. That was not even in the ballpark of anything she'd imagined Eve talking to them about. "What about you?"

"Like, how many people who come into the bar are your friends versus random customers," Adam told her.

"Hm, she asked me that too," Josie said.

"She also wanted to know how many of us are queer," Kaia added.

"What?" If Josie had been holding anything, she would have dropped it. What in the world?

"I'm not sure if that had anything to do with the bar or just, you know, personal interest." Kaia's lips twisted in a smirk.

"Personal interest?" Josie snuck a look at Eve, who was

still engrossed in her laptop, completely ignoring their conversation.

"In case you didn't notice, she's totally hot for you," Adam clarified with a grin.

Josie's cheeks heated. "I noticed."

"So what are you going to do about it?" Kaia asked.

"Nothing, probably. Yeah, I'm ridiculously attracted to her, but I'm not entirely sure I *like* her." Although, that was a lie. She liked Eve. Maybe she shouldn't, but she did. In fact, she had a feeling that icy exterior was armor, protecting her more tender parts. Or maybe that was wishful thinking on Josie's part.

Over the next few hours, she kept herself busy, chatting with Adam and Kaia between customers. Eve had grown very quiet at her end of the bar, working on her laptop. Around ten, Josie made her way down to check on her, to see if she wanted a beer or even some water. Eve had one elbow propped on the bar, head in her hand, facing away from Josie.

"Hey," Josie said, loud enough to be heard over the noise of the bar.

Eve jumped, looking up at her with bleary, unfocused eyes.

"Oh my God, were you asleep?" Josie asked, irrationally delighted by the sleep-drugged, disoriented version of Eve currently blinking at her, obviously trying to gather her wits.

"What?" Eve brushed at a flyaway strand of hair. "No."

Josie rested her elbows on the bar, leaning toward her. "Yeah, pretty sure you were."

Eve straightened on her stool, wincing as she stretched her back. "Might have dozed off for a moment."

"You should go home," Josie told her. "In fact, leave the

kittens here tonight. The bar's almost empty, and Adam can watch it for me while I feed them. I'll probably close early."

"Are you sure?" Eve asked.

She nodded. "Go get a good night's sleep."

Eve hesitated—surprising for a woman who'd spent the past week hassling Josie to find someone to take the kittens for her—before nodding. "Thank you."

"You're welcome." Josie watched as she shut down her laptop, packed it into her briefcase, and stood.

"I'll see you tomorrow, then."

"Yep."

And then Eve lingered for another moment, just staring at Josie, before she turned on her heel and walked out the door.

9

Eve breezed through Swanson's front door at five o'clock on Thursday looking as poised and impenetrable as she had when Josie first met her a week ago. Maybe she'd needed the sleep even more than Josie realized. She was feeling the effects of a night on kitten duty herself, although after years of it, she didn't really mind. She'd also become an expert at maximizing her sleep between feedings, something she didn't think Eve had been nearly as successful at.

"Hi," Josie said.

"Hello." Eve settled herself on her usual stool and set up her laptop. She was dressed all in black today, pants and a matching blouse. "How are they?"

"Fine," Josie told her. "You missed them, didn't you?"

"Not even a little bit." Eve powered on her laptop, keeping her eyes on the screen.

"They never crossed your mind," Josie teased. "Certainly, they weren't the *first* thing you asked about when you walked through my door."

Eve huffed in annoyance. "Forget I asked."

"Why can't you just admit you like them?"

Eve gave her a harsh look before returning her attention to her laptop.

"They're getting bigger," Josie said.

"I noticed."

"They're going to outgrow that box soon. Also...I named them." She dangled the bait, waiting for Eve to bite.

After a moment, she glanced up from her laptop. "And?"

"Our winning bidder is a Broadway aficionado. So we have Phantom the black kitten, Pippin the gray tabby, the gray-and-white kitten is Hamilton, and our little girl, the white one, is Blanche."

Eve's lips pursed, twisting slightly to one side, and then she smiled, a real smile that seemed to light up her whole face. "Blanche Dubois. I love *A Streetcar Named Desire*. Those are all great names, actually. Did you raise a lot of money?"

"About three hundred dollars. It should cover their first round of vaccines."

"Good."

"You're late today," Josie said, trying not to let on that she'd been watching the door for Eve's arrival all afternoon.

"I went to the office to check in with some of my other clients and start typing up my marketing plan for you. I really only stopped by to go over the schedule for the next week with you and pick up the kittens."

"Oh." Josie tapped her fingers against the bar. "You're finished observing me, then?"

Eve's gaze dropped to Josie's hands. "Yes."

"So what's next?"

"I'll bring the camera crew with me tomorrow afternoon before you open, and we'll shoot our meeting where I present my makeover plan for Swanson's to you. You'll remain open for business as usual through the weekend, and on Monday we'll begin our reno work. We'll shoot the makeover reveal on Thursday, and you'll have your grand reopening on Friday." As Eve rattled off this information, her gaze returned to the laptop in front of her.

"Wow, that's...a lot. And so soon." Josie had seen all these dates when she signed the contract, but it felt a lot more real now that she realized how quickly it was all going to happen. Eve would present her plan tomorrow. Josie's palms began to sweat.

"That's how the show works," Eve said.

"And you can't give me even the slightest idea of what you're going to do?"

"Sorry." Eve glanced up, and then she sighed. "But you have my word that everything I've done is with your best interest at heart, and Swanson's."

"Your idea of what's best may be very different from mine."

Eve's expression cooled, lips drawing into a slight frown. "You asked for this, Josie. You begged for it, as I recall."

"I did." She blew out a breath. "And I'm so grateful to you for taking me on. I'm sorry for being so neurotic about it. I just...this bar means a lot to me, that's all."

"I know that," Eve said. "You may find my ideas rather unexpected, at least at first, but I don't think you'll dislike them."

"Okay." Josie moved down to greet a couple who'd just taken seats at the bar. The next time she glanced in Eve's direction, her seat was empty.

She's gone upstairs to check on the kittens...the kittens she secretly cares about.

Josie grinned at the thought. A few minutes later, though, Eve was back...with the box of kittens. She set them on the bar as she packed up her laptop. Wow, she really had just stopped in to go over the schedule with Josie. And she was more than a little disappointed Eve was heading out already. Apparently, she'd gotten pretty used to her company over the last few days.

"Leaving so soon?"

Eve nodded, glancing over her shoulder at Josie. "It'll be easier to finish typing up my report at home. The hair-and-makeup team will be here tomorrow at one to get you ready, and I'll see you around two to shoot our segment."

Josie swallowed. The big reveal. "See you then."

JOSIE WOKE JUST past eight on Friday morning, still desperately tired after a late night in the bar, but too wired to sleep. She tossed and turned as her brain spun out of control, imagining all the potential scenarios that could go down later, from décor she hated to a rebranding of the bar that she wanted nothing to do with.

But, as Eve had so eloquently reminded her, she'd asked for this. Begged for it. And she would do her best to accept and be grateful for whatever Eve gave her. Eve was good at this, after all. The businesses she helped on *Do Over* almost always went on to achieve success...as long as their owners didn't screw up after she'd left.

Giving up on sleep, Josie climbed out of bed and fixed herself a cup of coffee, which she brought with her to the rooftop patio. It was peaceful up here, especially at this hour. She found a chair that was relatively clean and sat, closing her eyes. She used to come up here all the time with her dad. The rooftop had only been open to customers on the weekend, so on weekday afternoons, she would sometimes bring her homework and sit in the sunshine.

Her dad would sit with her and read a book or help with her homework. Sometimes, they'd put their feet up on the railing and just talk. They'd shared so many great conversations. In fact, she'd been sitting right here when she came out to him. He'd sat in silence long enough for her to start to panic before he'd crushed her against him in a massive hug and told her he'd always love her, no matter what.

She swallowed past the tears that threatened at the memory, taking a hearty sip of her coffee. It was so unfair that he'd been taken from her so soon, that she'd lost both of her parents so young. Sometimes, life was just cruel.

"I'm doing this for you, Dad," she whispered, looking around at the wasteland of discarded furniture around her, so different from the pristine rooftop in her memory. "To bring Swanson's back to what it was when you were here."

She kept that thought at the forefront of her mind as she got ready for her day. And she was still holding on to it when Eve arrived that afternoon with her camera crew in tow. She stood in the doorway, dressed in a pale pink silk shirt and white pants, looking so chic, so *hot*, Josie all but forgot how to speak.

"Ready?" Eve asked, setting a folder on the bar between them.

Josie glanced at it and then back at Eve. "Yeah, I...I guess."

Eve's gaze searched her face. "I see you've already sat with hair and makeup."

Josie scoffed, trying to stifle the nervous laughter that threatened to bubble out of her. The combination of her lack of sleep, the camera crew currently assembling in the bar, the folder resting in front of her, and her attraction to Eve was getting to her. "Should I be offended by that observation?"

She expected Eve to have little patience for her fragile ego, to come back with a curt response, but to her surprise, Eve very pointedly dropped her gaze to Josie's black tee and lilac pants before returning to her face. "Not at all. You always look good. I merely meant that you're obviously already wearing camera-ready makeup."

"Oh."

Eve's blouse strained slightly over her breasts, revealing enough cleavage to completely scramble Josie's brain. So much so that it took her entirely too long to realize she was staring. She yanked her gaze back to Eve's face, but the intensity in her eyes made it clear she'd seen Josie staring... and she liked it.

"You look good too," Josie said, sounding slightly breathless. They were flirting, definitely flirting, and her heart was about to beat its way out of her chest.

"I..." Eve looked down at her hands, which were clenched around the edges of the folder. She drew in a deep breath, uncharacteristically flustered.

"Where are the kittens?" Josie blurted.

"At the office with my intern."

"Oh." Josie gulped as the camera crew moved in, adjusting their positions and calling out instructions.

Eve opened her mouth, then seemed to falter, glancing down at the folder again and back at Josie. "I need to speak to you for a minute in private."

"What?" Josie's head was starting to spin. What was happening? Was Eve about to throw caution to the wind and kiss her? Of all possible moments, right now all Josie wanted was to find out what she'd planned for Swanson's.

"We'll be right back," Eve called to her crew as she led Josie down the hall to her office. Once they were both inside, Eve shut the door, turning to face Josie. "I asked my producer to let me give you a heads-up about this, and she... well, she wants your reaction on camera, but I can't do it. I have to follow my conscience. Which means..." She drifted off, giving Josie a somewhat desperate look.

"What?" Why did her voice sound so squeaky? What was Eve trying to say? Josie had never seen her look so rattled, and it was unnerving.

Eve pressed a hand to her brow, pacing from one end of the office to the other. "I think I need to start at the beginning."

Josie gulped, pulse skyrocketing from the situation and her proximity to Eve. "You're starting to freak me out."

Eve turned to face her, calm veneer back in place. "Okay, to make a long story short, my research showed something you probably already know. You've lost the majority of your customers to several newer, trendier bars that have opened in the neighborhood, most notably the gastropub down the street."

"Yes," Josie confirmed. "I suspected as much."

"Swanson's has become somewhat of a dinosaur. Your aesthetic is dated, you're one of the only bars in the area that doesn't also serve food, and you're suffering for it."

Josie winced. It hurt to hear, but she'd expected this. So why was Eve breaking protocol to tell it to her in private? "Okay."

"I also noticed something else," Eve said, and the hesitance in her eyes made it clear she was about to answer Josie's question. "And it has to do with your identity, so I'm breaking the rules here and giving you the chance to tell me to fuck off if you feel like I've overstepped."

"Okay." Josie gripped the back of the chair in front of her. What in the world...

"New York City has one of the most prominent LGBT

communities in the world," Eve said, and the bottom dropped out of Josie's stomach. "On any given night, approximately half of your customers belong to that community, largely because you've created such an inclusive space here."

"Eve..." Josie was already shaking her head. How *dare* she...

"Let me finish," Eve interrupted. "There isn't a gay bar within a ten-block radius. You have a unique opportunity to reposition yourself, to cater to a different demographic, a demographic you're already serving on a smaller scale. This is your niche, Josie. I can make you *shine*."

"No," she gasped, tears swimming across her vision. A gay bar? It was too much. She straightened, crossing her arms over her chest. "But I can't say no, can I? Because I signed your stupid contract. I gave you permission to do this to me, to do anything you want."

Eve's chin went up, brown eyes flashing. "I just told you I was giving you the chance to say no. I've come up with a detailed plan for renaming, remodeling, and rebranding the bar. We can proceed with my plans, minus the gay-bar aspect, if that's what you want."

"It's not what my dad would have wanted."

"Oh." Some of the fight went out of Eve's stance. "I'm sorry he wasn't supportive."

"No, he was," Josie said. "He was totally supportive."

Eve's eyebrows lifted. "Then I don't understand the problem."

"His parents—my grandparents—opened Swanson's forty years ago. This is their legacy. Swanson's is named after them, Eve. To change that, and to make it a gay bar? It just... it feels like you're undoing everything they worked so hard for."

"To be frank, you need to make drastic changes if you want to stay in business," Eve said, tone edged in steel.

Josie looked down at her desk, eyes blurring. "I guess I just wanted you to give me a pretty makeover and some business tips, and everything would go back to normal."

"That wouldn't be enough," Eve said softly. "You're captaining a sinking ship here, and you know it as well as I do."

Josie squeezed her eyes shut, tears rolling over her cheeks. "You made me cry, just like you do on every episode, but the cameras aren't even here to film it."

"A fact my producer will be most upset about."

"And you?" She opened her eyes, meeting Eve's gaze.

She stared back, unflinching as ever. "I told you I never intend to make anyone cry."

"Can I ask you to give me time to think it over?"

Eve's jaw clenched. "We're on an extremely tight schedule to fit you into season two. I can't postpone renovations, which will begin on Monday, but I could reschedule our interview to take place that morning and give you the weekend to make your decision."

"Okay." She nodded. "Thank you."

Eve turned, opening the door briskly. "I'll see you on Monday, then."

10

Eve needed a drink. Or, more likely, she needed anything *but* a drink, because the last thing she wanted to think about as she walked into her apartment that night was Josie. Or Swanson's. Or bars. Or anything to do with any of it.

She'd pissed off her entire team by rescheduling Josie's interview. If this segment fell through, she could kiss season three goodbye. And she'd worked hard for this, dammit. She loved *Do Over*, and she was good at her job. It kept her busy, fulfilled the restlessness inside her, and allowed her to afford this apartment.

The day she moved in, she felt like she'd made it. She'd arrived. Now, sometimes, especially on nights like these, it felt empty. Maybe that was the problem. She was craving human companionship tonight, the touch of another person. Usually, she preferred to be alone at the end of the day, but she had needs just like any other woman.

Unfortunately, her needs would have to wait, because there was a box of hungry kittens waiting for her. Heaving a sigh, she went into her bedroom to change, because wiping kitten butts in white pants seemed like a recipe for disaster. She resisted the urge to go straight for her pajamas, though, because she wasn't entirely sure she was in for the night. That empty, restless feeling lurking inside her would keep her up all night if she didn't attempt to tame it. Maybe dinner alone at one of her favorite restaurants would do the trick. She put on a pair of jeans and headed for the kitchen.

She mixed formula and sat on the couch, lifting the gray-and-white kitten into her lap. "Hamilton," she murmured as she positioned him for his bottle. She would never admit it to Josie, but it was nice to have names for them. Even she had grown weary of calling them by the color of their fur. And she liked their theater-inspired names.

Hamilton stared up at her through baby-blue eyes after he'd finished his bottle. His gray-striped head reminded her of the silly wigs men had worn back in his namesake's day, and it made her smile. She took care of his bathroom needs and then rubbed him for a minute, enjoying the feel of his soft fur beneath her fingers. She held him up in front of her face. "Don't tell anyone I said this, but you're pretty cute."

He meowed loudly, wriggling in her hands, so she put him back in the box. Hamilton crawled awkwardly across the blanket toward the stuffed animal that served as their substitute mother. Josie was right, they were going to need a bigger box soon. What would Eve do with them then? She couldn't keep a fucking playpen in her office.

She reached for the next kitten, Pippin, since he happened to be awake. She fed and cleaned him and then did the same for Phantom. Blanche, as usual, was last, snoozing away as Eve cared for her brothers.

"Time to wake up," Eve said as she reached for the white kitten. Blanche's meow was shrill as Eve lifted her, paws flailing. She settled the kitten in her lap and offered her the bottle. Blanche was still the smallest, but she was holding her own these days, guzzling hungrily from the bottle, paws kneading Eve's fingers as she drank.

She didn't look so fragile anymore, blinking up at Eve after she'd finished her meal. Now that her ears had lifted and her eyes opened, she looked much more like a tiny cat than the scrawny furball Eve had pulled out of a trash can nine days ago.

"Hi, Blanche," she said, giving her belly a rub as the kitten rolled across Eve's knees. As Blanche crawled over her legs, Eve leaned against the couch, surprised to realize she felt calmer now. Maybe it was good that the kittens kept her so busy. Or, at the very least, it wasn't all bad.

Still, she was hungry, and her options here at home were slim. She could run out and get something to eat and be back home before they needed their next feeding. They could go three hours without her now, thank God. Decision made, she placed Blanche in the box with her brothers.

Standing, Eve grabbed her purse and headed for the door. How was Josie feeling about things tonight? Had she decided to give Eve's ideas a chance? She had an uncomfortable feeling that, left to her own devices, Josie would talk herself out of it. She would convince herself to take the easy way out and just give the bar a makeover without fully embracing the vision Eve had created for her.

Surely, that was the reason Eve found herself boarding the F train toward Brooklyn. Maybe now that Josie had had a chance to calm down, she'd listen to reason, because Eve truly did have her best interests at heart.

Thirty minutes later, she pulled open the bar's front door and stepped inside. The noise hit her first, raucous voices that set her nerves on edge. Swanson's was busier than she remembered it being last Friday night, probably because of the buzz around the filming of the show. She'd seen it happen before.

This is such a bad idea. Leave now before she sees you.

But it was too late. Josie glanced toward the door, and their eyes locked. Eve walked toward her, stopping at an open space at the bar, hands resting on its smooth surface.

"I didn't expect to see you tonight," Josie said, her expression unreadable.

"I didn't expect to be here," Eve countered, fighting the unsettled feeling in her gut that said she'd made a horrible mistake. "I just thought maybe we should talk a little more about my vision for the bar."

"Hmm." Josie stared at her, lips twisted, fingers drumming against the bar. "I told you I'd think about it, and I've been thinking."

"I'm glad to hear that."

"Can I ask you a question, though?" Josie leaned closer, the overhead lights bringing out the green tones in her hazel eyes. "Since we're already breaking the rules. What's the new name? You know, for the bar?"

Eve resisted the urge to lean back, to restore an appropriate amount of space between them. "Dragonfly."

Josie's eyes widened, her mouth forming a tiny O of surprise.

"Like your tattoo, and for similar reasons. It can symbolize a transformation for Swanson's as well, a new start and a new image while we position you to a new clientele." She sucked in a breath. "I hope you don't hate it." Renaming a client's business without consulting them could be a tricky business, and it wasn't something she did lightly...or often.

"I don't hate it," Josie said quietly, her voice almost lost to the din of the bar.

"Those aren't your customers, Josie." Eve inclined her head toward a rowdy group of men, barely old enough to drink. "They drink beer, which earns you a smaller profit than liquor. They make a lot of noise and take up a lot of space. *Those* are your customers." She indicated a pair of women at one of the tables along the far wall, sipping martinis and leaning in close. "Dragonfly will have a more upscale vibe than Swanson's, soft lighting, smooth music, a custom cocktail list."

"Oh." Josie turned her head, looking around the bar as if trying to see the picture Eve was painting for her.

"We'll open the rooftop on weekends during the summer. Imagine strings of white lights twinkling against the backdrop of the city, high-topped tables where couples or groups of friends can gather with their favorite cocktails. In fact, my homework for you is to come up with at least one signature drink for your new menu, something served only here."

Josie closed her eyes, breathing deeply, lashes—still heavy with the makeup Eve's team had applied earlier—fluttering against her cheeks. When she opened them again, her expression was distant. "It's like an entirely different bar, Eve."

"That's kind of the point, isn't it?"

"Maybe." Josie looked at two middle-aged men in jeans and T-shirts a few stools down. "What about my regulars? Dougie and Sal have been coming here every night after work for as long as I can remember. They'd never step foot in a gay bar."

"And how many regulars like them do you have?"

"I don't know." Josie looked down at her hands. "A handful."

"You can't keep Swanson's open for a handful of people. Sometimes, you have to be willing to lose a few regulars to gain a new crowd."

Josie blinked, her eyes glossy. "That's really sad, and also...scary."

"I know, but don't let your fear hold you back from success."

Josie sighed, shaking her head.

The men at the end of the bar had gotten louder, good-natured banter giving way to an argument. Eve glanced at them, discomfort twisting inside her. This was exactly the problem with bars...too much noise, too much alcohol, drunk men heading out into the night, ramped up on alcohol and testosterone. At least here in the city, they were unlikely to get behind the wheel after they left.

Josie was watching them too, brow pinched in concern. As Eve's gaze swept the bar, she realized Josie was the only one behind it. "Where's Jason?" He usually tended bar with her on Friday and Saturday nights.

"On his dinner break," Josie replied. As they watched, one man shoved another, and a barstool went flying. "Dammit. I'll be back."

"Be careful," Eve warned as Josie headed toward them, intensely uncomfortable with the idea of Josie breaking up a fight between six large, drunk men on her own. The other customers in Swanson's had all turned to stare, some of them looking annoyed, others fearful. Eve pulled out her cell phone, placing it beneath her palm, ready to dial the police if the need arose.

"You have no idea what you're talking about," the man who'd been shoved roared, fists balling for a fight.

"No?" the man who'd shoved him responded.

"You guys need to settle down or take this outside," Josie said calmly, stepping between them, hands outstretched to keep them apart.

"The hell I will," the first man yelled, and then he punched the man who'd shoved him. Someone screamed. The rest of the group started yelling, fists flying as everyone seemed to pick sides and join the melee. And there was Josie in the middle of it all, still bravely trying to break it up.

Eve lifted her phone and dialed 911 to report the bar fight. "There's only one female bartender on staff at the moment," she told the dispatcher, feeling somehow as if she was betraying Josie with the admission, "and a half dozen large, drunk men fighting."

She hung up and approached the group, hoping to lend Josie a hand if possible. Eve might be small in stature, but she generally made up for it in attitude. As she reached them, one of the men staggered backward, knocking into Josie, who fell to her knees.

"Enough," Eve yelled, causing several heads to swivel in her direction. She extended a hand to Josie, helping her to her feet. "You guys need to knock it off. Now."

In the pause that followed, a few members of the group seemed to have second thoughts and jumped in to restrain the two men who had initiated the fight. Blood dripped from the first man's nose, staining the front of his T-shirt.

"Fucking asshole." He lunged forward, attempting to get at his opponent.

"That's rich, coming from you," the other man sneered.

Eve resisted the urge to roll her eyes at the ridiculous display of testosterone. She turned to Josie. "You okay?"

Josie nodded, but her face was pale, eyes glassy. Eve didn't think she was hurt, probably just shaken, not that Eve could blame her. Her own pulse was racing, her palms slick. She wasn't sure whether to mention that she'd called the police. It might encourage them to move outside, or it might escalate things. Eve didn't have much experience handling disorderly men. This was Josie's bar, and she should probably follow her lead.

"That's enough," Josie told them. "I'm calling individual cabs for all of you."

The first man broke free from the man who'd been restraining him, and fists started flying again. Eve gripped Josie's wrist, pulling her out of the way. Luckily, two NYPD officers entered Swanson's at the same time, and within minutes, everyone involved had been rounded up and escorted outside.

Jason returned from his dinner break and took over behind the bar while Josie wrapped things up with the police. Eve—still not quite sure why she was even here—ordered a beer and sat at the bar, waiting for Josie to come back inside so she could at least say goodbye before she left. But Josie didn't come back. And by the time Eve had finished her beer, she was starting to worry.

"Do you know where Josie is?" she asked Jason.

He shook his head. "I think she needed to clear her head after the commotion. I'm sure she'll be back in a minute."

Eve nodded. She slid off her stool and went down the hall to Josie's office, but it was empty. On a hunch, she checked the door at the end of the hall—the one leading to the roof—and found it unlocked. She stepped through and pulled it shut behind her, heels echoing against the wood as she climbed to the top.

Sure enough, Josie stood silhouetted against the skyline, arms wrapped around herself. Eve walked up behind her, grateful for the click of her heels to announce her presence.

She came to stand beside Josie, resting her hands on the railing as she glanced over at her. "You okay?"

Josie nodded, but her mascara was smudged, betraying her answer.

"Does that happen often?" Eve asked. "Bar fights?"

"No," Josie said. "Only a handful of times that I can remember in all my years here."

"Well, thank goodness for that."

"That was how it started," Josie said, her voice small. "The night my dad died."

Oh hell. She'd completely forgotten that Josie's dad was killed in a bar fight right here in Swanson's. No wonder she was so upset. "I'm sorry."

"I was sitting at the bar, about where you were sitting tonight. We had just made plans to see a movie together the next day."

"You were there?" Eve's stomach pitched as if the floor had just dropped out from beneath her.

Josie nodded. "He walked over to break it up, and someone pulled a gun, and..."

"Oh, Jesus." Eve tugged at her hand, pulling her in for a hug. "That's a hell of a thing."

Josie wrapped her arms around her, holding tightly to Eve, and she realized in a rush that *this* was what she'd come to Swanson's tonight looking for. She'd craved the touch of another human, but not any human, just the one currently wrapped in her arms, breath coming in warm gusts against her neck, hands fisted in the back of her blouse. She closed her eyes, breathing in the feeling, absorbing it, memorizing it.

"Thanks for having my back down there," Josie whispered.

"Of course." She inhaled the scent of Josie's shampoo,

something light and fruity. "You can't do this on your own anymore."

"I know." Josie drew back, staring at Eve in the darkness, arms still clasped around her. The glow of the city sparkled in her eyes and reflected the sheen of her lips.

Eve's heart was racing, even faster than it had downstairs as she'd attempted to control a half dozen drunk men. She felt just as drunk, just as out of control as her chin tipped forward, breath catching in her throat as Josie's lips crashed into hers.

She pressed forward, deepening the kiss, tongue sliding into Josie's mouth as her hands slid into the back pockets of her jeans, anchoring them together. Heat flooded her system, pulse pounding, skin tingling, desire bursting to life inside her like a hungry beast after a long hibernation. Josie nipped at her bottom lip, and *fuck*.

Eve swayed forward, hips bumping into Josie's, breasts pressed together as they kissed. Josie's hands slid up her back and into her hair, tugging gently as her tongue tangled with Eve's. This woman. God, this woman...

"You taste like beer," Josie murmured, breath feathering over Eve's cheeks, hot and damp, lighting every inch of her on fire. "God, Eve, I've been thinking about this since the first moment I met you."

"Mm, same." She rested her forehead against Josie's as she caught her breath, realizing in some distant, rational part of her brain that she should put a stop to this, but surely she could indulge for just another moment, because *God*, she couldn't remember the last time she'd felt this good, this alive, this utterly consumed with another person.

She pressed her lips to Josie's, and they were kissing again. Her hands slipped beneath Josie's shirt, sliding over her smooth, warm skin, eliciting a soft moan against her lips. "You feel so good," she whispered, skimming her fingers up Josie's spine.

In response, Josie tugged at Eve's blouse, untucking it from her jeans so that her hands could do some roaming of their own. She cupped Eve's breasts over her bra, thumbs brushing against her nipples, intensifying the need pulsing inside her until it was almost overwhelming.

"Lace under silk?" Josie gasped. "You really are trying to kill me."

"Josie..."

"It's okay. My heart's still beating." Josie gripped one of Eve's hands and moved it over her left breast so she could feel her heart pounding beneath her palm.

"We can't do this." Eve had to force the words past her lips as her body screamed for more, more, more. *Don't stop. Please don't stop.*

"Shh," Josie whispered, smiling against her lips. "Don't overthink this. Just kiss me."

"I can't," she managed, even as her lips met Josie's for another blistering kiss. "We can't. You signed a contract with the network. I could lose my job."

"Oh." Josie's hands, which had been toying with the waistband of Eve's jeans, stilled as she lifted her head to meet her eyes. "It's in the contract?"

She nodded, sliding her hand out from under Josie's shirt and instead reaching up to tuck a lock of turquoise hair behind her ear. "I'm bound by a code of conduct. I'm not technically supposed to have any contact with you outside of work until filming is complete."

"That's only next Friday," Josie said, not making any effort to pull away.

"Yes."

"So, after that..." Josie's arms tightened around her.

"We'll see," she hedged, because Josie was almost certainly looking for more out of their relationship than Eve was. But she'd cross that bridge when—and if—they got to it.

"Since we're already here, I don't see any harm in kissing just a little bit more," Josie said as her lips roamed over Eve's neck, licking and sucking, each stroke of her tongue sending bolts of fire through Eve's core.

"No harm," she echoed, helpless to pull away, completely lost to Josie's touch.

"Eve," she murmured as her tongue traced circles over a tender spot on her neck.

"Yes?" she gasped, hips arching against Josie's.

"Tell me why you hate bars."

And there was the metaphorical bucket of water she'd needed. Reality washed over Eve in a harsh, cold wave, and she shuddered, pulling free of Josie's grasp. "Not tonight."

"Yes, tonight." Josie gripped her hands. "We may not get another moment like this. Please."

Eve wrapped her arms around herself, acknowledging the truth of Josie's words. She didn't owe her this, didn't owe her anything, but in this moment, lips swollen and pulse racing from their kisses, it felt like she did. If Josie had asked for anything else, Eve would have given it to her in a heartbeat, but she'd asked for the one thing Eve held closest to her heart. "I..."

"Please," she whispered, brushing a hand over Eve's cheek.

She cleared her throat, tasting the bitter truth on her tongue. "It's because my wife was killed by a drunk driver."

11

Josie reeled as Eve's words registered. Of all the things she might say, Josie had never imagined anything as horrible, as painful, or as personal. She stepped forward, pulling Eve into her arms. "Eve...I am so sorry."

Eve was stiff against her, as cold as she'd been hot moments before. "The driver was on his way home from a bar where he'd been overserved. He never should have been behind the wheel."

"No, he shouldn't," Josie agreed. "That's...it's awful."

"I don't talk about it," Eve said, pulling free to walk to the railing. "It happened a very long time ago."

"Can't have been *that* long," Josie said gently. Eve was only a few years older than she was. A widow. Jesus Christ. That was tragic. And unexpected. She tried to imagine a young, happily married Eve. What had her life been like then? Had her wife's death caused her to turn into the icy workaholic that Josie had first met last week, or had she always been this way?

"Long enough," Eve responded, but her voice cracked

just slightly, and it was all Josie could do not to hug her again, to pull her close and never let her go.

"I had no idea."

"Of course you didn't," Eve said, sounding more like herself now. "No one does. And I'd appreciate it if you'd keep it to yourself."

"Yeah, of course."

Eve pressed a hand against the small of her back, turning away. *An old injury*, she'd told Josie.

"You were in the car with her," she whispered.

"I was." She glanced at Josie and sighed, as if resigning herself to tell the rest of the story. "I fractured my back, and they had to fuse two of my vertebrae together to stabilize it."

"Jesus," Josie whispered.

"It's fine," Eve said with a slight shake of her head.

"No, it's not."

Eve looked down at her hands. "Lisa was a teacher, but she tended bar part-time too. If you want the truth, *that's* the reason I avoid bars now. They stir up a lot of memories for me, nights when I hung out with Lisa while she worked."

Eve's wife was a bartender.

"That makes a lot of sense," Josie said.

"We were young, and we needed the extra cash. I had insisted she quit, because..." She drew in a deep, shaky breath, turning her face away from Josie.

Josie walked up behind her, leaning into her, offering silent support.

"That night, I had a few beers while Lisa worked, so she drove us home. We were T-boned on the driver's side. She died in the ambulance on the way to the hospital." Eve spoke in a monotone, her voice gone hoarse.

"I'm *so* sorry. I really thought, well, I don't know what I thought you were going to tell me, but it wasn't this. But I really appreciate you trusting me with it, and I'm so sorry for everything you've been through."

Eve kept her back turned. "Now you know."

"Thank you," she whispered into the soft depths of Eve's hair.

She nodded, tension radiating off her like a force field slowly pushing Josie away.

"Hey." She tugged at Eve's hand, not liking the wall she felt going up between them after everything they'd shared.

"I need to go home," Eve said, spinning on her heel and striding toward the door that led downstairs.

"Wait," Josie called, hurrying after her. "Eve, wait a damn minute."

She paused at the door, looking over her shoulder at Josie. Her eyes were dry, but Josie saw the raw emotion, the pain still lurking in their dark depths. She closed the distance between them and pulled Eve into her arms, squeezing her tight. Eve softened in her embrace, just for a moment, before pulling away.

"I left the kittens in my apartment," she said. "I didn't plan to be out this long."

"Okay." Josie brought her lips to Eve's, needing to end on something good, to feel the heat and the connection between them one last time before they said good night. Eve kissed her back, lips warm and seeking, as if she needed this moment as much as Josie did. "Night."

"Good night." Eve slipped through the door.

Josie let her go, deciding to stay up here another minute to collect herself before she went back down to the bar. She pressed her fingertips against her lips as she gazed out at the Manhattan skyline gleaming in the distance. *Holy shit.* That was one of the hottest kisses of her life, the kind of kiss she wanted to drown in forever and had every cell in her body screaming for more. Who knew the frosty Eve could light her on fire like that?

Josie knew. She'd known almost from the moment they met. She'd sensed a current running between them and the fire burning behind Eve's cool veneer. That woman had so many layers, Josie could spend a lifetime unwrapping her and maybe never reach her core. And yet, she'd give anything for the chance to try, if only Eve would let her.

ON SATURDAY, Josie opened Swanson's for business as usual, except...nothing felt like business as usual. And not just because she was still reliving her rooftop kiss with Eve. It was more like she was seeing her bar through a new lens. She watched a rowdy group of twenty-something guys in the back, telling crude jokes over spilled beer.

Those aren't your customers, Eve had told her before the fight broke out last night. Was she right? Josie panned her gaze around Swanson's, trying to imagine it as Eve had painted it for her, an upscale bar with soft lighting and fancy cocktails.

A gay bar.

Was that what Josie wanted? She didn't *not* want it. In fact, the longer she stood here, the more she thought it might be exactly what she wanted. Dragonfly. It was personal and meaningful. How did Eve know her so well in such a short time? Was she really that good at her job or did some of it have to do with the connection between them?

Maybe a little of both.

By the time Josie locked up the bar that night, she knew she would say yes. She was ready to put her future squarely in Eve's hands. Eve's wonderfully soft, capable hands. And yes, Josie really needed to get a grip, at least until filming wrapped next Friday...

Even though it was four in the morning and Eve was no doubt asleep, Josie sent her a quick text before she lost her nerve. *I'll do it. All of it. (and I'm sad there's not a dragonfly emoji, but pretend I attached one.)*

And then she went to bed. When she woke just before noon on Sunday, Eve's name gleamed on her screen.

Good. I'll see you tomorrow morning at 10 for the taping.

Right, then. Josie gulped at the finality of it all. Today was Swanson's last day in business. She went through the day in a daze, telling as many of her regulars as she could about the upcoming changes to the bar. By the looks on their faces, she didn't think she'd see Sal or Dougie again, which she'd already known but was still unspeakably sad about. They both hugged her and wished her well on their way out the door.

When she closed that night, she put out a sign explaining that the bar would be closed until its relaunch on Friday. A wave of intense nostalgia washed over her as she walked through the darkened bar on the way to her apartment. Swanson's as she'd known it, as her dad had known it and his parents before him, would cease to exist after tonight.

"I hope you would approve of what I've done, Dad," she whispered into the empty bar, sliding her hands over the weathered counter. "I think you would, because I think mostly you wanted me to be happy, but it's a big change."

So big, she was apparently talking to herself. She smiled, tapping her knuckles against the wood. Swanson's was evolving, much like Josie herself, symbolized by the dragonfly on her shoulder and soon to be on the sign over the door.

She went upstairs and climbed into bed, expecting to fall straight to sleep. She'd made peace with this. She was ready to embrace the changes she'd put into motion. But as she lay in her darkened bedroom with Nigel curled over her feet, her mind spun endlessly with a combination of nerves and excitement.

She finally dozed off as the sun rose outside her window, sleeping for a pitiful few hours before her alarm went off to rouse her for the day.

"This is it," she whispered to Nigel as he rubbed his face against hers, purring loudly. Eve and her crew would be here in a few hours to tape their segment, and then Josie had the rest of the week off. She needed to make herself scarce and let the *Do Over* team do their thing until the grand reopening at the end of the week.

Eve.

Josie's heart beat faster at the thought of seeing her again. She let that energy fuel her as she climbed out of bed, showered, and dressed. She blew her hair out straight and put a few loose waves in it with the curling iron, because hey, she was going to be on TV. And if she happened to look good for Eve at the same time, that was just an added bonus.

The hair and makeup team arrived at nine, further sculpting her hair and applying the extra makeup she'd need to go before the cameras. How did people do this every day? The false lashes made her want to claw at her eyes, but when she looked at herself in the mirror, she had to admit the end result was worth the discomfort...at least for today.

Tomorrow, she'd go back to her minimalist makeup and messy hair, but right now, she was ready for her moment in the spotlight. In fact, she was feeling one hundred percent more confident about her interview with Eve than she had been on Friday. And speaking of Eve, she pushed through the front door promptly at ten, box of kittens in her arms.

Josie met her halfway to take them from her. She caught Eve's eye, smiling. "Hi."

"Hello." Eve wore a black knit dress, accented by a long silver necklace and matching earrings, a warning flashing in her eyes.

As if Josie had forgotten. They couldn't mention Friday night, at least not while the crew was around. Still, she took a long moment to soak in the sight of Eve, looking good enough to eat in that dress and her camera-ready makeup, smelling like some kind of expensive perfume that made Josie want to press her face to Eve's neck and just breathe her in. Eve cleared her throat, and Josie realized she'd been staring...probably too long. Definitely too long. She dropped her gaze to the box of kittens in her arms. "Oh my God, wow. They've grown."

Four pairs of baby-blue eyes stared back, alert and curious. Phantom, Pippin, Hamilton, and Blanche, their little theater kittens.

"They have," Eve agreed. "Not surprising, considering how much they've been eating."

"I'll take them upstairs," Josie said, hoping Eve would follow so she could have a moment alone with her, but Eve merely nodded before walking over to talk to a member of the film crew.

Fine. She could act like nothing had happened, but she had opened up to Josie on Friday night. She'd held Eve in her arms, had kissed her until she moaned and pulled at Josie's clothes in desperation. They might not talk about it, but they would both be thinking about it. There was *no way* Eve wasn't thinking about it, no matter how cool and calm she looked right now.

So Josie took the kittens upstairs to her apartment. She set the box in its usual spot in her living room, pausing for a moment to watch them. Now that they were no longer being jostled around in transit, they were in the process of snuggling in an adorable pile to go back to sleep. According to the schedule taped to the side of the box, Eve had fed them an hour ago.

"We've got to figure out a new arrangement for you guys," Josie murmured, reaching in to rub them as they got settled. They needed a bigger living space. Soon, they'd need a litter box and food and water bowls. They couldn't keep traveling the city with Eve in this box.

Nigel strolled through the room, twining himself around Josie's legs as if to remind her of his presence. She reached down to rub him.

The distinctive sound of heels on the stairs met her ears, and she turned just as Eve appeared in the doorway. She stopped there, leaning one hip against the doorframe, expression casual. "I just wanted to remind you to act surprised when we shoot our segment downstairs, as if you're hearing it all for the first time."

"I know," Josie told her. "I'm not much of an actress, but I'm sure I can manage to look surprised."

"Okay." Eve turned as if to go.

"Wait." Josie closed the distance between them in several quick steps, not even sure what she was going to say, but once she was standing in front of her, she realized she'd just needed to feel the connection that ran between them whenever they stood this close. It hummed through her, causing goose bumps to pebble her skin as she looked into Eve's eyes. "You can leave them here this week."

"What?" Eve's gaze dropped to Josie's lips.

"The kittens. Swanson's is going to be closed all week, so

I should have plenty of time to look after them. I need to get them set up in a bigger space anyway, and this way, I can make a new YouTube video about them too."

"Oh," Eve said, glancing over Josie's shoulder at the box of kittens. "Okay."

"You know, for someone who endlessly harassed me about taking them off your hands, you don't seem all that excited that I'm finally able to help," Josie teased, reaching out to thread her fingers through Eve's.

Eve's chin went up, a muscle in her jaw clenching. "Believe me, I am."

"You won't miss them even a tiny bit?" Josie gave her fingers a squeeze.

"I'll be so busy this week, I'm not sure how I would have managed them anyway," Eve said, a deflection if Josie had ever heard one, but she'd never expected Eve to admit being fond of them. Josie didn't really need to hear her say the words. She'd seen the evidence for herself every time Eve interacted with them.

"Well, you can feel free to stop in and visit us any time."

"Mm." Eve's tongue slid over her bottom lip, pink against pink. Josie tugged at her hand where their fingers were still interlaced, and their bodies swayed together, so close she could feel Eve's warmth and see the pulse pounding in the hollow of her throat.

Heat bloomed in Josie's belly, radiating through her core. Her heart thumped wildly against her ribs, and she felt herself leaning closer, drawn to Eve almost against her own will, needing to feel her lips, even if just for a moment.

Eve inhaled sharply, pupils dilating as Josie dipped her head. "Don't," she whispered, just before Josie's lips met hers.

"Eve..."

"I told you, we can't do this." Eve's eyes slid shut, chest heaving, breasts dangerously close to Josie's on each inhale.

"Not today, anyway." Josie should take a step back. She knew she should, but she couldn't bring herself to do it.

"Not today," Eve echoed. And because she was apparently going to have to be the mature one in this situation, she turned, glancing over her shoulder at Josie as she headed for the stairs. "I'll see you downstairs for the taping."

12

"I'm confident we have a winning strategy in place for your relaunch," Eve told Josie as cameras filmed them from three different angles. She *was* confident. She never moved forward with a plan she wasn't one hundred percent sure about. But this was different, because Josie was different. Eve had let herself get personally involved, and now she genuinely cared if Josie liked her plan. More than that, she cared whether or not Josie succeeded.

"I trust you," Josie said, green flecks in her eyes gleaming with the reflection of the canopy lights in front of her. She was acting, putting on a show for the cameras, but there was something incredibly earnest in her expression at the same time. "And I'm really excited about your vision for Dragonfly."

"I'm glad to hear that."

"Cut," her director called. "That should do it. I think we've got everything we need."

Eve nodded, leaning over to put her notes away. Across

from her, Josie slumped against the bar, a silly grin on her face. "That was exhausting."

"Well, we aren't finished yet," Eve told her.

"We aren't?"

Eve shook her head, pulling a folder out of her briefcase. "I have some details to go over with you that didn't need to be included in the taped segment."

"Oh," Josie said, resting her elbows against the bar. "Okay."

"We've placed job listings for the new staff you'll need to hire, and I'd like you to help me interview people later this week. I've got details here for you, and as soon as we've narrowed down the candidates, I'll start setting up interviews."

"Staff. Right." Josie swallowed as she looked down at the paper Eve had slid toward her.

"Have you talked to Jason to see if he'd like to stay on at Dragonfly?"

Josie sighed. "Yes, and he doesn't, so we'll need to start from scratch with the bartending staff."

"All right." Eve jotted this down. "We'll cover costs for the first two weeks to help get you on your feet, but I'd recommend that you use your time off this week to get that loan I mentioned."

Josie nodded, her smile gone fragile.

"Remember, you have to spend money to earn it, okay?" Eve said. "We're also advertising on Facebook and other local media outlets to generate interest in your relaunch on Friday, and we'll continue to advertise through the end of the month to help you find your new audience."

"Advertising," Josie repeated, a wild look in her eye. "Eve, I don't know how to do any of this. Should I have been advertising the bar these last few years? I don't think my dad was doing that, but maybe he was."

"I've written up a detailed marketing plan for you, and we're going to go through it right now," Eve told her. "I'll be here to teach you everything you need to know, and remember, you can still call me after your relaunch. I work with all my clients for as long as they need me, and my services will still be free under our existing contract for two weeks after your relaunch. I want you to succeed, and I'm going to make sure you've got all the tools you need, okay?"

"Okay," Josie said, looking a lot calmer.

Eve spent the next few hours going over every detail of the marketing plan with Josie and laying out a checklist of things Josie should be working on this week while the bar was closed. By the time they'd finished, the film crew had packed up and left, and the renovation team had arrived. All around Eve and Josie, plastic was being rolled out.

"You have to stop giving out so many free drinks," Eve told her as they went over the budget.

Josie shook her head, turquoise curls bouncing. "I don't feel right taking money from my friends."

"This is a business, and you have to start running it like one."

"But—"

"Do you pay when you buy something in Kaia's store?" Eve countered.

"Well, she doesn't own it. She just works there, so if I don't pay..."

"She has to cover the cost for you, just like you do when you give her and Adam free drinks."

Josie frowned. "I don't want their money. I'm just happy to have their support."

"They're successful adults with full-time jobs. Take their money."

Josie slumped in her seat. "I'll think about it."

"Do that," Eve told her. "One last thing. I've noticed that you have a good relationship with several of the neighboring restaurants and often get takeout for yourself and your friends to eat here in the bar."

"Yeah," Josie said, brow wrinkling in confusion.

"As I mentioned once before, it was a significant disadvantage that Swanson's didn't serve food. So I propose that you approach your neighbors about creating an official arrangement. You would keep a list of approved restaurants' takeout menus here in the bar that your customers can order from and have delivered to enjoy while they're here. In return, you ask the restaurants to promote the deal on their end, maybe offer a discount if they send a customer your way."

Josie pursed her lips, tapping her fingertips against the bar. "Yeah, you know what? I love that idea."

"Perfect," Eve said. "You can get it set up this week before the relaunch."

"Okay."

"And also, get your cocktail menu ready. I want at least one signature drink on there, but I'll leave the particulars to you, as that's more your area of expertise than mine. If you can get it to me by Thursday morning, I'll have drink menus printed for the opening on Friday."

"Got it." Josie looked around at the crew already disassembling the bar. "Wow, this is all really happening, isn't it?"

"It sure is." Eve stood, resisting the urge to grimace at the pain in her back, not wanting to revisit her conversation with Josie on the roof the other night. "Get anything you want out of the bar now. I'll have my team put everything else in storage during renovations."

Josie nodded. She brought a crate out from the back room and began putting various liquor bottles inside it. "For creating signature drinks, not because I'm planning to go on a bender," she explained.

Eve nodded before picking up her briefcase. She went down the hall to Josie's office to keep herself out of the way while the crew worked. Today would mostly involve demolition. Swanson's old tables and chairs were already gone, and now the team was starting to tear down the bar itself. Josie poked her head in a few minutes later with what looked like half of Swanson's liquor supply in her arms before heading upstairs to her apartment.

Eve spent the rest of the day working quietly in Josie's office. When five o'clock rolled around and the crew headed out, she hesitated. Part of her wanted to go upstairs and check in with Josie. In fact, every part of her wanted to walk up those stairs. Which was exactly why she wasn't going to.

Because she didn't have any more business to cover with Josie today. She didn't even need to get the kittens, since Josie had offered to watch them for the week. Eve was free to go home, and that was exactly what she planned to do. She'd had precious little free time since pulling those kittens out of the trash a week and a half ago, and she was going to enjoy the hell out of a night to herself.

So she packed up and went out through the front door, locking it behind her. She rode the subway home, picking up a sandwich from the deli down the street on her way. In her apartment, she poured herself a glass of wine, put on some relaxing music, and settled on the couch to eat her dinner. Her mind kept calculating feeding schedules, wondering why the alarm on her phone hadn't gone off yet. But tonight, there were no kittens to feed, and the alarm wouldn't be going off until it was time to get up for work in the morning.

When she'd finished eating, she turned on her Kindle. She'd been trying to find time to finish reading this book for weeks. And if she caught her eyes wandering to the spot beside the couch where the box of kittens usually sat, it was only because she was a creature of habit. They had consumed so much of her life over the last ten days. It was only natural she'd feel somewhat off-balance tonight without them.

After successfully finishing her book, she did a few stretching exercises for her back. Then she poured herself a second glass of wine and went down the hall to take a bath. As she relaxed into the hot, scented water, her thoughts drifted to Josie. What was she doing on her night off? Was she feeding the kittens right now? Working on a signature drink for the bar? Taking advantage of the opportunity to go out with friends? A date, even?

Alone in her bathroom, Eve allowed herself to remember the heat of their kiss, the electric thrill of Josie's fingers beneath her shirt, the way Josie's tongue had painted an erotic landscape on her neck. Where else could she use that talented tongue? A warm ache spread between Eve's thighs.

This was a problem. She didn't make a habit of fantasizing about her clients, but her attraction to Josie had been there from the moment they met, long before she'd agreed to work with her, and now that they'd kissed...

It was almost inevitable that they'd wind up in bed together after filming wrapped. She could only hope it would be enough to burn out the flames simmering between them, because Eve never allowed herself more than one night, not anymore. Even one night with Josie might be more than her heart could handle.

She cleansed the thought from her mind, soaking in her scented bath until the water had cooled. Then she got out and wrapped herself in a robe, noticing it was only a few minutes past eight. What was she going to do with the rest of her evening?

She opened her laptop, debating whether to work for another hour or two, but there wasn't anything pressing waiting for her, and she'd vowed to enjoy this night off, after all. Self-care and all that. She checked her personal email and the social media accounts she never used, and then—refusing to let herself consider *why*—she opened YouTube.

Josie had uploaded three new videos since the night Eve first discovered her page. All three of them featured the theater kittens. The most recent video had been posted about an hour ago. She clicked Play. There was Josie, in the same outfit she'd worn for her *Do Over* segment that morning, a shimmery purple top and black jeans. She smiled for the camera, revealing her dimples, and Eve was so screwed where she was concerned. So fucking screwed.

"Hi guys! I wanted to give you an update on our theater kittens. Look how big they're getting." Josie held up Phantom, squirming and mewling loudly in her hands. "They're staying with me for the week, and I set them up in a playpen so they'd have more room to move around."

Josie turned the camera, showing the kittens in a clear-sided enclosure. They were crawling all over the place. *Holy shit.* They couldn't have changed that much since Eve left them that morning, which meant she simply hadn't been giving them the opportunity to move around like that. Her jaw clenched. They were better off with Josie. Eve had known this, had insisted on it from the start. Now, she had visual confirmation.

She closed her laptop and sat there for a long minute, disconcerted by the empty feeling in her chest. Once Dragonfly opened and Josie was running a fully staffed bar, she should be able to keep them. There was no reason for them to come back to Eve's apartment. And there was no reason for her to feel disappointed about this. No reason at all.

Josie paced her apartment on Tuesday morning, desperately wanting to see what was happening downstairs but knowing she wasn't supposed to interfere. Still, it was her bar, so maybe she should quit second-guessing herself and walk down there like she owned the place. No doubt, it was what Eve would do.

So she followed the sounds of power tools and the scent of fresh paint down the stairs. She found Eve seated at the desk in Josie's office, working on her laptop. "Morning."

Eve looked up, an almost-smile on her lips. "Couldn't stay away, hm?"

"Nope."

"Well, you're welcome to have a look, but there's really nothing to see yet."

"Thanks." Josie went down the hall and peered into the bar. The floor was covered with tarps, and several men on ladders were painting the walls with white primer. The area behind the counter had been stripped to its original exposed brick, which, as she'd seen on Eve's mockups, would remain visible in the new bar.

It would be an adjustment to get used to something other than Swanson's rich earth tones and heavy wood, but already the space felt lighter and brighter. She'd reserve judgment until she'd seen the finished product, but she was almost certain she was going to like it. She went down the hall to her office. "How are you surviving in here with all those paint fumes?"

Eve's nose wrinkled. "Well, to be honest, I was about to do some shopping to escape it."

"Okay." Josie stepped back into the hall, irrationally disappointed Eve was leaving, even though she could hardly blame her. The fumes had to be giving her a headache.

"I have an appointment at a gallery uptown to pick out some prints for the walls." Eve closed her laptop, glancing at Josie. "Would you like to come with me?"

Her stomach gave a funny swoop. "Yeah, I'd love to."

"All right." Eve stood, reaching for her purse.

"I should feed the kittens before I head out. Want to help?"

"Sure." Eve followed her to the stairs, heels clicking against the hardwood floors, a sound Josie would forever associate with her. Today, she wore a gray blouse with black slacks and matching strappy heels.

Josie was developing a serious fetish for business attire, or maybe it was just the woman wearing it. She led the way into her apartment. "Wait until you see their new setup."

"Oh?" Eve walked to the playpen, staring down at the kittens, and Josie watched her visibly soften at the sight of them, a warmth gleaming in her brown eyes that hadn't been there before. Currently, they were in a pile against their stuffed animal "mother," fast asleep.

"Did you miss them?" Josie asked as she went into the kitchen to start preparing bottles.

"Not nearly as much as I enjoyed a full night of uninterrupted sleep."

It wasn't the flat "no" Josie had expected, and she looked at Eve in surprise. "Nothing like a good night's sleep."

"Mm." Eve joined her in the kitchen, prepping a bottle with practiced ease. "I didn't know they could move around so much."

"Amazing, isn't it?" She looked over at the pile of sleeping kittens as realization dawned. "Wait, did you watch them on YouTube?"

Eve's eyes widened slightly, as if she hadn't intended to admit this fact, and Josie's heart absolutely melted. "I was curious to see how they were doing," Eve admitted.

"They were really active last night when I recorded them."

Eve walked to the playpen and picked up Hamilton.

Josie lifted Phantom, gently waking him for his meal. "They grow up fast. In another month, they'll be running all over the place."

"It's good that they have someone knowledgeable taking care of them now."

There she went again, downplaying her role in their lives. "You nursed them through the most critical week of their lives. Not everyone would have done that for them."

"Well, I couldn't let them die." Eve stroked Hamilton's gray-and-white fur.

"You'd be surprised how many people would have taken them to the shelter, even knowing what you knew."

Eve looked over at her, something heavy in her expression, before she stood to put Hamilton back in the playpen. She went to the kitchen for a fresh bottle and picked up Blanche. Josie replaced Phantom with Pippin, and together, they finished up their bottle-feeding session. Once the kittens were settled, they went to the kitchen to clean up and wash their hands.

"So, prints for the walls?" Josie asked.

Eve nodded. "The network has a decorator who's handling most of the décor, but I know the guy who owns this gallery. I told him what we're looking for, and he's going to put together a selection of photographs to choose from."

"Cool." Josie felt a flutter of excitement at being involved in the process, as well as the chance to go shopping with Eve.

"Ready?"

Josie nodded, grabbing her purse and leading the way to the door. They went out the back, walking down the street together toward the subway. As she watched the breeze ruffle Eve's hair and the confident way she navigated the street, it hit her that she'd never left the bar with Eve before. How was that possible?

Well, mostly it was possible because Josie herself had rarely left the bar over these last few months. She and Eve swiped their MetroCards and descended the steps to the platform, boarding a train to take them to the Upper West Side.

"I have bartender interviews scheduled tomorrow afternoon," Eve told her as they stood together in the crowded car, holding on to the silver pole between them for balance. "I'd like you to sit in."

"I might have fought you if you tried to keep me out," Josie told her with a smile. The train slowed abruptly, and her shoulder bumped into Eve's. Their eyes locked, and Josie felt it in the pit of her stomach. It had been *so* long since she'd been this attracted to anyone. Honestly, she'd struggled lately to form any kind of lasting connection with a woman and had almost given up on feeling anything like...this.

They stood in silence for the rest of the ride, occasionally bumping into each other as the train lurched beneath their feet. Eve made no effort to move away, and neither did Josie.

"This is our stop," Eve announced, and together, they stepped through the doors and climbed the steps to the street above. They came out on West Ninety-sixth Street, and Eve led them briskly down the sidewalk, eventually stopping in front of a sleek building that reminded Josie of the one where Eve worked.

She held the front door open for Josie, following her inside. They stood in a white-walled room full of photographs, many of them shots of Manhattan. At the tinkling of the bell, an older man with dark brown skin and a neatly groomed beard walked out to greet them.

"Eve," he exclaimed warmly, leaning in to air-kiss her cheeks.

"Michael," she responded with a smile before gesturing to Josie. "This is my client, Josie Swanson. Josie, this is Michael Danvers."

"Hi," Josie said, extending her hand. "It's so nice to meet you."

"Likewise," Michael said, giving her hand a firm shake. "Eve and I go way back, and I'm thrilled for the chance to find some prints for your bar."

"Are these your photos?" Josie asked, glancing around the studio.

"I've taken some of them, but I also work with several other local photographers. Come on back." He gestured for them to follow him down the hall to a small room. "Can I offer you ladies anything to drink?"

"No, thank you," Eve told him.

"I'm fine," Josie said.

"All right, then." He walked to a laptop on the desk and tapped it to life. Immediately, a black-and-white photo of a dragonfly filled the TV screen mounted to the wall above. "I've put together a gallery of images I think might suit what you're looking for. Once you've decided which—if any—you're interested in, we can discuss size and framing."

"Okay." Josie looked up at the dragonfly displayed on the screen. It had been captured in such detail, its wings seemed to shimmer. A beautiful shot, but she wasn't sure she envisioned it on the wall of her bar.

He clicked the touchpad and another photo appeared. This one was a closeup of two women's hands, clasped tightly.

"Oh," Josie said. "I really like this one." She could immediately picture this photo as a framed print on the wall of her brand-new gay bar. For a moment, she had the irrational urge to grab Eve's hand like the ones in the photo.

"I do too," Eve agreed. "It's exactly what I had in mind."

"That's one of mine," Michael said with a pleased look before moving on to the next photo.

They scrolled through his collection, eventually settling on two nighttime shots of New York City, the handholding photo, and a closeup of a dragonfly tattoo that could have passed for the one on Josie's shoulder. Collectively, she thought they represented Dragonfly's vibe. They finalized all the details for framing, and Michael promised to have the prints delivered on Thursday.

She and Eve stepped outside into the warm sunshine. Eve reached into her purse and slipped a pair of sunglasses into place.

Josie checked the time on her phone. "Want to grab lunch, or do you need to get back?"

Eve hesitated a moment before nodding. "Sure. That's fine."

"Cool. What are you in the mood for?"

"How do you feel about sushi?" Eve asked. "There's a good place not far from here."

"Sounds great."

Ten minutes later, they were seated across from each other at a little table in the middle of the restaurant.

"How do you know Michael?" Josie asked, toying with her water glass to keep from staring at Eve.

"Business," she answered. "I used to work with his wife."

"Your marketing business?"

"Before that," Eve said. "When I was working for a larger company."

"Have you always lived here in Manhattan?" She knew she might be pushing her luck, but she couldn't resist the chance to get to know Eve a little better.

"Only for the last five years." Eve lifted her water glass and took a sip.

"Where did you grow up?"

"Indiana," Eve answered, giving Josie an amused look. "So many questions."

"Sorry," she said with a shrug. "I'm just curious. How did you get from there to here?"

Eve stared at her for a long moment, as if deciding how to answer that question. "I had a falling-out with my family."

"When you came out?"

Eve nodded, a shadow passing over her expression. "They're not supportive."

"I'm sorry," Josie said. She had a lot of friends with

similar stories, and it made her even more grateful for her own family. "That's shitty."

"It is what it is," Eve said with a shrug. She exhaled deeply, staring at her water glass. "I'd always been fascinated with New York, but I couldn't afford to live here at first, so I accepted a marketing position in New Jersey."

"New Jersey, huh?" she asked with a smile. "I can't quite picture you in the suburbs."

"Well, I always had my sights set on the city."

"That doesn't surprise me. And is that where you met Lisa? In New Jersey?"

Eve cleared her throat. "Yes."

"How long were you together?" She knew she was prying now, but Eve never volunteered this kind of information on her own, nor would she have any qualms about putting an end to it if she became uncomfortable with Josie's questions.

"We lived together four years, married for one." She looked up. "We got married the day after they legalized it."

"That's badass," Josie told her, and boy was she in trouble, because she liked Eve more and more with every new tidbit she learned about her.

A smile toyed with Eve's lips. "It was a good day."

"I'm glad."

Their sushi arrived then, interrupting the conversation. And Josie watched as Eve buttoned herself up—metaphorically speaking—soft smiles and personal confessions vanishing behind her professional veneer. When she next spoke, it was to remind Josie about the bartender interviews she'd scheduled for the following afternoon.

Their conversation continued in this vein as they ate, although Josie didn't really mind. She knew these glimpses into Eve's personal life weren't things she shared often or with many people. So she chatted happily about the weather, the prints they'd selected, and the relaunch on Friday as they finished their meal.

But as they walked outside into the sunny April afternoon, she reached for Eve's hand and gave it a quick squeeze, just to thank her for it. And Eve squeezed back before shaking her hand free and leading the way toward the subway.

13

"Another round!" Josie slammed her shot glass on the table and threw her head back with a laugh. Rum spread a delicious warmth through her belly, scrambling her thoughts. She was at one of her favorite bars—just for fun, because she didn't own this one—with two of her favorite people, and it was exactly what she'd needed tonight.

"I'll get it." Adam pushed back from the table and headed toward the bar while Kaia sipped her martini, staring into it thoughtfully.

"You're awfully quiet tonight," Josie said, nudging her friend with her elbow.

"Actually, I was thinking about the girl I went out with last week," she said with a shrug. "I thought we had a really good time, but she hasn't texted."

"Maybe she's waiting to hear from you first?" Josie suggested.

"Nope. I texted her a few days ago, said I had fun, and suggested we get together again. Crickets."

"Ugh," Josie said. "I'm sorry."

"I mean, we only went out twice, so it's no big deal." She swirled her martini glass. "But I just thought we had a connection, you know?"

"Yeah, I do." She thought of Eve.

"Speaking of connections," Kaia said, perking up. "Any new developments between you and Eve?"

"Not really." Her cheeks flushed hot. "I mean, nothing's happened since that kiss on Friday night, but..."

"You both want it to," Kaia finished for her.

"I know *I* do," Josie admitted.

"I hope you guys aren't gossiping without me," Adam said as he arrived at their table with a fresh round of drinks. He plunked glasses in front of Kaia and Josie before going back for his own.

"Josie was just about to tell us how much she wants to jump Eve's bones," Kaia told him with a wicked grin as she took another sip of her martini.

"Pretty much can't stop thinking about it," she agreed, knowing the alcohol had loosened her tongue and not much caring.

"Damn, girl," Adam said with a playful lift of his eyebrows. "Tell us how you really feel."

"I feel *good*," she said as she tossed back the shot in front of her. "I've been so overwhelmed and stressed out about everything at Swanson's. I really needed this."

"I'll drink to that," Adam said, raising his glass. "You were definitely overdue for a night out. So a gay bar, huh?"

"Yeah." She looked at her two best friends, sobering. "It's a pretty big change."

"A good one, I think," Kaia said. "There really weren't any good gay bars in this part of town, which is why so many of us hung out at Swanson's in the first place."

"It's exciting, but also...terrifying, and a little bit sad," Josie said.

"Explain that last part," Adam said.

"I've lost all my regulars," she told him. "I know I didn't have many, but I had a few, and I'll miss them. And this morning, my Uncle Timothy—my dad's brother—reamed me out on the phone for destroying Swanson's legacy."

"Hold up." Kaia placed her hands on the table. "I thought your family was always super cool and supportive."

"They are." Josie shrugged with a sigh. "I guess I should have expected a few ruffled feathers about turning Swanson's into a gay bar, though. It all happened so fast, I didn't have time to discuss it with them before I made my decision."

"Which is fine, because the bar is *yours*," Adam said adamantly. "You're the one working your ass off night after night, the one paying the bills, the one whose name is on the deed."

"I know." She nodded. "Everyone else has been great, and I'm sure Uncle Timothy will come around. It's...I don't know, big change like this is always scary, and I'm not used to moving so quickly. Eve and I are going to be interviewing new bartenders tomorrow."

"Ooh, hire me," Adam said, tapping his glass.

"What?" She gave him a skeptical look. "Really?"

"Yes. I cover for you all the time. It's fun, and I could use the extra cash."

"But you have no real bartending experience, and you already have a job."

Adam made a face. "Being a bank teller isn't all that. I'm honestly starting to hate it. Just try me out on weekends or something and see how it goes. Maybe, if I'm having enough fun and making enough money, I'll quit my job and work for you full-time."

"Well, okay," Josie said, reaching out to take the hand he'd extended toward her, shaking on their deal. "In that case, you're hired." She grinned as she imagined working with Adam every day. Really, what could be better?

"I don't want a job, but I'll bring you lots of new customers," Kaia said. "And no more free drinks."

Josie flinched, remembering her conversation with Eve.

"I mean it, Jo," Kaia insisted. "From now on, I pay."

"I guess, but...I'll still slip you a beer on the house when I can," Josie said, resting a hand on Kaia's arm. "And thank you."

"Of course," Kaia said.

"Hey, speaking of drinks, I'm working on a new signature cocktail for the bar. What would you want to see on the menu? What do you look for in a drink?"

"I want something so smooth, I don't even taste the liquor," Adam said.

"And I like to feel the burn," Kaia said. "Just enough flavor to get it down."

"Wow, that's helpful," Josie said, rolling her eyes at them. "Fruity?"

"Fruity is always good," Adam agreed. "But everyone's doing that. What if you made something different, something minty, maybe? Like a mojito, but not."

"Hm, interesting." Josie pressed her fingers against her lips. "I like that."

"Or a bitter drink like a Manhattan," Kaia suggested.

"And if you do go fruity, make it something fancy like pomegranate or passionfruit," Adam said.

"This is going to be fun," Josie said. "I'll have you guys over to taste test for me later this week."

"Just say the word," Adam said.

"All right, well, as much as I hate to end our night early, I've got foster kittens at home who're ready to be fed."

"You and your foster kittens," Kaia told her with an affectionate look. "Is this the litter Eve found?"

She nodded. "I was finally able to take them, while the bar's closed."

"I would say bummer, but I know you actually live for this shit," Adam said. "So, good for you."

"I do," Josie confirmed, standing from her chair, and *whoa*, she was drunker than she'd realized. "I'm glad to have them."

"They're lucky to have you," Kaia said as she stood. "And I'm happy to see you getting back to the things you enjoy."

"Me too." Josie led the way outside, letting the cool evening air serve as a slap to the face to restore her senses for the subway ride home. Briefly, she wondered if she needed to be slapped back to her senses when it came to the other monumental changes in her life, but she'd set this train in motion, and she was going to ride it to the end of the line, no matter where it took her.

Eve was in bed, reading on her Kindle, when her phone dinged with an incoming text message. She frowned. Who in the world was texting her at eleven o'clock on a Tuesday night? She picked it up, revealing Josie's name on the screen, and then her frown deepened as she fought her body's instinctive reaction, the warmth already flushing her skin and the tingle deep in her belly.

Josie had no business texting her at this hour. It was completely unprofessional, and Eve should just ignore it until she got to work in the morning. She put her phone on "Do Not Disturb" mode and set it on the table beside her bed, then stared at it for a moment in frustration before snatching it back up. Her finger swiped across the screen, bringing up the text.

Someone misses you.

Josie had attached a selfie holding Blanche beneath her chin. The kitten's eyes were wide, her chin wet from a recent feeding. Josie was fake pouting into the camera, eyes twinkling mischievously, wearing a shimmery tank top that matched the turquoise streaks in her hair.

Eve pressed a hand against her heart, which was racing at the sight of her. And maybe there was a tiny pinch in her chest at the sight of Blanche's little white face. The kitten had a habit of falling asleep on Eve's belly after her feeding, and it was sweet. Comforting.

I doubt that, she texted back. Such a boring thing to say, but how else could she respond? There was no way she was going to flirt with Josie over text message. If anyone at the network ever got wind of it... She set her phone down, but it dinged with another message before she'd even had a chance to let go of it.

Josie had attached another selfie. This time, she was holding up Blanche's little paw in a faux wave. And seriously, what was Eve supposed to say? What *could* she say? The whole thing was ridiculous.

And her body was humming with electricity.

She huffed out a breath, annoyed with herself for allowing her infatuation with Josie to get to this point, annoyed with Josie for sending silly selfies, annoyed with everything that had led to this moment. She picked up the phone and dialed. "What are you doing?"

"Sending you cute pictures of your favorite kitten?" Josie answered.

"We've been over this, and you can't—"

"They're just kitten pictures, Eve," Josie said, giggling. She sounded like she'd been drinking. That might explain the sparkly top too. Had she gone out tonight? With who?

Stop sending them was what she meant to say, but what came out was "Are you drunk?"

More laughter. "A little bit."

"Maybe you should drink some coffee before you feed the kittens."

"Aw, look at you, being all overprotective of them," Josie teased. "I'm not that drunk. Believe me, I would never endanger them, but it's very sweet that you care."

Eve sighed into the phone, annoyed that she found even drunk Josie charming. "All right, then. I'll see you tomorrow."

"'Kay. Oh, I hired a bartender tonight," Josie said.

Eve rubbed at her brow. "What?"

"Adam wants the job, at least part-time."

"Adam." She tried the keep the skepticism out of her tone. "Does he have any bartending experience?"

"Not officially, but what he lacks in experience, he makes up for in charisma. The customers love him."

"We'll talk about it tomorrow."

"Okay." Josie's voice was soft and dreamy. A tiny meow drifted over the line, and the sound stirred something in Eve's chest that felt an awful lot like longing.

"Good night, Josie."

"Night."

She ended the call, put her phone back on "Do Not Disturb," and set it beside the bed. She glanced at the place where she usually put the box of kittens at night. Thank goodness she wouldn't have to wake up three times tonight to feed them. Good luck to Josie dealing with that while fighting a hangover.

Yep, Eve definitely got the better end of this deal, all by herself in her comfortable bed. Unfortunately, she'd never been a very good liar, not even to herself.

14

Come up before you leave. I need your opinion on something.

Eve stared at the text from Josie, trying to think of an excuse to say no. She'd purposely avoided Josie's apartment today, not wanting to be alone with her or to see the kittens. Better to keep her distance on both fronts. She and Josie had spent the afternoon interviewing bartending applicants and had successfully filled the available positions, although Eve hadn't been able to talk her out of hiring Adam. In her experience, hiring friends was a recipe for disaster, but maybe Josie needed to learn that lesson for herself.

At any rate, Eve had planned to make a quiet exit tonight for everyone's sake. She had no idea what Josie wanted to see her for, and it was probably better that she didn't find out. She composed a text telling Josie she had a commitment after work, and then she deleted it with a sigh. What if Josie's request was work-related? So Eve climbed the steps to her apartment a few minutes after six. She rapped her knuckles lightly against the door, half hoping Josie wouldn't hear her and she could just go straight home as planned.

"It's open," Josie called from inside.

Eve gripped the knob and opened the door, where she found Josie sitting cross-legged on her kitchen counter, a row of cocktail glasses in front of her.

"Hey," she said with a smile.

"What's all this?" Eve asked, stepping closer.

"Contenders for my new signature drink." Josie gestured to the glasses in front of her. "But I need your opinion on which one you like best."

"That sounds more like a job for Adam and Kaia than for me," Eve said. Taste-testing drinks in Josie's kitchen was definitely not a good idea. To distract herself, she wandered into the living room, watching the kittens as they staggered around their playpen like little drunks.

"I already did," Josie told her. "But they wildly disagree on which one I should pick, so I'm counting on you to be the tiebreaker."

"Which one do *you* like best?" Eve hedged as she knelt and lifted Blanche. The kitten wriggled in her hands, blue eyes wide, belly round with milk.

"Well, I like all of them, obviously."

"Mm." Eve set the kitten down and walked to the counter, resting her palms against it as she looked at the row of glasses in front of her. "Do you want to tell me what's in them first?"

"Nope. Just try them and let me know what you think."

"All right." Eve lifted the first glass. It contained an amber liquid and had a vaguely spicy scent. She sipped, feeling the burn of whiskey down her esophagus. "Strong."

"Too strong?" Josie asked, watching her closely.

"Maybe." She lifted the next glass, giving it a gentle

shake. The liquid inside was a milky white, swirling like smoke inside the glass. "Pretty."

Josie smiled.

Eve sipped, tasting mint and lemons ahead of the warmth of liquor. It was light and refreshing but also packed a punch. "I like it."

Josie clapped her hands together, looking pleased.

The third glass contained a pink drink that was so sweet, it made Eve's cheeks hurt. Next up was a clear concoction that she couldn't identify but didn't like. The last glass contained a liquid with a purplish hue. She sipped, tasting rum and something fruity. "This one's good," she said. "Sweet, but not too sweet."

"Which one's your favorite?" Josie asked.

She went back for another sip of the minty drink. "It's a tie between this one and that last one. Sour and sweet. I like them both."

"That one was Adam's favorite, and Kaia liked the pomegranate one at the end."

"I haven't helped much, then." Eve looked up and met her eyes as liquor warmed her stomach and blurred her inhibitions.

"Just pick one."

She took another sip of both drinks. "Actually, I think you should add them both to your drink menu, and maybe that whiskey one too, but tone it back a bit."

"You think?"

"They're all good and very different from each other." She lifted the sour drink and swirled it again, watching it spin like smoke. "Have you named them?"

Josie shook her head, sucking her bottom lip between her teeth.

"Want suggestions?"

"Absolutely." She leaned forward, hands clasped in her lap.

Eve lifted the purple drink, picturing the bar's new lavender logo and décor. "This one has got to be The Dragonfly."

"Wow, yeah," Josie said. "I can't believe I didn't think of that. Done."

"And this one..." Eve gave the sour drink another swirl. "When I hold it up to the light, it reminds me of clouds passing by the moon. I'd call it Midnight in Manhattan."

"I love it," Josie whispered.

Eve downed the rest of the drink and plunked the glass on the counter, leaning forward. "Rumor has it, if you drink one at midnight, you'll fall in love before the end of the year."

"What?" Josie's brows wrinkled adorably. "You just made that up."

"Of course I did. But people love that stuff. Put it on the menu. I bet you'll have customers lining up at midnight to drink one. It's just marketing."

"Okay," Josie said, eyes twinkling dangerously. "So are you going to fall in love?"

"It's not midnight," she said with a wink.

"It's midnight somewhere." Josie lifted the whiskey drink. "And this one?"

"Whiskey Kiss."

Josie's eyes widened as she set down the glass. "Damn, you're good at this. Done, done, and done."

"All right, then." She gripped the counter in front of her. The alcohol was definitely going to her head, because all she could think about was...

Josie leaned forward, hands cupping Eve's cheeks as she brought their lips together. *Yes.* Eve exhaled in relief as Josie kissed her. This was what she needed, what she'd been needing all week. Her whole body relaxed as she slid her tongue into the welcome heat of Josie's mouth, tasting a mixture of the same flavors she'd sampled from each glass on the counter.

Maybe they were drunk, or maybe they just needed this kiss. She pushed the glasses to the side and moved closer, belly pressed against the counter. Josie scooted forward to meet her, legs wrapping around Eve's waist, enveloping her in the warmth of her body.

"Man, that Whiskey Kiss really works." Josie's hands were in her hair, tugging gently as she brought their mouths back together.

"Mm."

"You taste better than all my drinks combined," Josie murmured into her mouth, and Eve moaned, gripping her ass, pulling her closer, unable to get her close enough to satisfy the need clawing inside her. "I want—"

"Shh," she whispered, silencing Josie with a kiss. She slid her hands beneath Josie's T-shirt, fingers skimming over each notch of her vertebrae, eliciting a shiver from Josie.

There was a desperation to the kiss as Eve tried to absorb every moment of pleasure she possibly could before reality stepped in and she had to force them to stop. But they were already kissing. That line had already been crossed, so there was no real harm in prolonging the moment just a little bit. Not when it felt this good. And God, it felt *so good*.

Josie wiggled in her arms, settling herself closer, hips pressed against Eve's, intimate enough to ignite a fire between her thighs, throbbing in time with her frantic pulse, but not intimate enough to offer any satisfaction.

She closed her eyes, just feeling...Josie's heels on her ass, her breasts pressed against Eve's, their chests heaving in an alternating pattern that seemed to have them breathing into each other, bodies synced in a rhythm as intoxicating as the liquor buzzing through her system.

This. Yes. More.

Josie's hands slid down her back, nails scraping gently against her skin over her blouse, causing goose bumps to rise on her arms and a needy gasp to escape her throat.

"You like that," Josie whispered, dragging her nails down to the waistband of Eve's pants.

"Yes," she whispered, hips jerking against Josie's as the aching need in her core intensified.

"How important is that contract?" Josie asked, fingers tracing circles over Eve's skin, distracting enough that she almost missed the question, but...*dammit*.

She pressed her forehead against Josie's, panting for breath as she attempted to restore some reason into her sex-addled brain. "Important."

"Some rules are made to be broken."

"Not this one." She lifted her head, steadying her breath.

"But it's okay to kiss me?" Josie cocked her head to the side, smiling so widely, her dimples showed, a lock of turquoise-tipped hair hanging over her left eye. Her lips were swollen and glossy, cheeks flushed, and she looked so adorable, so fucking sexy, Eve could hardly believe she wasn't already dragging her toward the bedroom.

"I didn't mean to do that either," she admitted. "I signed a contract with the network, but *Do Over* is an extension of my business, and I hold myself to my own standards of conduct, none of which involve sleeping with clients."

"In that case, I may have to fire you on Friday after taping wraps," Josie said, making no move to let her go.

"That might be hasty." Eve made no effort to let go of her

either. "From where I'm standing, you need as much of my help as you can get."

"No arguments here," Josie said. "But I also need *you*."

Eve forced herself to step back. Josie's big orange cat came out of nowhere, darting between her feet, and if she didn't know better, she'd say it was a deliberate effort to trip her. She stumbled, her head swimming with a combination of alcohol and arousal. "I should go."

The cat glared at her, standing beside the door as if he agreed with her decision.

"Okay." Josie hopped down beside her, leaning forward to place another quick kiss against her lips. "Thanks for helping me pick my signature drinks."

"You're welcome. Email me tomorrow with all the details so I can have the drink menus printed up."

Josie nodded. "Will do."

"Good night." And before she could do anything else she'd regret later, she turned and walked out the door.

JOSIE FELT like she'd swallowed a swarm of butterflies. Maybe dragonflies, given the circumstances? Or bees, because there was a definite sting somewhere deep inside her belly as she made her way downstairs to the bar. Not Swanson's. It was gone, just another piece of her past. She swallowed the pang of nostalgia that had risen in her throat. She was about to see Dragonfly for the first time, and she could hardly breathe.

A cameraman descended the stairs ahead of her, recording every emotion that crossed her face. Would the video capture the shake of her hands? The sheen of tears in her eyes? She resisted the urge to press a hand against her belly.

The cameraman walked backward down the hallway, leading her into the bar. Josie followed, pulse quickening as she stepped over the threshold. She looked around, breath caught in her throat. Swanson's wood-paneled walls had been stripped and refinished, painted a pale gray with aqua undertones and offset by the brick wall behind the bar. The prints she and Eve had picked out hung on the wall opposite the bar, matted a deep lilac to match the new Dragonfly logo. Overhead, strings of white lights ringed the room, making everything seem to glow in their warm light.

"What do you think?"

She turned at the sound of Eve's voice, spotting her at the far end of the bar, and now she understood why Eve had insisted on keeping things professional—or at least semi-professional—between them until after filming wrapped. Because just the sight of her knocked the air from Josie's lungs, and it was a good thing she was already breathless from seeing Dragonfly, because hopefully it masked her reaction to Eve from the cameras. "I...I love it."

Eve smiled, a wide, approving smile, the kind she only used when the cameras were rolling. "I'm glad to hear that."

Josie preferred the small, genuine smiles she'd received in private, but right now, she didn't much care. She spun, taking it all in, not even trying to contain her excitement, because that was what the *Do Over* team wanted for their episode, after all. They wanted to see a happy customer, and right now, she was very, *very* happy.

"It's warmer than I had expected, and it feels so modern." She blinked back the tears hazing her vision. "I think my dad would have loved it."

"I'm sure he would have."

"I mean, he never would have done anything like this in a million years. There wasn't a trendy bone in his body. This place isn't him. It's me. But he'd love seeing me here, now that it's mine...if that makes sense." She wrapped her arms around herself. "And it doesn't really make sense, since it's only mine because he died."

"It makes perfect sense," Eve said smoothly.

"It's just...wow, I can't quite believe this is the same place." She walked slowly through the room, taking in the new furniture, the freshly polished floor, the sleek track lighting overhead. Nothing about it felt like the building she'd grown up in.

This space might occupy the same street address, but it was a different bar. Out of nowhere, a rush of sadness washed over her, and she wiped away a tear that ran down her cheek. She might have felt embarrassed or tried to hide it, but she knew the show loved when business owners got emotional. They wanted to see her tears.

She looked over at Eve, surprised and yet *not* surprised by the calm air of professional detachment she wore like an extra layer of clothing. Josie wasn't hurt by it, though, because she knew that this was simply how Eve acted on camera. It was the reason Josie had been so intimidated by her when they'd first met.

Somewhere beneath that cool exterior, though, Eve stored all the warmth and passion she'd shared last night in Josie's arms, bodies pressed together and gasping for breath. Josie looked away, forcing her attention back to the bar before her feelings showed on her face.

"That should do it," the director called, and all around the room, red lights blinked off as the cameras stopped recording. "Break for five while we set up for the next shot."

Josie exhaled, slow and deep, resting her hands against

the bar. It was new too, a lighter-colored wood, sleek and glossy beneath her fingers.

"You did well," Eve said, coming to stand beside her.

"Thanks. It helped that I didn't have to fake my reaction. I really do love it."

"Are you sure?" Eve asked quietly.

Josie nodded as fresh tears spilled over her cheeks, betraying her words. "I just need a minute."

She turned away and went down the hall to her office. She dropped into the chair behind her desk and rested her face in her hands, gasping past the urge to cry. Even her office felt different. A hint of Eve's perfume lingered in the air, and when Josie lifted her head, Eve's laptop sat in front of her on the desk.

"Josie."

She looked up to see Eve standing in the doorway. "I'm okay, really."

"You don't like it?" Eve asked, and Josie couldn't tell if she was imagining something tender behind her neutral tone.

"I do. I *love* Dragonfly, but I miss Swanson's too. It's just... an adjustment, that's all."

"Okay," Eve said from her position in the doorway.

"Come in and close the door," Josie said.

Eve stiffened, jaw clenching, and Josie had to fight the urge to laugh. Oh, how she wanted to kiss that prim look right off her face, but that wasn't even what she'd had in mind when she made her request. After a moment, Eve shut the door.

Josie stood and walked over to her, pulling her in for a quick hug that she knew Eve would never tolerate in public. "Thank you," she said quietly. "Dragonfly is perfectly me. I wouldn't change a single thing."

"Oh," Eve breathed, eyes locking on Josie's.

"I just had to grieve Swanson's for a minute, but that doesn't mean I have regrets, because I don't."

"Okay."

Josie stepped back, opening the door before she gave in and kissed her. "Why are they setting up for a second shot?"

"Because I have something else to show you." Eve gestured for Josie to follow her into the hallway. A black sheet hung over the opposite wall. Josie had noticed it peripherally on her way into the bar, thinking it was an odd decorative choice, but now she realized it was concealing something.

She gulped as Eve stood beside her. The camera crew assembled around them, red lights blinking on as the director counted them down. Josie inhaled, looking to Eve for guidance.

"We saved a little piece of Swanson's for you," Eve said in her TV host voice as she reached out and gave the curtain a solid yank. It fluttered to the floor, revealing framed photos and news clippings spanning the hallway from one end to the other, above a solid wood panel that was as familiar as her own skin.

"Oh," Josie whispered, stepping forward to run her fingers over its well-worn surface. "The old bar top."

"Yes," Eve said, sounding pleased.

"And my family..." Josie's eyes welled with fresh tears as she took in the photos. Starting at the far end of the hall, she saw her grandparents—young and in love—as they first opened Swanson's. The photos progressed to show her parents, her father standing proudly behind the bar, and baby Josie in her mother's arms beside him. Here and there, newspaper headlines announced Swanson's various accolades. At the end was a photo of Josie and her father behind the bar, taken a few weeks before he died.

"You told me once that dragonflies symbolize transformation," Eve said. "And this wall represents Swanson's evolution into Dragonfly."

"Eve, this is...it's perfect."

"You have a lot of history in this building," Eve said.

Josie nodded, blinking to clear her vision. "I do."

"And a lot more history to make."

"Cut," the director called, and again the red lights went out. The camera crew went through the door that led to the rooftop, leaving Josie and Eve alone in the hallway.

"Okay?" Eve asked.

"Better than okay," Josie told her. "I was struggling a little with saying goodbye to Swanson's, but this makes it a lot easier." She touched the old bar top again.

"I hoped it might," Eve said, leading the way to the stairs.

They filmed a short sequence on the rooftop, which had been cleaned up and furnished with a variety of seating, from bar-height tables to cozy couches. Afterward, Josie retreated to her office. She sank into the chair behind her desk and sat there, head in her hands, until the click of Eve's heels announced her arrival. Josie looked up. "What now?"

"Now, we get ready for the grand opening." Eve sat across from her, spinning the laptop to face her.

And so they went over every detail together, from local media coverage to the drink menu. Later that afternoon, Josie trained her new bartenders. On weekends, Adam would be with her at the main bar and her new hire, Elizabeth, would work the rooftop bar. During the week, the rooftop would be closed and another new hire, Lauren, would tend bar with Josie downstairs.

She tested out her new delivery agreement with the

Italian restaurant next door and ordered food for the whole staff, including the *Do Over* crew. Eve sat at a table with two of the cameramen, keeping a professional distance. In between bouts of laughter at Adam's nonstop jokes, Josie found herself thinking about what her life would be like after the grand opening tomorrow. A bar with a full staff, a bar that hopefully brought in enough income to keep her afloat.

The freedom to ask Eve out on a proper date.

Where would they go? Appearance would suggest she should take Eve somewhere fancy, somewhere she could wear one of her sleek dresses and they could order a bottle of champagne and sit at a table for two with a little decorative candle in between them. But Josie also entertained a fantasy that involved her and Eve crammed into one of the booths at Bertie's Tavern, sharing burgers and beer and making out on the cracked vinyl seat.

"Earth to Josie." Adam snapped his fingers in front of her face.

"Sorry." She lifted her beer and took a hearty swallow. "Just...thinking."

He leaned in so that Elizabeth and Lauren, who were sitting across from them, wouldn't overhear. "And do those deep thoughts involve a certain brunette who's been very deliberately not looking over at our table all night?"

She didn't even try to hide her smile. "Maybe."

"Do tell," he said, looking delighted.

"If you must know, I was thinking about asking her out after filming wraps tomorrow."

He tapped his beer bottle against hers. "To your love life. May it flourish, and your new bar too."

15

Josie was going to have a nervous breakdown. She gasped against the tightness in her chest, gripping the bar as she waited for the whooshing noise in her ears to recede.

"Breathe." Adam's hand landed on the small of her back, rubbing up and down.

She nodded, sucking in a shaky breath. "What if no one comes?"

"They'll come," he said. "Even if they don't give a shit about Dragonfly, they'll come tonight because of the *Do Over* taping. If anything, we'll be turning people away at the door to keep from going over capacity."

"You're right," she said, forcing another slow, deep breath into her lungs.

"Everyone wants their fifteen minutes of fame, especially in this town. Tonight's going to be fabulous. There's really no way around it," he told her, completely sincere.

She turned to fling her arms around him. "I'm so glad you're here."

"Me too." He squeezed her back. "We're going to make

an awesome team. Basically, you made the best decision ever by hiring me." He pulled back with an exaggerated wink.

"You better not make me regret it." She gave him a playful shove. "It *is* going to go well tonight, right?"

"It is. I mean, look at us?" He waved his hand dramatically between them. They both wore black T-shirts with the new logo—a lavender dragonfly identical to Josie's tattoo—on them. Adam's hair was carefully styled with so much gel, it probably wouldn't budge if he stood outside in a hurricane. He'd let the *Do Over* team go a little crazy on his makeup too, but he looked fantastic, and his enthusiasm was sure to keep the customers happy.

Eve had been here earlier but had left a little while ago to go home and change. Doors opened to the public in forty-five minutes, and the camera crew had been milling around all afternoon, getting ready. The anticipation was slowly getting to Josie. She just needed to get on with things. Once the bar was full and she was busy pouring drinks, she'd relax. Hopefully.

Kaia pushed through the front door, wearing black leather pants and a purple top with a matching streak through her hair. She crossed to the bar, looking around wide-eyed. "Holy shit, Jo. It looks amazing in here!"

"It does. Eve and her team did a great job." Josie swept her gaze around the room.

"And here you are behind the bar looking all official," Kaia said, leaning over to kiss Adam's cheek.

"That's because I *am* official," he said proudly, patting the logo on his chest.

The front door opened again, and Eve walked in. She had on a knee-length black sheath dress with a gold zipper running down the front, extending the entire length of the dress. Its tab nestled between her breasts, just begging for someone to tug it down and unzip her.

Josie swallowed roughly. "Fuck me."

Adam choked on a laugh. "No, thanks, but it's obvious you want to fuck *her*."

"That dress," she muttered.

"It's hot," Kaia agreed. "And you should make sure she knows it, just saying."

"Oh, I think she knows it," Adam said, waving as Eve glanced in their direction.

She walked over to stand beside Kaia, her brown eyes meeting Josie's, as calm and steady as Josie was frazzled. "Ready?"

Josie nodded. "As I'll ever be."

Eve's lips quirked with the hint of a smile. Her hair was down tonight, glistening beneath the track lighting overhead. Her lips were painted a deep red, eyes highlighted with a bronze eye shadow that shimmered when she blinked. "You'll be fine," she said softly, resting her hand momentarily over Josie's on the bar.

A bold move, coming from Eve. Josie sucked in a breath, trying to play it cool in front of her friends before she realized Adam and Kaia were no longer there. Apparently, they'd made themselves scarce to give her a moment alone with Eve, something she'd have to thank them for later.

Grinning, Josie leaned forward, gaze dropping to the gold zipper tag dangling between Eve's breasts. "You look ridiculously gorgeous tonight," she whispered. "That dress is *hot*."

Eve sucked in a visible breath, and when Josie dragged her gaze back to Eve's face, her cheeks were an adorable shade of pink. "I love your hair."

Josie lifted a hand reflexively, touching her newly lavender locks, the same shade as Dragonfly's logo. "Yeah?"

Eve nodded. "This is how it looked the first time I ever saw you, in that video about bottle-feeding kittens."

"I change it up a lot, but this felt right tonight, you know?"

"Very on-brand." Eve's gaze lingered on her a moment longer before she turned to scan the room. "Your friends aren't exactly subtle," she said with a frown.

"Nope," Josie agreed with a laugh. Adam and Kaia stood at a table in back, talking to a member of the crew and shooting delighted glances in Eve and Josie's direction.

"Tell them to knock it off, would you?" Eve said, tapping one hand against the bar before she walked off, hips swaying inside that dress, and what had she just said? Josie's whole brain had just gone up in smoke.

"You have got it so bad for her," Adam announced, reappearing magically at her side.

"I know." She gave her head a slight shake. "But I've got to get a grip, because we open in..." She glanced at the clock above the door and gulped. "Thirty minutes."

"That's right," he agreed. "Time to get serious."

"Yes." She braced her palms against the bar. "Okay. You stay here and go over that drink menu one more time. Make sure you know where everything is. I think we can expect to sell a lot of the new signature drinks tonight. I'm heading up to check on Elizabeth before we open."

"Got it," Adam said, turning to study the recipe chart on the counter behind the bar.

She ducked around him and headed up to the rooftop. It was a clear evening, just cool enough to warrant a light jacket, perfect weather for their grand opening. The rooftop, as Eve had envisioned, had been set with twinkling strands of white lights, with larger lamps around the perimeter of the space to provide sufficient lighting for their customers.

High-topped tables were scattered across the patio, and the bar was freshly painted and fully stocked, with her brand-new bartender Elizabeth standing behind it, texting on her phone. Elizabeth's short-cropped black hair and full-sleeve tattoos gave her an edgy vibe, offset by her wide smile and the laugh lines around her eyes.

"You all set?" Josie asked.

Elizabeth nodded. Unlike Adam, she had extensive bartending experience. "Ready to rock and roll."

"You've got your recipe sheet?"

Elizabeth pointed to it, taped to the backside of the bar where only she could see it.

"Great," Josie told her, eyeing the camera crew already milling around the patio area. "Just text me if you need me, okay? And I'll come check on you when I can."

"Don't worry about me. I've got everything under control," Elizabeth said, lifting her right hand to bump her knuckles against Josie's.

"I'm not worried about you," Josie said, relieved that it was true. "Okay, I've got to get back downstairs before the doors open. See you in a bit." With a wave, she headed for the stairs, nearly colliding with Eve in the doorway. "Hey."

"You should be downstairs," Eve said, looking over Josie's shoulder, scanning the rooftop. "People are lining up outside. We're about to open the doors."

Josie gulped. "People are lining up?"

She nodded. "You've got a good crowd building."

They're here for the cameras, Josie reminded herself. It wasn't going to be like this tomorrow night. "Okay, I'm ready."

"Good." Eve turned to follow her downstairs.

They were quiet as they went down the back stairwell. Josie could feel herself hyperventilating again. This was by far the biggest moment in her professional life. When she'd taken over Swanson's after her father's death, it had been a quiet transition. No cameras. No fanfare. No crowd waiting outside the front door. Just a few tears and the support of her friends. Those last two things would likely repeat tonight. She was almost certain to cry at some point, and Adam and Kaia would be there to dry her eyes, just like they had two years ago.

She paused at the bottom of the stairs, drawing in a shaky breath. She'd almost forgotten Eve was behind her until she felt a hand on her shoulder.

"It's going to be fine," Eve said.

Josie felt herself nodding, but her throat was too tight to respond.

"Breathe," Eve said quietly, giving her shoulder a light squeeze. "You've been a natural in front of the camera so far, and you know you're a great bartender. If there are any bumps, my team will make them disappear before the episode airs, so you've got nothing to worry about. We look good when you look good."

"Thank you," Josie whispered, reaching up to press her hand over Eve's.

Eve's hand slid down her back, making Josie shiver in anticipation, but her fingers merely switched on the mic pack attached to the waistband of Josie's jeans. They were all wired for the cameras, and it was unnerving to know everything she said for the rest of the night was being recorded.

"Now go on out there so I can open the door," Eve said.

"Yep." Josie swallowed again before leaving the stairwell. She ducked behind the bar as Eve crossed to the front door.

"Thought you might need this," Adam said, sliding a shot glass her way.

She managed a dry laugh. "You know what, I don't usually drink while I'm working, but this might be exactly what I need right now." She picked it up and tossed it back, feeling the warmth of whiskey as it coated her esophagus and slid down to her stomach, loosening the knot of tension lodged there.

Eve glanced over at her, and Josie nodded that she was ready. Eve turned to the camera crew, pausing as they assembled around her. Josie watched as she slid into her television persona, her petite frame seeming to grow impossibly taller in her black stilettos as she drew herself up, smoothed her hair over her shoulders, and put her camera-ready smile in place.

The director shouted a few last-minute instructions, and then they were rolling. Eve spoke earnestly into the camera in front of her, introducing the segment as she gestured around the bar. Josie gulped, glad for that shot of whiskey to take the edge off her nerves.

Eve opened the door, pulling it wide as she welcomed the first customers inside. Many of them stopped to shake her hand and speak to her, probably fans of the show. But they were also here for a drink, and before Josie had even adjusted to the idea of the doors being open, the bar had filled with the sounds of laughter and conversation, bodies sliding onto the barstools in front of her.

"Josie!"

She turned at the singsong voice to find her Aunt Cecily standing there, arms outstretched. "Thank you so much for coming," Josie said as she leaned across the bar for a big hug.

"Aww, I wouldn't miss your big night," Cecily said. "Your dad would have been so proud."

"Thanks." Josie blinked back tears, peripherally aware of the cameras moving in to capture this family moment. "Can I get you a drink? A White Russian?" It had been her aunt's favorite for as long as Josie had been mixing drinks.

"Absolutely." Her aunt slid onto an empty stool, brushing a hand over her silver hair as she looked around the bar. "It looks great, Josie. So different, but sometimes change can be a good thing."

"I hope so," Josie said as she combined vodka and Kahlua in a shaker before pouring it into a glass of ice. She bent to take heavy cream out of the fridge beneath the bar, adding a splash to the top of the drink. As she turned to hand it to her aunt, Cecily leaned forward with a conspiratorial smile.

"I've never been in a gay bar before," she said. "Do you think I'll get hit on by any women tonight?"

Josie grinned, overwhelmed with affection for her aunt. "I don't know, Aunt Cec. Try flirting with someone and see what happens."

Her aunt tipped her head back and laughed. "I'll do that."

From there, Josie's night began to blur. She and Adam slid from one end of the bar to the other, mixing drinks while the *Do Over* team filmed them in action. To streamline things on opening night, she wasn't launching her new takeout delivery option until tomorrow, but she had plenty of snack mix on hand for the current crowd. Meanwhile, Eve interviewed customers to get their opinions on the new bar, effortlessly working the room in that black dress.

"Dammit," Adam muttered, and Josie tore her gaze from Eve to find him cleaning up a beer he'd overfilled. Well, he couldn't be expected to get through his first full night of bartending without a few mishaps.

The crowd tonight was...odd. Overall, the customers were a lot straighter than Josie had expected. In fact, most people seemed to be here for the *Do Over* taping instead of the chance to check out a new gay bar, and maybe that was okay for tonight. But as she watched a woman deliberately knock her drink on the floor before turning toward the cameras with a dramatic shriek, Josie hoped she wasn't in trouble once the cameras had left.

She hurried out from behind the bar to clean up the mess, as the woman who'd spilled her drink seized her moment of fame, chattering excitedly for the cameras. Behind her, Josie heard a man say, "Excuse me, but I think you poured me a lager instead of a stout."

"So sorry about that," Adam said. "I'll pour you a stout right away. Next one's on the house."

Eve glanced over, an "I told you so" in her eyes, and while Josie still didn't regret hiring Adam, maybe she should have started him out on a quieter night. She kept a smile pasted on her face as she fixed a new martini for the woman who'd spilled hers. Sucking in a breath, Josie turned to greet a woman who'd just taken an empty barstool in front of her. "Hi. What can I get you?"

"You're Josie, right?" the woman said.

"That's right," Josie told her. She didn't think they'd ever met, but occasionally someone came into the bar who'd watched her videos on YouTube.

"I'm Jules Vega," she said warmly. "I had the winning bid to name your new kittens."

"Oh!" A genuine smile spread over Josie's face. "My theater kittens?"

"That's right." Jules nodded. She was about Josie's age,

with long, honey-brown hair. "I'm a Broadway actress and a lifelong theater lover, so I couldn't resist."

"Really? That's so cool," Josie said. "Would I have seen you in anything?"

Jules laughed. "You might have, but you probably wouldn't remember me. I'm usually a member of the ensemble, although I've got a small supporting role in *Paradise* right now. I guess you could say I'm still waiting for my big break."

"Aren't we all?" Josie agreed, taking an immediate liking to Jules. "Can I get you something to drink?"

"I'll try the Whiskey Kiss," Jules said.

"Coming right up."

"Actually, I was hoping to meet you tonight," Jules said as Josie mixed her drink. "I've been watching your videos, and I guess I've gotten kind of attached to those kittens since I named them."

"Thinking of adopting?" Josie asked as she set a tumbler on the bar in front of her.

"I am, actually." Jules lifted the glass to her lips and sipped. "Mm, that's good."

"Well, they aren't officially available for adoption yet," Josie told her, "but I'm always willing to make exceptions in unique situations."

"Unique situations?" Jules gave her a hopeful look before taking another sip of her drink.

"Such as when the person who donated a bunch of money to name them takes the time to come to my bar's grand reopening," Josie told her. "It'll be a while before they're ready to go home with you, but I'd be happy to give you the pick of the litter, assuming you pass my adoption screening."

"Yes." Jules fist-pumped the air.

"Don't leave tonight without me getting your information, okay?"

"You got it."

Josie looked up to see Eve watching her from across the room, eyes narrowed, and then she was walking straight toward her. And if Josie wasn't mistaken, she looked pissed.

16

Eve turned off her mic pack as she crossed the room to where Josie was leaned against the bar, laughing and talking with a very attractive woman. Flirting. It looked like flirting, and while it was certainly Josie's prerogative to flirt with whomever she wanted, she didn't need to do it in front of the cameras. Or in front of Eve.

She slid into an opening at the bar, catching Josie's eye. "I sent the crew on their break if you want to turn that off for a little while." She gestured toward Josie's mic pack.

"Yeah, sure," Josie said, reaching behind herself to switch it off. Her lavender hair shone beneath the overhead lighting like she was some sort of fairy, a very adorable fairy who made Eve's heart beat too fast every time she looked at her.

"Everything okay over here?" Eve asked.

Josie nodded enthusiastically, waving a hand toward the woman Eve had hoped to ignore. "Actually, I wanted to introduce you to Jules."

Reluctantly, Eve turned toward her with a polite smile, extending a hand. "Eve Marlow."

Jules's eyes widened as she took it and shook. "It's a pleasure to meet you. I love your show."

"Thank you."

"Jules named our kittens," Josie told her. "And now she's thinking of adopting a couple of them."

"Oh?" Eve had to think for a moment to figure out what she was talking about. She'd forgotten all about Josie's fundraiser to name the kittens. "That's great."

"Eve's the one who found them in a trash can," Josie told Jules. "And she raised them for the first week or so until I was able to take them in."

"Wow," Jules said. "I had no idea you'd found them. That's so horrible. I can't imagine how someone could throw them out like that."

Eve nodded.

"Anyway, I hope you put up a new video of them soon," Jules told Josie. "I'll give you my number before I leave." With a friendly wave, she picked up her drink and went to join several other women at one of the high-top tables along the wall.

"Isn't that cool?" Josie said, pulling out a cloth to wipe down the bar. "I hope it works out for her to adopt them."

"Yes." Eve drummed her fingers against the smooth wood, not particularly thrilled by the idea of the kittens going home with Jules or about Jules giving Josie her number, however petty that was of her.

"Want something to drink?"

"Just water," Eve said. "I'm working."

"Gotcha." Josie grabbed a glass and filled it, plunking it down in front of her. "How do you think things are going so far?"

"Really well." She swallowed some water and set down the glass. "Turnout has been good, and your guests all seem to be enjoying themselves."

"Are *you*?" Josie asked, leaning closer. "Enjoying yourself?"

"I'm working."

Josie rolled her eyes playfully. "Yes, I can tell. Are you guys going to be filming all night?"

"No. When the crew gets back from their break, I want to get some footage on the rooftop, and then I'll interview you if you're not too busy. That should pretty much do it. We'll get out of your hair."

"Or," Josie said, eyes narrowing. "You could stick around, drink something stronger than water, and have some fun."

"I could," Eve agreed, meeting her eyes. "We'll see how the evening goes."

Josie leaned even closer. "Anything I can do to help sway your decision?"

Don't take that woman's number. But she'd never say it out loud, because it was a ridiculous request. A ridiculous thought, even. She wasn't interested in more than a night with Josie, if they even made it that far. Which meant Josie was free to get anyone's number that she wanted to. Eve darted a glance toward the far wall to see Jules deep in conversation with her friends.

"Oh my God," Josie whispered. "Are you jealous?"

"What?" Eve picked up her glass and took another swallow. "Of course not. I don't care if you take her number."

"It's so I can contact her about adopting the kittens," Josie said, grinning. "Not for me to ask her out."

"I don't care what you do with it," Eve insisted.

"Yes, you do." Josie looked delighted. "You're jealous."

"Don't be ridiculous."

"If you only knew," Josie said quietly, biting her lip as her gaze raked over Eve's body. She felt it like a physical touch, heat blazing everywhere Josie looked, burning her beneath her dress.

"I'll come back in a little while with the camera crew for your interview," Eve said, turning away before things got any more out of hand. "Thanks for the water."

"OH MY GOD, I'm so tired." Josie resisted the urge to rub at her stinging eyes.

"No kidding," Adam agreed, resting his elbows on the bar. "I feel like I just ran a marathon, or at least what I imagine that feels like."

She laughed quietly. It was past three, and the crowd had finally thinned. The *Do Over* crew had gone home hours ago, except for Eve, who lingered at the end of the bar, sipping whiskey and talking with a couple of men Josie didn't recognize. The camera seekers were long gone, as well as her Aunt Cecily, leaving behind a crowd that felt more like the one Josie hoped to attract after tonight.

"Can you hold down the fort for me for a few minutes while I go upstairs and feed the kittens?" she asked Adam.

"You bet." He waved her off, turning his attention to their remaining customers.

Josie went upstairs and let herself into her apartment. Working a long shift was nothing new, but she hadn't served a packed house in a long time. And it was even more draining, having the camera crew around. Her cheeks hurt from so much smiling. A few minutes alone with her theater kittens was exactly what she needed.

She stopped in the kitchen to prepare their bottles

before settling herself on the floor beside their playpen. Eve had done their last feeding while Josie was busy downstairs, and there was her neat handwriting on the feeding chart, indicating how much each kitten had eaten. Kaia's swirly script was above Eve's, and Josie was so grateful to them both for stepping in to help her tonight. It took a village to raise these tiny creatures.

"I met someone tonight who wants to adopt you," Josie said as she lifted Phantom into her lap, stroking him gently until he woke, stretching, blue eyes blinking up at her from his fluffy black face.

Nigel stalked by, giving her a haughty look for checking on the kittens without greeting him first. He was always great with her foster babies, though, once they were old enough to leave their playpen and romp around the apartment with him. He was like the cool older brother, showing them all the best playground hacks while he feigned annoyance when they tackled him and batted at his tail.

"Get over here, you," she said, extending a hand in his direction, and he walked over, purring as she gave him a neck rub. "You know you're my boy. The little ones are only temporary."

It was a tough but necessary rule for any animal rescuer. If she kept the kittens she saved, she wouldn't have room to save more. But she loved helping them find perfect homes. She still had to vet Jules as an adopter, but her gut said whichever kitten or kittens she adopted would be lucky to have her.

Josie fed the remaining kittens as quickly as she could without rushing them. Then, she hurried downstairs to rejoin Adam behind the bar. They poured more drinks, and for the first time in weeks—maybe months—she had enough customers to warrant last call.

She walked over to Eve, who was sitting by herself now, still sipping whiskey as she looked at something on her phone. "You're still here."

Eve looked up. Something in her had softened over the course of the evening as her camera-ready makeup wore off, exposing the woman Josie had gotten to know over the last two weeks. "Thought I should stick around in case anything went wrong."

"Is that so?" Josie cocked a hip against the bar.

"Who's going to help you break up the next bar fight?" she said, lips curving into a sardonic smile.

"Somehow, I don't think this group is the fighting type." Josie swept her gaze around the bar. Two women were kissing in the back, while a couple of men slow danced together on an imaginary dance floor in the center of the room. She never would have imagined turning this place into a gay bar. She'd balked at the idea when Eve first presented it to her. But now that she was standing here looking at the results? "Thank you for pushing me on this and for having the vision to see it in the first place."

"You're welcome."

"We're closing in a few minutes."

"I know," Eve said, draining the last of her whiskey.

"Don't go anywhere, you know, just in case..." She winked, but she wasn't thinking about bar fights, and she didn't think Eve was either.

"I won't."

Josie cleaned up behind the bar, a ritual she'd completed a thousand times. Tonight, she had Adam at her side, watching and helping, learning what needed to be done. She wished her last customers good night as they headed out into the night.

"We'll be back," one of the men told her, pulling her in

for an impulsive hug. "This is exactly the kind of place I've always wanted to see in this neighborhood."

"I'm so glad," she told him, feeling the prick of tears behind her eyes.

Elizabeth came down from the rooftop. They finished closing up together, and more hugs were exchanged before she sent Elizabeth and Adam home. And then she was standing in the middle of her empty bar, this brand-new space that already felt like home in a way Swanson's never had.

And she wasn't alone. Eve rose quietly from her barstool, walking over to join Josie in the center of the room. Music still played over the sound system, an instrumental version of one of Josie's favorite pop tunes. In the sudden absence of conversation, the music seemed much louder.

"Okay?" Eve asked quietly, reaching out to brush the tears from Josie's cheeks. She hadn't even realized they were there until Eve's fingers were rubbing them away.

She nodded, blinking as more tears fell. "Really okay. Better than okay."

"Good."

Josie wrapped her arms around Eve, hugging her tightly. Cheek to cheek, they held on to each other, swaying to the rhythm of the music. Josie hadn't had any alcohol tonight except for that one shot Adam had given her twelve hours ago, but her head was spinning, drunk off the euphoria of a successful night, the aftereffects of the adrenaline that had fueled her through her shift, and the woman in her arms.

Eve sighed, and Josie felt the tension go out of her spine as she settled closer against her, relaxing into their embrace. She felt so small in Josie's arms. So petite. So...mortal. She'd been this larger-than-life presence all night, effortlessly and tirelessly managing the *Do Over* crew while she mingled with customers, interviewing them and answering their questions about the bar. Eve Marlow, business mogul, television host, all-around badass.

Right now, she was just Eve. Josie trailed her fingers up and down her spine, rewarded by a shiver and a hitch in her breath. Eve turned her face, lips pressed to Josie's cheek.

"Eve," she whispered, arms tightening around her. "You're fired."

"What?" Eve drew back to meet her eyes, confusion etched between her brows.

"The *Do Over* contract is complete, right?"

Eve nodded.

"So I'm firing you from that consultation period you mentioned. I'll hire you again on Monday, which leaves us free to do whatever the fuck we want to this weekend. Deal?"

"That's warped logic if ever I heard it," Eve said, but her pupils were blown with lust, chest heaving against Josie's.

"Come upstairs with me." She brushed her lips against Eve's. "Spend the night in my bed."

"It's almost five a.m.," Eve whispered, eyes sliding shut.

"Then spend the morning with me." She kissed her again, more urgently this time, tasting the whiskey on Eve's lips. "Please."

Her hands fisted in the back of Josie's T-shirt as she yanked their bodies together. "Yes."

17

They were surprisingly civilized as they climbed the stairs to Josie's apartment, Eve's heels echoing through the building with each step. Josie opened the door, gesturing Eve in ahead of her. She stepped into Josie's living room, eyes tracking automatically to the kittens in the playpen by the couch. They were—thankfully—asleep.

She turned toward Josie, and for a moment, they just stared at each other. Eve searched her lust-drunk mind for a reason not to do this, a glimmer of sanity to remind herself that—no matter what Josie had said downstairs—Eve would still be advising her over the next few weeks and ought to keep her hands to herself.

But she didn't want to keep her hands to herself. She wanted them all over Josie's beautiful body. She wanted to kiss her until her lungs screamed for oxygen, fuck her until she couldn't walk, drink her in until her thirst for all things Josie had been quenched.

"Get over here and kiss me," Josie said, licking her lips so that they glistened in the muted light from the lamp in the living room.

Eve stepped forward, hands sliding into the purple depths of Josie's hair as she brought their lips together. Josie opened to her, mouths meeting messily as they dove headlong into the kind of kiss there was no pulling back from, the kind of kiss that had Eve's blood pumping hot and fast, need throbbing between her legs, her body screaming to be touched.

In her heels, she and Josie were about the same height, and she leveraged it to her advantage as she wedged a thigh between Josie's, fitting their bodies together. Josie rolled her hips, gasping into Eve's mouth, palms against Eve's back as she pressed them closer together.

Yes. Eve tilted her hips, thrilled by the scrape of Josie's jeans against her bare thighs. They kissed, bodies moving, hands groping, hips rocking, until Eve's breath came in ragged gasps, knees shaking from the energy building inside her.

"This dress," Josie whispered, fingers toying with the clasp at the top of the zipper.

"You like it?" Eve arched her back, pressing her breasts into Josie's hands.

"I've been dying to touch it all night." She moved the zipper down a few inches and back up, the hiss of metal on metal the only sound in the room. "Wondering if this was a real zipper, if I could just pull it down and...unzip you."

Eve's pulse skyrocketed as she watched. "It's real."

"So I see." Josie inched it down until Eve's breasts spilled from the bodice of the dress, revealing the top edge of her bra. Behind them, a kitten mewled, and Josie smiled, tugging the zipper back up. "Come on."

She took Eve's hand, leading her into the bedroom. As

soon as they stepped into the darkened room, they were on each other again, kissing and groping, bodies pressed together. "Eve," Josie gasped, head lolling back as Eve sucked at a sensitive spot below her ear.

She pressed her tongue against Josie's racing pulse as her hands slid beneath the hem of her T-shirt, skimming over her hot skin before lifting the shirt. Josie pulled back long enough to tug it over her head, tossing it to the floor.

Eve blinked, but it was too dark in Josie's bedroom to see a damn thing. And she wanted to. She wanted to see and remember every detail. She fumbled behind her for the lamp on the dresser and switched it on, illuminating the bedroom in its soft glow.

Josie blinked at her owlishly. "You like to watch, hm?"

She gazed appreciatively at Josie's black satin bra. "I want to see every inch of you."

"And it would be a shame for me not to see what's underneath this dress." She tugged at the zipper again, drawing it down a few inches.

Eve went for the button of her jeans, popping it open and lowering her zipper, a much shorter journey than the one on her dress. She pushed at the denim, and Josie helped her out, wiggling the jeans over her hips and down her legs so she could step out of them, leaving her in matching black boy-shorts.

Eve cupped Josie's breasts over her bra, so much fuller and heavier than her own. Josie bit her lip as she watched, nipples pebbling through the satin. Then Josie was reaching for her again, one hand going to the zipper of her dress. She lowered it at a maddening pace, so slow Eve thought she could hear each individual metal tooth slide through the mechanism that released it.

The dress gaped open, revealing her black lace bra. Josie

sucked in a breath, cheeks flushed as her gaze followed the zipper's journey. Eve focused on her own breathing, pulling air in and out of her lungs as Josie's knuckles grazed her skin, shooting sparks through her body.

"Fuck me," Josie whispered as the zipper purred past Eve's hips and kept going, releasing the bottom of the dress with a gasp and a metallic clink. Cool air kissed her newly bare skin, and she shivered, letting the dress slip from her shoulders like a cape. It puddled at her feet, leaving her standing before Josie in nothing but black lace.

"That is the sexiest thing I've ever seen," Josie said reverently.

Eve reached for her, bringing their bodies together as she stepped out of her heels, relinquishing the height advantage to Josie. Her hands slid over Eve's bare skin, fingers teasing the edge of her thong. Eve squeezed her eyes shut, silently urging her on. Josie's fingers skimmed over her, stroking her through the lace, and Eve couldn't contain the needy gasp that escaped her lips, although she was able to restrain herself from grinding against Josie's hand.

And then, Josie's fingers were gone. Apparently, she was a woman who liked to take things slow, liked to touch and tease for as long as either of them could stand it, but Eve couldn't wait, not tonight. She'd let herself go too long without this, and now that she was in Josie's bedroom, her patience was running short. Their chemistry was stronger than anything she'd felt in years, and she was so turned on right now, she could hardly stand it.

She pushed Josie onto the bed, straddling her. Their hips rocked together, and she gasped in relief to finally have some friction against her clit. Below her, Josie flung her head against the pillow, lavender hair everywhere, so beautiful, she took Eve's breath away. So beautiful, she stilled her hips, stopping before she'd found release. Not like this. Not with Josie.

Eve didn't always undress all the way for sex, preferring to keep things as impersonal as possible, but that wasn't an option tonight. This was personal. Deeply personal. And Josie deserved more than Eve grinding against her until they'd found release, and then heading for the door. Josie deserved everything, so much more than Eve could give her. But she could give her this night.

She ignored the desperate throbbing in her core, pressing her thighs together as she helped Josie slide out of her bra and panties. "So worth turning the light on for," Eve murmured as she dipped her head to take one of Josie's perfect rosy nipples into her mouth.

"Touch me," Josie gasped, hips jerking up to meet Eve's. "Please touch me, Eve."

"My pleasure," she whispered as she slipped a hand between Josie's legs, sliding through her wetness. And oh, she was so wet, every bit as wet as Eve herself. She circled Josie's clit, drawing a strangled sound from her throat as her hips pressed against Eve's hand, meeting her movements thrust for thrust.

Eve arched her back, keeping enough space between their bodies that she wouldn't be tempted to ride Josie's leg, pushing her own need aside as she focused on Josie's pleasure.

"Eve," she gasped, drawing her in for a messy kiss as Eve's fingers slipped and stroked. Carefully, she slid a finger inside Josie, pumping in and out, feeling Josie's body grip her. "More."

She added a second finger, filling her as her palm pressed against Josie's clit, giving her the friction she needed. Her thighs clamped around Eve's hand, hips moving, and then she was coming, release pulsing through her, her inner walls tightening rhythmically around Eve's fingers as a long moan tore from her throat.

She gripped Eve's ass, pressing her hips down to meet Josie's, replacing her fingers with her body. They rocked together, separated only by the lace of Eve's thong as Josie rode out the last waves of her release. At last, she went limp, arms flung wide against the sheets, eyes closed and mouth parted in silent relief.

Eve held herself still, desperately aroused and just as mesmerized by the vision of postcoital Josie displayed beneath her. *Breathtaking.* She felt an uncomfortable pinch somewhere in the vicinity of her heart.

"Wow," Josie breathed, one arm sliding around Eve's waist, drawing her down for a kiss. "You have no idea how much I needed that."

"I think I do."

"Do you?" Josie murmured, kissing her slow and deep as her fingers teased Eve over the lace of her bra.

"Josie," she gasped. "I'm dying here."

Josie laughed as she rolled them, landing with one thigh between Eve's. "Is that so?"

"Yes." She shifted restlessly beneath her.

Josie slid a hand between them and inside Eve's underwear, fingers sliding through her wetness. "Yeah, I guess you are," she whispered, stroking her, and Eve exhaled in relief. Josie's fingers retreated, and then she was pushing down her underwear, stripping them away, followed by her bra. Their bodies pressed together, hot damp skin against hot damp skin.

"Don't worry, I've got you." Josie's fingers were back where she needed them, stroking and plunging as she rocked their bodies together, pressing Eve's body into the sheets with each thrust.

"Fuck." She squeezed her eyes shut, overcome by the energy building inside her.

Josie's fingers swirled over her clit, circling until Eve was dizzy with desire, whimpering and writhing beneath her, and then Josie pushed two fingers deep inside her. All Eve could do was hold on for the ride. As the pressure inside her finally reached its breaking point, Josie's fingers stilled. Eve wanted to scream.

"Look at me," Josie whispered.

Eve opened her eyes, staring into the swirling green-and-gold depths of Josie's eyes as she thrust her fingers again, sending Eve flying. She came with a cry, hips bucking as the orgasm washed through her, cleansing her of the emptiness she'd held on to for so long, filling her with a breathtaking rush of emotion.

She wrapped her arms around Josie, and they lay like that for several long minutes, arms and legs entwined, Josie's weight resting warm and solid over Eve's body. She might have thought she'd feel smothered by it. Eve was a woman who liked her space, after all. But in this moment, with Josie's body pressing her into the mattress, Josie's heart beating against her chest, and her breath feathering over Eve's neck, she felt grounded inside herself in a way she hadn't in a very long time.

Right now, beneath Josie's warm weight, Eve couldn't think. She could only feel. The languid aftershocks of her orgasm, the hum of satisfaction in her veins, the way every cell in her body felt achingly, exquisitely alive. Her arms tightened around Josie, heart thumping against her ribs, tears sliding over her cheeks and trickling into her hair.

She kept her breaths even, swallowing the sob that rose

in her throat, desperate to hide this unexpected surge of emotion from Josie. She closed her eyes, breathing past it, focusing on the way Josie's fingers slid up and down her arm, making goose bumps rise in their wake.

"I could lie here like this all night," Josie whispered, "except I'm absolutely famished." As if to emphasize her point, her stomach rumbled loudly.

Eve chuckled. She'd hadn't consumed anything but whiskey tonight either, although she hadn't really realized it until Josie pointed it out. "That's a problem."

"It's not, if I can just find the energy to walk to the kitchen," Josie said with a soft laugh. "I've got sandwich stuff in the fridge. I'm usually hungry after a long shift, but last night was so crazy, I never had dinner. I'm not even sure I ate lunch."

"We should feed you, then." Eve trailed her fingers up Josie's spine.

"Come on." Josie sat up, giving Eve's hand a tug. She turned toward the dresser beside the bed, and Eve used the moment to wipe the moisture from her cheeks, emotions now firmly in check. Josie pulled open a drawer and tossed Eve a hot pink T-shirt.

Eve lifted it, eyeing the rainbow-colored cat face on the front. "Really?" she deadpanned, arching an eyebrow.

"Would you rather wear this one?" Josie asked, holding up a purple shirt that said I LIKE PUSSY in big letters across the front.

"Nope. This one is good." Eve tugged it over her head and slid off the bed. The shirt hit her mid-thigh, possibly the most ridiculous thing she'd ever worn.

Josie took one look at her and doubled over in laughter.

"I know you own other shirts," Eve said.

"Maybe I just wanted to see you in that one." Josie

winked as she led the way to the kitchen. "Do you like roast beef?"

Eve nodded, accepting the package Josie held toward her. They worked in comfortable silence in the kitchen, fixing sandwiches, which they brought into the living room to eat. Outside the window, the sky was brightening with dawn. The clock read 6:04.

"You live like a vampire," Eve said, taking a big bite of her sandwich. No wonder she felt so delirious. She'd been up a full twenty-four hours at this point, had worked a half day at the office yesterday before Dragonfly's grand opening.

"It's not always this bad," Josie told her with a grin, wiping mustard from her cheek. "We're only open until four on Friday and Saturday nights. The rest of the week, we close at two, and if I'm really lucky, I'm in bed by two thirty. But yeah, this job has definitely turned me into a night owl."

"Were you not a night owl before?"

Josie looked wistful for a moment. "I guess I've always been a bit of a night owl, but I definitely kept a more normal schedule."

"What did you do for a living before you inherited Swanson's?"

"For about a year beforehand, I had been supporting myself on the income from my YouTube channel." Josie looked down at her plate. "I was a full-time kitten rescuer."

"Oh."

"I mean, it helped that I was renting this apartment from my dad, and he was cutting me a deal on rent," Josie said, her expression a million miles away.

Eve had the uncomfortable impression she'd hit on a sore subject, although she wasn't quite sure why, unless Josie was just missing her dad. "Did he live here too?"

"He had the apartment on the top floor." Josie gestured

above her head. "It's much bigger and nicer. I rent it out now. Well, you know that."

Eve nodded. She had known that. She was just so tired, she couldn't think straight. As part of her work for *Do Over*, she'd been over every inch of Josie's financial records. *Which is why you shouldn't be here now, in a rainbow pussy shirt, eating sandwiches in her living room.*

"That income helped keep me afloat this year, but you know that too." Josie smiled sadly.

"I think it's best if we don't talk business while we're dressed like this."

Josie glanced over at her. "Yeah, right. I didn't really mean to talk about business, just answering your question."

Eve turned her attention to her sandwich as an air of awkwardness descended between them, reminding her of all the ways she'd fucked up by sleeping with Josie. This was so much more than sex. She was so screwed. "My mistake for bringing it up."

18

Josie practically shoved the sandwich down her throat, feeling reenergized now that she had food in her belly. Beside her, Eve had gone quiet, posture stiff, staring fixedly into her water glass. The sight of her here in Josie's living room, hair mussed, makeup smudged, wearing Josie's ridiculously big and super-gay T-shirt...well, it was the most beautiful thing Josie had ever seen, but maybe it was too much. Maybe she'd pushed her too far.

She leaned over, nudging her shoulder against Eve's. "I'm glad you're here."

Eve's shoulders rounded as she tossed a small smile in Josie's direction. "Me too."

"You know I don't give a shit about mixing business with pleasure," she said, hoping to put to rest whatever was bothering Eve. "And I don't for a minute expect you to go easy on me when you come in to consult next week."

"Good, because I won't."

"I know you'll still be brutally honest, because that's just who you are, and honestly, I wouldn't want it—or you—any other way."

Eve was quiet, but the fight seemed to have gone out of her. Now, she just looked tired. Josie could relate. They needed to sleep before it got any later.

"I don't know about you, but I'm about to keel over," Josie said, rubbing beneath her eyes, suddenly desperate to scrub off what remained of the makeup the *Do Over* team had applied.

Eve nodded. "We should sleep. But we should probably feed them first." She tipped her head toward the kittens. Hamilton and Phantom were awake, crawling around their playpen on wobbly legs.

"Sometimes, I think you know their schedule better than I do," Josie teased as she stood and went into the kitchen to prepare bottles, bringing their dinner trash with her. Her body felt sluggish, like she was walking through mud, fatigue weighing her down now that she'd finally slowed down enough to feel it.

"I have a knack for schedules." Eve joined her in the kitchen to help. The T-shirt swamped her petite frame, effectively obliterating the razor-sharp armor she wore day-to-day with oversized cotton and a rainbow-colored cat.

"That you do." Josie leaned in to kiss her, and Eve sighed as she relaxed into the kiss, her body swaying against Josie's. Josie slid her hands over that hot-pink cotton, soft from countless washings. It was her comfort shirt, her sleeping in on a Monday morning shirt, and she'd never wear it again without picturing it on Eve.

She also had a feeling she wasn't going to be ready for this thing between them to end on Monday, but that was something to puzzle over later. She and Eve carried bottles into the living room, each lifting a kitten from the playpen.

Eve held Hamilton, positioning him effortlessly over her knees as she gave him the bottle. She was good at this, although Josie wasn't sure she'd appreciate having it pointed out to her. Instead, she focused on Phantom. When he was fed and cleaned, she rolled him over, tickling his tummy as he wiggled around on her legs, yawning contentedly.

And then Josie was yawning. "It's contagious," she said, giving him a quick kiss before she set him back in the playpen.

"Don't start that," Eve warned as she swapped Hamilton for Blanche. "At least not until we've finished feeding them."

Josie watched her, wondering if Eve realized she always reached for Hamilton and Blanche first. *You like them*, she wanted to tease. And suddenly, she pictured Eve taking them home in a few months. Adopting them. Full circle from the moment she'd pulled them out of that trash can.

Josie lifted Pippin, stroking his gray belly until he woke. He was sluggish this morning, much like Josie herself, and by the time she'd finished with him, Eve was already done feeding Blanche. She'd leaned against the couch with Blanche on her stomach, eyes closed. Blanche had curled up beneath her breasts and was fast asleep, toes twitching.

Josie pressed a hand to her mouth. If she wasn't so absolutely, positively sure Eve would hate her forever, she would have grabbed her phone and snapped a picture. Instead, she sat there for a moment, just watching them. Eve had to adopt Blanche. It just had to happen.

"Finished yet?" Eve asked groggily without opening her eyes.

"Mm-hmm."

"Let's go to bed." She sat up, sliding Blanche onto her palms and depositing her into the playpen in a move so practiced, it couldn't have been the first time she'd done it.

And the mental image of Eve at home in her apartment, snuggling with Blanche on her couch, was now permanently etched into the mushy, romantic part of Josie's brain.

"She likes you," she couldn't resist saying as they stood.

"Who does?" Eve asked, looking confused. "You mean Blanche?"

She nodded, taking Eve's hand as they walked to the bedroom.

"She'd like any warm body at this point, I think," Eve said, and then she softened. "That first night, it was so hard to get her to eat. She was so much smaller than the others."

"I always have a favorite too," Josie said, giving her fingers a squeeze. These moments when Eve let her guard down and offered little bits of raw honesty felt like being given a huge compliment, like she'd received something rare. "It's hard not to."

"They're just kittens," Eve deflected, and Josie let it go.

They took turns in the bathroom washing up. As Josie crawled onto the bed beside her, Eve's ankle tattoo caught her eye. She traced her fingers over the infinity symbol, thrilled with the newfound freedom to touch her.

"Lisa and I got them together," Eve said quietly. "Matching tattoos."

"Oh?" Josie had wondered at the meaning behind it. She paused with her fingers pressed against Eve's inked skin, hoping to encourage her to continue.

"There was a long time when we weren't sure when or if we'd be able to get legally married, so we got them to show that our love was forever."

"That's beautiful." Josie slid up to press her lips against Eve's. Maybe it should bother her that Eve had her love for another woman tattooed on her body, but it didn't. It seemed like a fitting tribute to the woman who would forever be a part of Eve's heart. "Thank you for telling me."

Eve nodded, giving her a quick kiss in return. She was quiet, but her body was relaxed, her eyes calm. Josie rolled over to turn off the light before pulling the sheet over them. Nigel hopped up, landing between them, but she nudged him onto the floor. *Not tonight, dude.* And then, with Eve curled at a polite distance on the other side of the bed, she closed her eyes, falling almost immediately asleep.

When the alarm on her phone buzzed three hours later, the first thing she registered was an arm tucked around her waist, a warm presence at her back, and the whisper of breath in her ear. Josie grinned. Who would have guessed the ice queen liked to snuggle in her sleep? Careful not to wake her, Josie silenced the alarm and slipped out of bed, tiptoeing to the living room to feed the kittens.

She kept the lights off—although it was fully daylight outside at this point anyway—running through the routine the way she always did in the middle of the night. When she climbed back into bed, Eve had rolled over and was mumbling in her sleep. Josie set another alarm, in case neither of them woke before the next feeding, and drifted back to sleep.

The next time she woke, the bed was empty, and the smell of coffee permeated the apartment. Josie squinted, bringing the clock into focus before her sleep-blurred eyes. It was almost one o'clock in the afternoon. Ugh. Going to bed at sunrise really threw off her whole day. But, judging by the sounds coming from the kitchen, Eve was still here, and...that changed everything.

Josie stretched, smiling despite the fatigue still clinging to her body. It hadn't been a good night's sleep, but there was a very good reason for that, so she really couldn't complain. She hauled herself out of bed and went into the bathroom to freshen up. Then, stifling a yawn, she headed into the living room to find Eve—still wearing the pink T-shirt—on the couch feeding Pippin. Nigel sat beside her, watching her intently.

She looked up. "Good morning...or afternoon, depending on your perspective."

"Yeah. I'm all out of whack." She dropped onto the couch next to Eve. "Who still needs to be fed?"

"No one. He's the last." She rubbed Pippin's gray head as she looked at Josie, and wow, barefaced-fresh-from-bed Eve was breathtaking. There was a youth and an innocence to her with sleep-mussed hair and Josie's oversized T-shirt hanging off her left shoulder.

"Thanks for feeding them."

"Well, since you let me sleep through their last feeding, I figured the least I could do is return the favor." Eve finished up with Pippin and set him in the playpen, glancing at Nigel, who was still watching her every move. "I'm not sure your cat likes me."

"Nah, he's just nosy," Josie said with a grin.

Eve gave him a skeptical look, then stood to clean up the feeding supplies.

"Want breakfast?" Josie asked as she followed her into the kitchen.

"It's past one," Eve pointed out.

Josie shrugged. "It's what happens when you spend the night with a bartender. We have dinner at six a.m. and breakfast at one."

"I need to go," Eve said, rinsing bottles at the sink.

"Got plans today?"

She hesitated just long enough for Josie to realize that if she'd gotten up five minutes later, Eve would have been long gone. "Look, I don't do this." She gestured around the apartment at large, glancing at Josie with an apology in her eyes. "Not anymore."

Josie folded her arms over her chest, argument dying on her tongue. *Not anymore.* Because Eve had done this before, all of it. As hard as it was for Josie to picture her as part of anything as domestic as this morning after, borrowed T-shirts and awkward conversations, Eve had been married. She'd lived a life a million times more domestic than anything Josie herself had experienced.

"You can leave now if you want, but that doesn't make me one of your one-night stands," Josie said quietly.

Eve kept her back turned as she wiped down the kitchen counter.

"I have muffins in the pantry. Or I'll see you on Monday for work. Tuesday, actually, because the bar's closed on Monday. Your choice."

Eve smoothed her hands over the front of the T-shirt before reaching up to tuck her hair behind her ears, flattening it beneath her palms. She turned to face Josie. "What kind of muffins?"

Josie hid her smile. "Coffee cake and chocolate chip. I have a sweet tooth in the morning."

Eve's lips twitched as if she were hiding a smile of her own. "I don't usually, but today I think I might."

"I'm rubbing off on you." She nudged her shoulder against Eve's as she walked to the pantry and pulled out the box of muffins. She set it on the counter so Eve could help herself and reached up for two coffee mugs, since Eve had already brewed a pot for them. *She was planning to leave, but she still made me coffee.* Josie grinned as she poured herself a cup. She got out the milk and sugar, and they prepared their breakfast quietly, carrying muffins and coffee into the living room to eat. "I have to be back downstairs in just a few hours."

"Weekends are busy for you," Eve said, breaking off a little piece of her muffin and popping it into her mouth. Of course she'd eat it that way.

Josie lifted the whole thing and took a big bite, chewing thoughtfully. "Weekends are exhausting."

"I bet."

"Will I see you? You know, before Tuesday?" she asked cautiously. "I mean, just for the record, I had a really good time last night, and I'd really like to do this again...preferably when we could actually spend a whole night together instead of going to bed at daybreak."

"Latest night I've had in ages," Eve agreed, carefully avoiding the question.

"Well, you know where to find me, if you decide you want to," Josie said, realizing she had no idea where Eve lived. It was disconcerting when she thought of how often Eve had been in her apartment over the last two weeks. Granted, it had been primarily for the sake of the kittens, but still.

"I do," Eve agreed, and well...it wasn't a no.

"Do you live far from here?" she asked.

"The East Village," Eve answered.

Josie immediately pictured her in one of the sleek, high-rise apartment buildings in that part of town. "What's that, about a half an hour from here?"

"About that, yes."

Eve looked at the kittens, currently snuggled against their surrogate mother, fast asleep. "Can you keep them permanently now that you have a full staff?"

Somehow, they hadn't discussed this yet, although Josie figured they were both assuming that she would. "It's not ideal, but they're too big now to sit in a box behind your desk, so yeah, I'll make it work."

"Good," Eve said with a decisive nod, and Josie wondered if it was wishful thinking on her part that she looked vaguely wistful.

"You know you're welcome to visit them anytime," she said.

Eve shot her a warning look.

Josie laughed. "You don't even have to see me if you don't want to. You know the code to the door. Just text me and let me know you're stopping by."

"That's ridiculous," Eve said.

"Coming up without seeing me is a little bit ridiculous, yeah, but visiting them isn't. You're invested, Eve. Of course you are. You saved their lives and nursed them through their first week."

Eve looked down at her hands. "I need to go."

"Okay. Hey..." She tugged at the pink sleeve of Eve's shirt, drawing her in for a lazy kiss. With a sigh, Eve relaxed, kissing her back. "I really am glad we spent last night together...or this morning...whenever."

"Me too," she murmured against Josie's lips before she pulled back and slid to her feet.

"You can borrow anything you need, clothes, toiletries, whatever," Josie told her, wrapping her arms around her knees.

"Thank you." Eve went into the bedroom, closing the door behind her.

Josie sat on the couch, sipping coffee and trying not to imagine what she was doing in there or whether she'd ever get to see Eve in one of her T-shirts again, whether she'd kiss her, hold her, strip her naked. Somehow, she had to believe the answer was yes. Yes to all of it.

Eve might like to think she was unaffected by the power of their connection, but Josie had held her, trembling and begging, as Eve came apart in her arms, and she didn't think it had been just sex for her either. She came out of Josie's bedroom a few minutes later, wearing a floor-length black T-shirt dress that was a size too big for her, hair neatly brushed and purse over her shoulder. Naturally, she'd managed to find what was probably the only dress Josie owned.

"I'll return it the next time I see you," Eve said.

"Sure."

She walked to the door but paused there, looking over her shoulder at Josie. "Thanks."

For what, Josie wasn't sure, but she smiled anyway, because whatever Eve meant, she was grateful for it. "Any time."

And with a nod, Eve was gone.

Josie sat there for a few minutes in silence, just absorbing everything that had happened in the last twenty-four hours. Dragonfly's grand opening. Her night with Eve. It was a lot to process, but it was all good. She refused to entertain the worries nagging at the back of her brain that the bar might be empty tonight without the draw of the cameras, that Dragonfly would still keep her from investing herself in her rescue the way she wanted to, and that Eve might go back to all business now that they'd released the sexual tension between them.

Josie shook her head and picked up her coffee mug. None of that. The new bar was exciting. There would definitely be fewer patrons tonight without the lure of cameras, but Eve had helped her set up a lot of advertising, so people would come. And even if Eve returned them to a strictly business relationship, she'd still be grateful for the night they'd shared.

One thing Josie had learned over the years was that life rarely went in the direction she expected. She finished her coffee and carried the mug to the kitchen. It was almost two, and she had a lot to do before Dragonfly opened for its second day. On that note, she showered, dressed, and went downstairs. She sat in her office and spent some time on social media, adding photos from last night and responding to customer comments.

Before she knew it, Adam was poking his head in the doorway. "Hey, boss."

She laughed. "Ugh, don't call me that. It just feels weird."

He dropped into her guest chair with a grin. "Even weirder when I ask about your night, because hot damn, girl, you and Eve looked like you were about to go at it right there in the bar when I left. Please tell me you took her upstairs once you got her alone."

Josie's cheeks flushed hot. "I did."

He whooped, leaning forward to give her a fist bump. "And?"

"And it was great...like, *really* great." She sighed as she remembered the feel of Eve's naked body pressed against hers and all the intimate things they'd shared, both in and out of bed.

"I'm happy for you, Jo. It's been a while since I've seen you this taken with someone. How did you leave things?"

"Well, I told her I wanted to see her again, but I don't know if she's going to take me up on it or not."

"She'd be a fool not to," he said. "But what's the hang-up? You like each other. Your gig on her show's finished. You had a great night together. Why wouldn't you go for round two?"

She shrugged. "She's more of the 'one night' type, or so she says."

"I guess I can see that about her," he said, looking thoughtful. "And believe me, I have nothing against one-night stands. But they're usually more of a spontaneous thing, whereas you guys were simmering for weeks. Definitely feels like the start of something more."

"Yeah, well, she's been hurt in the past, so I think she's afraid to go there again," Josie said quietly. "And I can't blame her. She's been through a lot."

"Is she still in the closet?" he asked.

"No, it's not that. It's just...something personal I don't feel comfortable sharing without her permission."

"Gotcha, but I'll just add this...sharing deep, dark secrets isn't something one usually does with a one-night stand either," he said, eyebrows raised dramatically.

"I know." She closed her laptop with another sigh. "I really like her, and I'll do what I can to nudge her in the right direction, but if she truly doesn't want a relationship, then I have to respect that."

He leaned back in his seat. "Ugh, you're so good."

"I know," she said playfully as she stood from behind her desk. "Ready to help me open? I've got to run back upstairs and feed the kittens first, though."

"Want a hand?"

"Always."

So she and Adam fed the kittens together. Elizabeth arrived to work the rooftop bar again tonight. And soon enough, the doors were open. No line waited outside tonight, but by five thirty, they had a handful of customers, and by seven, the place was packed. This was busier than any Saturday night in Swanson's recent history. And already, she loved Dragonfly's crowd so much more. Her bar was filled with a virtual rainbow of people. Her people. It filled her with joy every time she looked around the room.

Just after midnight, her gaze caught on a brunette at the end of the bar, wearing skinny jeans and a flowy black top. Josie's heart gave a weird double beat that made her head swim. Eve had come after all.

19

"Welcome to Dragonfly. I'm Josie."

Eve stared into Josie's laughing eyes, unsure what to make of the introduction. Was she trying to have a little fun, or was something else going on?

"House specialty," Josie said as she set a glass on the bar in front of Eve. "It's called Midnight in Manhattan, and since it's actually midnight in Manhattan—and also here in Brooklyn—you should try one."

"I didn't order it," Eve pointed out, reluctant to play along with this game Josie had started. But then again, a little role-play might keep her from having to address other uncomfortable topics...like why she was here tonight in the first place.

"You look like the kind of woman who would appreciate a romantic drink," Josie said, leaning her elbows on the bar with a satisfied smile.

"Romantic?" she asked.

Josie winked dramatically. "Rumor has it, if you drink one at midnight, you'll fall in love by the end of the year."

"Hm." Eve lifted the glass and gave it a swirl. "I'm not much of a romantic, so I guess I'll take my chances." She lifted it to her lips and sipped.

Josie looked delighted. "What do you think?"

"It's very good," Eve told her honestly. "Has it been popular?"

"Yeah," Josie said, smile softening as she dropped the act. "It's the most popular drink on the menu, by far. I may have to send Adam out for more lemons before the end of the night."

"And how are things going tonight, compared to last night?" she asked, falling easily into her role as marketing consultant. It was a hell of a lot easier to pretend she'd stopped by to check on Josie for professional reasons than admitting she couldn't get her out of her head no matter how hard she tried. And she'd tried pretty damn hard.

"It's quieter than last night," Josie said. "But we knew it would be. I think it's a good crowd for a Saturday night. Don't you?" Her voice slipped up in register at the end, doubt leaking into her tone.

"I do," Eve told her. "You're doing great."

"I hope so," Josie said. "Be right back."

She moved down the bar, lavender hair gleaming as she mixed drinks, smiling and laughing, sharing jokes and conversation. So beautiful. Josie was always energetic and outgoing, but she really seemed to shine when she worked. Eve could watch her all night. In fact, she'd be perfectly content to do just that. She sipped her drink as she watched Josie mix cocktails for a couple a few seats down.

"She's good, isn't she?"

Eve turned her head to find Adam standing in front of her, a knowing smile on his face. "Yes, she is."

"Can't seem to keep you out of this place," he said playfully.

"Well, I'm invested in its success," Eve said with a shrug. She liked Adam well enough, despite her doubts about his skills as a bartender, but she had no desire to discuss her personal relationship with Josie with him.

"And in Josie," he said, eyebrows rising for emphasis.

"Yes," she answered evenly, holding his gaze.

His grin widened. "Good." He slapped his palms against the bar, seemingly satisfied with her answer, and moved off to serve a couple of women who'd just come in.

Eve lifted her glass and drained it, savoring the warmth of liquor in her belly. She was going to need liquid courage to make it through the rest of the night, four hours until the bar closed...if she wanted to be here when Josie got off work.

"Want another?" Josie said, appearing in front of her.

"Sure."

"Coming right up." Josie turned to the counter behind her, deftly mixing ingredients. She gave the tin a shake before pouring its contents into a fresh glass, which she placed in front of Eve. She looked down at it, a wrinkle appearing between her eyes. "Does it still bother you to be here? You know, in a bar?"

Eve straightened reflexively. "No."

"Honestly?" Josie looked up, her eyes searching Eve's.

She hadn't consciously thought about it, but her reasons for being uncomfortable tonight had nothing to do with the past and everything to do with the future. "Honestly. You've desensitized me to it, I guess."

Josie flinched. "I'm not sure I want to be responsible for desensitizing you to anything."

"It was a silly hang-up of mine, but I'm past it now."

Josie rested a hand over Eve's. "There was nothing silly about it."

Eve sucked in a lungful of air and blew it out. "I hadn't been in a bar since the night she died, and it brought back some very visceral memories. I'm sorry for letting it affect my judgment when it came to the show."

"Don't you dare apologize. I'm just...I'm really glad you're here." The alarm went off on Josie's phone, and she swiped it from her pocket with a frown. She silenced it, glancing at the packed bar. Adam was here, but he mixed drinks at about half Josie's usual speed.

"I'll do it," Eve said, sliding off her stool. "Just put my drink behind the bar so no one touches it."

"Thank you," Josie told her earnestly. "I appreciate it."

She nodded, turning to weave her way through the people in the bar. It really was a good turnout for Josie's second night and boded well for Dragonfly's future success. Eve slipped out the back, punched in the code to the stairs, and headed up to Josie's apartment. It was dark inside, lit only by the small lamp in the living room that she left on for the kittens.

Eve had come up countless times over the last two weeks to feed them, but suddenly, it felt strange to be here alone. Because now, she was thinking about kissing Josie against the kitchen counter, stripping her naked in the bedroom, sitting on the couch in her pink T-shirt as they shared muffins and coffee.

She pressed her hands against her flushed cheeks. God, she needed to get a grip. But her grip had slipped the moment she decided to walk into Dragonfly tonight. Because Josie surely knew as well as Eve did that she was here because she wanted to wind up in Josie's bed again tonight. They'd barely gotten a chance to explore each other last night. It hadn't been enough. She needed more. Surely another night would do the trick.

She walked into the kitchen to prepare bottles, and then carried all the supplies with her into the living room. Hamilton and Blanche were awake, crawling around their playpen on wobbly legs. They'd gotten so much bigger—and stronger—in the two weeks since she'd pulled them out of that trash can.

"Hey, you," she said, lifting Blanche into her lap. "Hungry?"

Blanche meowed, heading straight for the bottle like a little pro. So different from that first night, when Eve hadn't been able to wake her, when she'd feared the kitten might die in her hands. Tonight, Blanche latched onto the bottle and drank hungrily. When she'd finished eating, Eve cleaned her up and let Blanche snuggle in her lap while she cared for the other kittens.

Josie's orange cat sat on the couch beside her, staring at her while she worked. It was unsettling. Eve did her best to ignore him. Once the three boys had been fed and cared for and returned to their playpen, Eve looked down at the little white kitten. Blanche was nestled against her stomach, face pressed against her shirt, fast asleep. For a few minutes, Eve just sat there, fingers stroking her soft fur. Her gaze caught on a droplet of spilled formula on her blouse.

Dammit.

Tears flooded her eyes, and since no one was here to see, she let them drip silently over her cheeks as she thought of the daughter she'd never met, the middle-of-the-night feedings that had never happened, the loss that sometimes got swallowed up in the enormity of Lisa's death. Eve had lost her whole world that night. The fear, the pain, *so much blood*, as she'd held on to Lisa's limp body in the seat beside her, praying for the paramedics to arrive in time to save her, to save them both.

She sucked in a shaky breath, forcing the memories away. She lifted Blanche from her lap and laid her against the stuffed animal in the playpen where her brothers were piled up, sleeping peacefully. Nigel still sat there, watching her.

"Get lost," she snapped, turning her back on him.

It was ridiculous, letting herself get worked up like this over a drop of spilled formula. *Crying over spilled milk.* Eve wasn't looking for a family, not anymore, and she didn't want to be reminded of the one she'd lost. She stood, drying her cheeks before walking into Josie's bathroom to fix her makeup. She shouldn't be here. Josie—and the damn kittens—stirred things in Eve that she didn't want stirred.

She removed all evidence of her tears, cleaned up the bottle-feeding supplies, and headed downstairs to the bar. Dragonfly's noise and crowd was a welcome distraction, silencing the ghosts in her head as she slid onto her stool. She sat there, letting it fill her, the music, the buzz of conversation, the liquor still warming her blood. And she relaxed, resting an elbow against the bar.

A glass appeared in front of her, and she looked into Josie's smiling face. "Babies all cared for?"

"They're kittens, not babies." Her voice came out harsher than she'd intended. She took a hearty gulp of her drink, avoiding Josie's unflinching gaze. "But yes, they're fine."

"Good," Josie said, seemingly unscathed by Eve's sharp edges. She leaned closer, purple hair falling around her face like a protective curtain, sealing Eve in a space where no one existed but the two of them. "Wish I could speed up the clock."

"Why?" Eve asked, hoping she sounded more nonchalant than she felt.

"Because I'm impatient to take you upstairs and get you naked."

"Who says I'm here for sex?" Eve said, toying with her glass as she leveled Josie with her coolest stare. Second nights allowed for unwanted baggage. She needed to get over herself and leave right now, before she made this thing between them any more complicated than it already was.

Josie laughed. She *laughed*, damn her. Eve might have tossed her drink in Josie's smug face if she wasn't so ridiculously aroused by the sight. Josie leaned in again, something wicked dancing in her eyes. "You're cute when you lie."

Josie had been trying to speed up the clock all night, and now that it was finally closing time, she wanted to slow it back down. Because Eve wasn't here. She'd gone upstairs almost an hour ago to feed the kittens a second time, and she must have slipped out the back, because she hadn't returned to the bar. And Josie was irrationally disappointed about it.

Worse, it was her fault. She shouldn't have teased Eve earlier. It was a big fucking deal that she'd shown up at all, and Josie should have respected that. She should have appreciated how difficult this was for Eve. Instead, she'd turned it into a joke, and Eve had bolted.

And she might not come back. She'd taken an emotional risk, and Josie had laughed in her face. Ugh. She could cry she was so upset with herself.

"You okay?" Adam asked as he bent in front of the dishwasher.

"Yep. Just tired."

"Where'd Eve go?"

"Home," she told him, trying to keep the frustration out of her voice.

"Bummer," he said, thankfully knowing better than to pry right now.

"Yep." She went through the rest of her routine methodically, wiping down the bar and tabletops, cleaning and straightening, transferring all the money from the cash register to the safe in her office, setting everything to order. She said good night to Adam and Elizabeth, and then she trudged upstairs to her apartment...alone.

It was just as well, because she was so tired, she could hardly see straight. Weekend bartending hours were no joke. She locked the door behind herself, grateful that at least the kittens had been fed, so she could fall face-first into bed for a few hours before she'd have to get up and feed them again.

She was halfway across the room before she saw her. Eve was on the couch, slumped on her side, fast asleep with Nigel curled up beside her, keeping watch. Josie slapped a hand over her mouth, swallowing her surprise. Tentatively, she walked closer, making sure the image before her was real. It was no trick of her sleep-deprived and eternally optimistic eyes.

Eve was really on her couch, feet on the floor, keeled over as if she'd passed out while feeding the kittens. *Oh shit.* Josie stepped closer, checking to make sure all four kittens were in the playpen, because even a petite woman like Eve could easily crush one to death if she rolled onto it in her sleep. But the kittens were all where they were supposed to be. Eve was responsible even in her exhausted state.

Josie hesitated for a moment, wondering whether to

wake her. But that position didn't look comfortable, especially for a woman with fused vertebrae, and ultimately, it should be Eve's choice whether she stayed the night. Josie shooed Nigel away and sat beside her, running a hand gently down Eve's arm. She jerked beneath Josie's touch, blinking up at her in confusion.

"Hi," Josie whispered.

"Why are you..." Eve pushed herself upright, wincing as one hand went to her back.

"You fell asleep on my couch," Josie told her. "I thought you'd gone home when you didn't come back to the bar after feeding the kittens."

"Oh." Eve ran her hands through her hair, clearly disoriented.

"I just closed up." Josie tugged at her hand. "Come on. It's late. Let's go to bed."

Eve followed her quietly to the bedroom, standing there in the darkness, her body humming with something unspoken as she came more fully back to her senses. Josie wasn't sure what it was, but she felt it hanging heavily in the air between them. Carefully, she went to Eve, cupping her face in her hands and giving her a gentle kiss. "We can sleep now and save the rest for tomorrow, if you want."

"I'm not *that* tired," Eve responded, hands sliding around Josie's waist.

"Could have fooled me," Josie teased gently.

"Well, I'm awake now," Eve murmured. Her hands slipped beneath the waistband of Josie's jeans, brushing against her bare skin.

Josie pressed forward, kissing her the way she'd wanted to since she first saw Eve at the bar earlier tonight, the kind of kiss that scrambled her brain and had their bodies moving against each other, seeking contact, creating friction, igniting the fire that always seemed to be simmering between them.

They fumbled with each other's clothes, pushing down zippers and popping bra clasps, mouths separating only to lift shirts overhead. It was like a messily orchestrated dance as their hips sought every opportunity to press together, moving rhythmically. When they were naked, Josie pushed Eve onto the bed, following her down.

They lay facing each other, still kissing as their hands roamed and teased. Josie palmed Eve's breasts, loving the way they fit in her hands, small but perfect. Eve's nipples pebbled beneath her touch, a gasp of pleasure escaping her lips as Josie toyed with them, wanting to memorize every inch of her.

It was so late—or early, depending how she looked at it —and she was tempted to hurry, knowing they both desperately needed sleep. But she didn't want to hurry. She wanted to spend hours finding out everything Eve liked, the most sensitive spots on her body, all the different ways to make her come.

"Sometime," Josie murmured as she trailed her hand down Eve's stomach, "we have to do this when it's not daybreak, so we can take our time and fuck each other properly."

"This isn't proper enough for you?" Eve responded, one hand sliding between Josie's legs.

She gasped, hips arching instinctively into Eve's touch. "You know what I mean."

"Yes." Eve stroked her, hips jerking as Josie returned the favor. "I do."

"Good." Josie matched the rhythm of Eve's fingers, hips moving together as they brought each other closer to release. "Because it's going to happen."

Eve didn't respond to that, didn't commit to anything beyond the pleasure of her nimble fingers as they drew circles around Josie's clit, making her hips buck and her breath hitch. She pressed closer, giving as good as she got, fingers stroking and plunging. She focused her attention—or at least as much as she could manage—on providing pleasure, making a silent pact with herself to bring Eve to orgasm before she herself broke.

And sure enough, Eve tensed against her, a cry of pleasure escaping her lips as she came, her body tightening and releasing around Josie's fingers. She held herself still, letting Eve ride out her release, feeling her own body tighten with each wave of Eve's pleasure.

Eve's fingers moved erratically against her before settling back into her previous rhythm with a vengeance. She swirled and stroked, making Josie see stars. The pressure inside her built steadily, and she pulled Eve closer, needing to feel every inch of Eve's skin joined with hers as she floated toward release.

"I'm so close," she panted. They were connected everywhere, foreheads touching, breasts nestled together, hands between each other's legs, all the way down to their toes, which were arched against each other as Josie used the leverage to thrust her hips into Eve's.

And then she was coming, release rushing through her, cleansing her of a long, exhausting day, shimmering inside her as if she'd been filled with sequins. She held on to Eve as tightly as she could, gasping for breath as she absorbed every last moment of pleasure.

They stayed like that, facing each other, arms and legs entwined, until sleep began to soften the edges of her brain. And then—because she had tiny lives depending on her—she broke free long enough to set the alarm on her phone before sliding back into Eve's arms, drifting blissfully into sleep in the comfortable warmth of her embrace.

She woke a few hours later when her phone buzzed, fed the kittens without waking Eve, and slipped back into bed, still desperately tired. The next time she woke, sunlight streamed through the window, and the bed was empty.

She smiled, imagining a replay of yesterday. Again, the smell of coffee permeated the apartment. Josie sat up, still wearing the T-shirt she'd put on to feed the kittens earlier that morning. The clock showed that—like yesterday—it was already past one. She went into the bathroom to freshen up before wandering into the living room.

The kittens slept peacefully in their playpen, but Eve was nowhere to be seen. A piece of paper lay on the coffee table.

Fed them at 10:30. Didn't want to wake you.

Unlike yesterday, Eve was gone.

20

If you have plans tonight after work, cancel them. I'm taking you on a real date.

Eve stared at the text from Josie. Then she set the phone on her desk, returning to the email she'd been composing before the interruption. For some reason, the polite but firm rejection that should have been her automatic response—that was *always* her response to an invitation from someone she'd already slept with—failed her. The words wouldn't come.

Instead, she found herself mentally running through her closet, imagining what dress, what heels, what lingerie Josie might like best. Which was ludicrous. She and Josie had already had their night together. Two nights, in fact.

Since Eve left her apartment yesterday morning, she hadn't spoken to Josie and had done a pretty damn good job at not thinking about her either. But now, with Josie's invitation lingering at her fingertips, she was *all* Eve could think about.

Maybe they deserved to go on a real date and spend an entire night together. Maybe that was the reason Eve was shifting restlessly in her office chair, imagining all the things she and Josie hadn't yet explored with each other. It was Monday, and Dragonfly was closed. This was her one chance to go out with Josie, something Josie herself had obviously already figured out. Eve picked up her phone.

Awfully presumptuous of you, she replied.

I'm very presumptuous where you're concerned.

That should have pissed her off. Instead, it turned her on. She crossed one leg over the other, spinning in her chair to face the window. *When and where?*

Bohéme at 7.

See you there.

Eve put down her phone, drew in a deep breath, and got back to work. She successfully managed not to think about Josie for the rest of her workday. In fact, she didn't let herself think about their upcoming date until she was on the subway headed home.

What would Josie wear tonight? Somehow, Eve couldn't picture her in anything but jeans. Would her hair still be purple? Probably. It had only been a day since they'd seen each other, after all.

Eve walked into her apartment, pausing before she switched on the light to absorb the darkness, letting it sink into her pores. Sometimes, she preferred the dark so she didn't have to see the emptiness that surrounded her. For a very long time, she hadn't wanted anything—or anyone—in her life. She was married to her career now. Wasn't that what people said?

She'd always had big career ambitions. Owning her own marketing business had been her dream since college. And then, barely out of grad school, she'd fallen head over heels in love, and everything had changed. She'd taken a detour, and she would have continued happily on that course if fate hadn't intervened. But it had. Losing Lisa had nearly broken her. She could never go through anything that painful again.

She flipped on the light, exhaling slowly as she adjusted to its glare. She had about an hour before she needed to leave to meet Josie. Her back had been bothering her all day. Too much activity, and too little sleep. She did a few stretching exercises and then went into her bedroom to get the heating pad, the same one she'd used to warm up the kittens that first night. She plugged it in and stretched out flat on her bed, letting warmth seep into her body, soothing her sore spots. Eyes closed, she melted into the comforter beneath her.

Twenty minutes later, she hauled herself upright before she fell asleep and stayed there all night. While it was tempting to do just that—to back out of their date and seal herself in the seclusion of her apartment—she needed this. She needed an entire night with Josie, time to fully explore the chemistry between them and get it out of her system.

Heat rolled over her skin as she thought of the night ahead. *Yes.* God, she needed it.

She went into the closet, pushing past the selection of dresses she wore to the office to the "night out" dresses she wore far less often. Even these were usually worn to client dinners and business events. In fact, it had been years since she'd gone on a real date, even longer since she'd felt anything like the anticipation humming through her veins as she pulled a slinky, plum-colored dress off its hanger and carried it to the bed.

She dressed, brushed out her hair, freshened her makeup, and added a dab of perfume behind her ears. In deference to her back, she put on strappy black flats. And then, deciding she didn't have patience for the subway right now, she called an Uber. Fifteen minutes later, she arrived at the restaurant.

Josie stood just inside the entrance, wearing a snug black top with a shiny silver-and-purple pattern woven into the fabric and black pants that highlighted her curves. It was perfectly Josie's style and also really, *really* hot.

She looked up, breaking into one of those grins that brought out the dimples in her cheeks, stepping forward to lace her fingers through Eve's as she drew her in for a quick kiss. "You look hot," she whispered.

"Funny. I was just thinking the same thing about you."

"You have the best clothes. Seriously." Josie looked her up and down, gold flecks in her eyes dancing beneath the restaurant's lighting.

"It's important to look the part for my job," she said, then smiled. "And also, I like shopping."

"And you're obviously good at it." Josie gave her another kiss. "Ready?"

Eve nodded, not objecting when Josie kept her fingers threaded with Eve's as they walked to the hostess desk. They were seated at a small table along the wall. Eve pushed the drink menu in Josie's direction. "This is your area of expertise."

"What are you in the mood for tonight? Wine? Cocktails?" Josie picked it up, scanning the list.

"Wine sounds good."

"Red?" Josie asked, glancing up.

"Yes. Pick a bottle. Whatever you like." Eve didn't usually give her dates this much decision power, but she loved seeing Josie's confidence and competence when it came to her job.

"The Brandlin Estate Cabernet Sauvignon is really good. It's rich but not too dry, just fruity enough to soften the flavor," Josie said, an adorable wrinkle between her eyes as she looked over the menu.

"Sounds perfect."

The waitress approached, and Josie ordered their wine, leaning back in her seat with a satisfied look on her face. "I'm so glad to be here tonight, you have no idea."

"Here, as in, not in the bar?" Eve asked, watching her closely.

"Well, yes," Josie said. "But I meant here, in this restaurant, with you."

"I'm glad too," Eve admitted. Sometimes she forgot how nice it was to go out with someone whose company she genuinely enjoyed, to share a romantic meal, wine, conversation, and the anticipation of the night ahead.

"I really needed this." Josie reached out and squeezed her fingers. "I've been on so many bad dates lately, and this one is already a win, just because it's with you."

Eve wasn't sure how to respond to that. Luckily, the waitress saved her by arriving with their bottle of wine, pouring a taste for Josie to approve. Eve smiled slightly. Usually, she was the one who approved the bottle, the one in charge. Not tonight.

Once the wine had been poured, Josie leaned forward, forearms on the table as she took a sip and settled her gaze on Eve. "So tell me, what do you do when you're not working? Hobbies? Activities?"

Eve swirled her wine, inhaling its rich scent before she took a sip. "Nothing terribly exciting. I try to make it to the gym a few times a week, and I do some yoga at home."

"Yeah, I can tell." Josie dragged her gaze appreciatively over Eve's body, filling her with a delicious warmth. "And what do you do for fun?"

"Believe it or not, I enjoy my job, which is good because I

work long hours." At Josie's skeptical look, she shrugged. "I also enjoy art. I like to wander through museums and galleries, and I buy way too much for the amount of wall space I have."

"Interesting," Josie said with a smile. "See, I just learned something new about you. And now I want to wander through a museum with you, because I know nothing about art, and my walls—as you've probably noticed—are pretty bare."

"Not true," Eve told her. "You've got kitten and cat pictures everywhere."

"Well, okay, I suppose I do." Josie laughed. "But maybe I could use some art too."

"Maybe." Eve took another sip of her wine. "Your turn. Tell me what you do for fun when you're not working."

Josie sighed, looking wistful. "Honestly? I just really like to go out with my friends. I like to go out for drinks somewhere I don't work. I like to go dancing. And I like caring for orphaned kittens. I don't know why. It's my calling, I guess."

"Even if it means endless middle-of-the-night feedings?" Eve didn't mind doing it for the theater kittens. They were temporary. Already, they were growing, able to go longer between feedings. But the idea of taking in new kittens, an endless cycle of needy, helpless creatures? That sounded overwhelming and exhausting.

"Yes." Josie shrugged. "I can't explain it."

"How did you get started?"

"I used to volunteer at the shelter, and someone brought in a litter of orphaned kittens just a few weeks old. And I found out they were going to be euthanized, these tiny, innocent babies, because no one had the time or ability to care for them. It broke my heart. I took them home, and I raised them until they were old enough to be adopted. And then I did it again. Eventually, I realized there was a gap in the system, and these babies were falling through it. So I formed my own rescue to save them."

"That's pretty inspiring, I have to say," Eve told her. "Not many people would do what you did."

"And I can't blame them. It's a *lot*. If you work a full-time job, it's almost impossible to care for them properly, as you found out."

Eve nodded as she remembered the box of kittens behind her desk.

"I had a network of volunteers I worked with, and we were saving so many kittens. My YouTube channel was really taking off. It was all working out the way I'd imagined. And then my dad died." Her expression clouded. "And my priorities shifted."

"I understand what that's like." Eve related to Josie's words to the very bottom of her soul.

"I guess you do," Josie said. "When you lose someone you love, it changes everything."

"Yes, it does."

"I don't believe in that 'everything happens for a reason' bullshit, because my dad shouldn't have had to die like that, and neither should your wife, but I do believe everything that happens in our lives molds us and shapes us into the people we become."

"That's true," Eve said. "And it changes us. I could never go back to being the person I was before."

"You don't think you'll settle down again?"

"No." She lowered her shoulders and softened the curve of her back, trying not to appear as tense as she felt.

"I've never really thought about settling down," Josie said, deflecting the conversation away from Eve, although she wasn't sure whether she'd done it on purpose. "Lately,

I'm lucky to find someone I even want to have a second date with." She caught Eve's gaze. "But I already know I'd like a second date with you."

JOSIE WATCHED an invisible lens slide over Eve's eyes, hiding her behind its protective shield. She hadn't really meant to blurt out her intentions like that, but the opening had been too good to pass up. "I know you're not looking for a relationship. Neither am I. We're both up to our ears in work. You of all people know how ridiculous my schedule is."

Eve reached for her wine, the hint of a smile ghosting her lips.

"So maybe we try something casual, dinner on my night off, maybe occasionally you find your way into my bed after work..." She winked, trying to lighten the mood.

"Maybe," Eve said quietly.

"I'll take maybe," she told her with a grin. "And I have a few ideas for later that might help persuade you."

"Is that so?" Eve's eyes met hers, heat simmering in their chocolate depths.

"Oh yeah. I mean, a whole night together? The kittens are a bit of a mood dampener, but if you want to know the truth..." She leaned forward, lowering her voice. "You look pretty hot in my T-shirt with a kitten in your lap."

"Not sure I can agree with that last part," Eve said, but her tone had softened, a playfulness there that made Josie's grin widen.

"Well, I'd probably find you sexy in just about anything, so there's that."

Eve laughed, and the conversation slipped back into comfortable territory as they ate. After their entrees, they shared a crème brûlée as they finished up their bottle of wine. Josie was comfortably buzzed as she led the way outside, pausing to push Eve against the side of the building and kiss her, tasting wine and caramelized sugar on her tongue, the promise of endless pleasure in her fingertips as they brushed over Josie's thighs before gripping her waist.

Someone whistled, followed by several men shouting lewd suggestions. Josie lifted her head just in time to see Eve flip them off, eyes glinting in the darkness.

"Hot," Josie whispered in her ear.

"Let's get out of here." Eve untangled herself, leading the way briskly toward the subway entrance at the end of the block before the situation could escalate. The men in question were still shouting and making rude gestures, but Josie refused to give them even a moment of her time. Nothing was going to spoil tonight for her.

She followed Eve down the steps into the subway, where they both swiped their MetroCards and headed for the platform.

"Sorry," Eve said. "I would have called an Uber for us, but I didn't think we should hang around that crowd."

"Agreed."

Eve gave her a small smile, but it was one of those genuine smiles that made Josie feel like she'd won the lottery or just saved a whole shelter's worth of kittens. As they waited on the platform, Eve stood close beside her, so close their arms brushed together and the scent of Eve's perfume drifted over her.

They boarded the A train, sitting side by side as it whisked them toward Josie's apartment. Someday, she wanted to see where Eve lived, but with the kittens needing to be fed in a little over an hour, there was no question whose bed they'd wind up in tonight.

They were mostly quiet as they rode, quiet as they climbed the steps to the street, quiet as Josie unlocked the back door to her building, letting them in. It wasn't an uncomfortable silence, though, more of a calm before the storm, because she felt the energy between them building with each step toward her apartment door.

As soon as they'd stepped inside, Eve had her pinned against the wall, bodies pressed together, mouths meeting hungrily. "How much time do we have?" she asked, tipping her head toward the playpen in the living room.

"About an hour."

"Perfect." Eve spun them, stepping Josie backward into her bedroom, lips on Josie's as her fingers worked open the button on her pants, and *whoa*. Josie's head was spinning, heat building beneath Eve's fingers as she pushed down her fly, brushing against the front of Josie's underwear.

Eve pushed her down on the bed, rocking their hips together as she slipped a hand beneath Josie's top, sliding up to pop the clasp on her bra. She was a woman on a mission, hands everywhere as they rid Josie of her clothes, touching and teasing as she worked.

Josie tried to even the playing field, eager to get her hands on Eve's dress, to run her fingers over it and beneath it and, even more importantly, get her out of it. But Eve had other ideas, ignoring Josie's attempts to undress her.

"Eve..." she murmured against her lips as Eve palmed her breasts, fingers skimming over her sensitive skin. Her back arched involuntarily, pressing her more firmly into Eve's touch.

Eve hummed her approval as she dipped her head, replacing her fingers with her tongue, swirling and flicking Josie's nipple until it had tightened before repeating the process on her other breast as her fingers trailed down

Josie's belly to dip between her legs. She gasped as Eve's fingers slipped through her folds.

Josie closed her eyes, surrendering to her touch. This time, the night was young. They had all the time in the world to touch and explore each other, and apparently, Eve had already embraced this concept. Her fingers kept stroking as her teeth skimmed against the delicate underside of Josie's breast, making her shiver with pleasure, hips arching into her touch.

Eve placed a series of openmouthed kisses over Josie's belly, and *oh God*, it felt so good. Every nerve in her body was on high alert as Eve's fingers ignited a fire deep inside her, growing hotter with each stroke. And then, Eve was moving, dress slithering seductively over Josie's skin as she crawled down to position herself between Josie's thighs.

"Oh," Josie gasped as Eve placed a scorching kiss at the crease of her inner thigh.

She looked up, eyes smoldering into Josie's. "Yes?"

"Yes," she whispered. Need pulsed through her, centered in her aching clit, and *yes, yes, yes,* she wanted to feel the heat of Eve's mouth there.

Eve dipped her head, tongue skimming over Josie's thigh, licking and kissing, tantalizingly close to where she needed her. And while part of her wanted to scream in frustration, to thread her fingers through Eve's dark hair and guide her, she found herself gasping as Eve kissed her way down the tender flesh of Josie's inner thigh.

It was intimate, so incredibly intimate, and surprisingly erotic. Had anyone ever kissed her there before? If they had, it hadn't been memorable, but the hot press of Eve's mouth was sure as hell memorable. She could note it in her calendar, *inner-thigh kisses from Eve*, but she wouldn't need to. This moment was forever etched into her brain.

Eve's tongue swirled over her skin, followed by the brush of her teeth, and Josie thought it could last forever and never be enough. It was one of the most exquisite things she'd ever felt. And then Eve was kissing her way back up Josie's thigh, and she could hardly breathe. She gasped, her whole body tensing in anticipation.

Eve paused, her eyes meeting Josie's. With one hand, she swept her hair over her shoulders, the other resting against Josie's thigh. Still staring into Josie's eyes, she lowered her head and gave one long, slow lick that had Josie arching off the bed, eyes slamming shut, a breathy moan escaping her lips.

Eve's tongue circled her clit, swirling until Josie had forgotten all about the inner-thigh kisses, their date, the kittens in the other room. Hell, she wasn't sure she even remembered how to speak. She sure as hell couldn't form coherent words. Instead, she moaned and gasped, hips moving against Eve's mouth. Eve's lips closed over her clit, and she sucked hard. Josie cried out, hands clenched in the sheet beneath her.

Yes, yes, yes. Please don't stop.

Josie kept her eyes shut, just absorbing the sensations, the heat and the thrill of Eve's mouth. She moved away from Josie's clit, licking and kissing, exploring every inch of her while Josie lay there, legs shaking, panting for breath, her skin coated in a fine sheen of sweat as Eve brought her closer and closer to her release.

She pressed a finger against Josie's entrance, stroking her, testing her before slipping inside, pumping in and out as her tongue flicked against Josie's clit, and *oh God*. Her body seemed to vibrate with the power of the orgasm building inside her, thighs shaking, pulse pounding in her ears.

That was all she could hear, that and the wet sound of Eve's mouth against her skin. She kept stroking, kept licking, kept sucking as the pressure inside Josie built until she thought she might explode. And then she was coming, release pulsing out from her core, rolling through her in a scorching wave that left her limp and breathless in its wake.

Finally, she opened her eyes, looking down to see Eve with her head resting against Josie's thigh, hair spilling over Josie's skin in a dark wave, watching quietly with a satisfied smile on her face.

Josie reached down for her, realizing in a rush that Eve was still fully clothed. She traced a finger along the bodice of her dress, meeting her gaze. "My turn."

Eve's breath hitched as she bit her lip. "Please."

21

Eve drifted awake, recognizing the floral scent of Josie's shampoo and the soft cotton of her sheets before she'd opened her eyes. She rolled to her back, blinking up at the wood-beamed ceiling overhead. Muted sunlight filled the room, and a quick glance at the clock told her it was just past six. Her internal clock had woken her ahead of her alarm.

She looked over at Josie, still peacefully asleep, lavender hair spread across the pillow like a halo. She'd certainly taken Eve to celestial places last night. Despite getting in bed before ten, they'd still been up late, exploring their seemingly insatiable chemistry. Case in point, Eve's body ached in some interesting places as she sat up to turn off the alarm on her phone.

Her foot bumped something solid and warm, and she looked down to see Nigel the cat curled up on the end of the bed. Should she wake Josie or leave her a note? Eve had to be at the office this morning, but Josie should enjoy the chance to sleep in since she'd be bartending until two tonight. This was the third time in four days Eve had woken in Josie's bed, a habit she was already finding hard to break. Last night, Josie had suggested a casual relationship, no strings sex until the spark between them burned out.

Staring at her now in the soft morning light, Eve could think of no rebuttal. The idea of walking out now, of not kissing her, sleeping beside her, or experiencing the delicious pleasure of her body ever again felt unbearable. As Josie had pointed out, neither of them had the time or interest for something serious right now. Just sex.

It's already more than sex.

But maybe that was okay. She could like Josie, as long as they never went near that other "l" word. And with their opposite work schedules, there was little chance of ever sharing more than a few scattered nights together. Eve leaned over to check Josie's phone. The alarm for the kittens' next feeding was set for twenty minutes from now. She dismissed it. The least she could do was feed them before she left. And if Josie hadn't woken by the time she'd finished, she would leave a note and let her sleep, because this wasn't their last night together.

Decision made, she slipped out of bed and opened the middle drawer of Josie's dresser, familiar by now with where she kept her stash of T-shirts. She grabbed a plain black one, pulled it over her head, and went into the bathroom to freshen up. Then she walked to the kitchen to turn on the coffeepot and start warming up kitten formula.

Fifteen minutes later, she was just finishing up as Josie walked into the room, still blinking the sleep from her eyes. Eve set Blanche in the playpen and stood to give Josie a kiss, managing to aggravate her back in the process. She winced. "Good morning."

"Morning," Josie said, her voice scratchy, arms slipping around Eve's waist.

"I have to go to work." Eve rested her forehead against Josie's. "You should go back to sleep."

"I will," Josie murmured. "But I wanted to see you before you left."

"You've seen me." She gave her another kiss, lingering long enough to leave them both breathless, blood pumping, desire tingling low in her belly.

"How soon do you have to be at work?" Josie asked, fingers wandering below the hem of Eve's T-shirt, finding the evidence of her desire.

She exhaled against Josie's lips, resolve crumbling beneath her talented fingers. "I can be a few minutes late," she whispered.

Josie pushed her onto the couch, and Eve couldn't help the hiss that escaped her lips as her sore back collided with Josie's upholstery.

"Sorry," Josie murmured, hovering over her. "Your back?"

Eve nodded. She reached up, intending to pull Josie against her, but the movement sent a spasm of pain up her spine, and she dropped her hand with a grimace.

"Shit." Josie sounded concerned now. "Did I hurt you?"

She shook her head. "I tweaked it just now. It'll be okay in a minute."

"Can I do anything?" Josie's fingers traced gently over Eve's sides.

She shivered with pleasure. "No."

"How does ibuprofen and a back rub sound?" Josie asked, her fingers stroking slow circles over Eve's ribs.

She exhaled, imagining those fingers working their magic over her sore muscles, and... "Yes," she breathed. "Please."

"Can you sit up?" Josie asked.

Eve pushed her elbows into the cushion beneath her, raising herself partway before Josie's hands slid around her, lifting her smoothly into a sitting position. She went into the kitchen, returning with two pills and a glass of water. Eve swallowed them and followed Josie into the bedroom. She pulled Eve in for a gentle kiss as she helped her out of her T-shirt, hands rubbing gently up and down her back. And *fuck*, that already felt amazing. Eve carefully arranged herself facedown on the bed.

She heard Josie squirting lotion onto her hands, and she released a slow, deep breath in anticipation. Then Josie's hands were on her, warm and slick, sliding over Eve's shoulders, and it felt *so good*. She closed her eyes, feeling herself flinch as Josie's fingers pressed into her sore spots.

"Sorry," Josie whispered.

"No," she breathed. "Keep going."

"You're so tense... Jesus, Eve."

She wanted to cry as Josie's thumbs pressed into a knot between her shoulder blades, but it was a good kind of pain, the kind that promised relief on the other side, the kind that reminded her how long it had been since she'd gone for a session with her chiropractor or even a massage. And this was so much more intimate...so *comfortable*, despite the pain. She kept breathing, inhaling the rose-petal scent of Josie's lotion as her fingers worked out all of Eve's kinks.

By the time she'd finished massaging Eve's lower back, she felt like a whole new woman, her muscles as soft and pliant as freshly kneaded dough. "You are one thousand times more talented than my heating pad," she mumbled into the sheet.

Josie laughed. "And I'm at your disposal any time you need me. You had some pretty badass knots in your muscles."

"Blame the kittens."

"Never," Josie whispered, "but I'm sorry I let you lug that box all over town if this is what it did to you."

"Well, it didn't cause the problem, only aggravated it."

"Will you always have this pain?" Josie asked, trailing her fingers down Eve's spine to circle the small surgical scar over her fused vertebrae.

"Probably, but it's not usually this bad. I haven't been keeping up on my exercises. Someone's been distracting me." She rolled over, pulling Josie in for a kiss.

"Sorry," Josie murmured against her lips.

"Don't be," Eve told her. "I'm not." She pushed herself upright, sighing in relief at the improvement in her back. "Thank you for the back rub."

"You're welcome. I made you late for work for an entirely different reason than I'd planned."

"Mm-hmm." Eve kissed her again, slow and deep. "I'll make it up to you another time."

"Damn straight." Josie's eyes twinkled playfully.

"I really have to go, but my day will be a lot more comfortable now, thanks to you."

"I'm glad." Josie leaned against the headboard, one hand toying with the lavender tips of her hair.

Eve slid out of bed and dressed, and with another kiss, she was on her way. She rode the subway to her apartment, where she showered, put on fresh clothes, and headed to work. It felt like an eternity since she'd left the office yesterday, before her date with Josie and the night that followed.

Eve caught up on emails at her desk before making her way down to Greta's office for a scheduled meeting. By now, her producer would have reviewed the footage from Dragonfly's grand opening on Friday night and have feedback on how she thought it had gone. Eve rapped her knuckles against Greta's door.

"Come in," her producer called, and Eve pushed the door open. Inside, Greta sat behind her desk, glasses perched on her nose, typing briskly on her laptop. She looked up at Eve. "Your gay bar seems to be a success so far, eh?"

"Looks that way." She perched on the guest chair, opening her laptop to take notes.

"Not exactly a surprise. All the businesses you help tend to do well, unless their owners completely fuck things up after you leave."

"I don't think Josie will fuck things up," Eve said.

"Doesn't really matter to me one way or another," Greta said. "Sometimes, a little drama is good for ratings. And speaking of ratings, yours are still not where we'd like to see them as we consider your renewal."

"Okay," Eve said, sitting up straighter. God, she was tired of the constant fight for ratings. This was an aspect of television she'd never considered before becoming a part of it. "I'll take another look at our advertising budget and see if there's any room left to reallocate."

"You can try, but at this point, things are pretty well set. Your episode with Josie Swanson's bar is going to be our season two finale, so you need to focus on generating as much buzz for that episode as possible. We need drama. We need tears."

"We have both of those things," Eve assured her.

"What about the friend she hired as a bartender against your advice? He had a few mishaps on opening night. Let's try to follow up on that. I mean it, Eve. You need to pull out all the stops on this one if you want a third season."

Pain radiated through Eve's lower back as that all-too-familiar tension crept back in. "I'll see what I can do."

"You'll be filming your follow-up segment at the bar sooner than usual, since we're on such a tight production schedule. I'd say it needs to be completed by next month this time. That gives us two weeks to get everything finalized before it airs."

"Got it," Eve said, noting the dates on her calendar.

"And if you get any whiff of drama between now and then, use that to your advantage during filming. Get us that million-dollar video teaser we can use in our promo for the episode. Remember, drama draws ratings."

"I'll see what I can do." Eve swallowed the urge to tell Greta where she could shove her request, because she would probably agree with her if she hadn't spent last night in Josie's bed. Despite her shower and change of clothes, the scent of Josie's lotion still teased her every time she inhaled, and *this* was the problem with mixing business and pleasure. There was no way for Eve to be objective about anything to do with Josie or Dragonfly anymore.

Josie had owned Swanson's for over two years, but she'd never had a busier or more overwhelming week than Dragonfly's first week in existence. She'd gotten fairly comfortable working with Adam and Elizabeth over the weekend, but on Tuesday, she worked her first shift with Lauren, and it felt like starting all over again.

They seemed to hit their stride together easily, though, which was good since they would be working the main bar together on weeknights. Lauren was energetic and experienced, and she had a great rapport with the customers.

By the time Dragonfly's second Saturday rolled around, the crowd had thinned considerably, but Josie was still doing a steady business. The signature drinks had been popular, and a lot of customers were taking advantage of her delivery agreement with neighboring restaurants, having their dinner delivered to Dragonfly and drinking her liquor while they ate. That had been a stroke of genius on Eve's part.

As for Eve, she'd been strictly business all week. Josie had seen her for two scheduled marketing meetings, but she hadn't allowed so much as a kiss, even when they were alone. Josie had been so consumed by her work at Dragonfly this week, she hadn't had time—or energy—to protest too hard, though. She'd spent every spare moment setting up ads the way Eve had shown her, maintaining her social media presence, and managing all the behind-the-scenes details that went into running the bar.

Still, Josie missed her. As she poured wine for a couple of women who'd just come in, she found herself hoping Eve might show up tonight the way she had last Saturday.

"You do still own this place."

Josie looked at the woman in front of her as she set two glasses of shiraz on the bar. She'd definitely seen her in Swanson's before, although not in a while, and Josie couldn't remember her name, if she'd ever known it. "I do," she said with a smile.

"I'm glad," the woman said. "When I saw the new name out front, I thought you'd sold. I used to live around the corner."

"I knew I remembered seeing you in here," Josie said. "New name. New brand. What do you think?"

"I love it," the woman answered. She had shoulder-length brown hair and a friendly face. "Much more my style.

I'm Nicole, by the way, and this is my wife, Fiona." She gestured to the blonde beside her.

"Nice to meet you," Fiona said in a crisp British accent.

Josie found herself enchanted by the pair of them, sipping wine in matching turquoise wedding bands. "Do you still live nearby?"

"Unfortunately, no," Nicole told her. "We split our time now between our house in New Jersey and a cottage in the French countryside. This one hates cities." She nudged Fiona, who smiled into her wine. "But I still make her come here with me a few times a year. I can't help it. This city is in my blood."

"I don't hate it as much as I used to," Fiona said, giving her wife an affectionate look.

Josie laughed. "This city has a way of winning people over if you spend enough time here."

"It sure does," Nicole agreed. "And maybe Fi will be easier to convince next time, now that we know this place is here."

"Perhaps," Fiona agreed, glancing appreciatively around the bar.

"Well, I certainly hope so," Josie told them. "Because I'd love to see your faces here at Dragonfly again."

"I'm sure you will," Nicole said with a laugh.

Josie was still thinking about them as she climbed the stairs to her apartment that night. She'd never been in love or even had a serious relationship, never given marriage much of a thought one way or the other. But Nicole and Fiona seemed so...happy, so relaxed, so at ease with each other and the world around them.

And yeah, maybe Josie did want that for herself someday.

As she crawled into bed with the sun rising outside her

window, she was missing Eve like crazy. It felt like an eternity since she'd shared Josie's bed, since they'd even shared a kiss. So when she woke just past noon on Sunday morning, she sent Eve a quick text.

How's your weekend?

It took several long minutes for Eve to respond. *A lot quieter than last weekend.*

Was that an invitation? Josie decided to treat it as one. *Stop by tonight?*

Tempting, but I can't.

Hot date? Josie asked, adding a winking emoji so Eve knew she was joking.

I'm attending a gallery opening.

Josie took a moment to imagine Eve wandering through a gallery in one of her exquisitely sexy dresses, art admiring art. And Josie wished for the opportunity to experience it with her, to see her in her element, to let Eve educate her on the finer points of fine art. If only Josie didn't work every goddamn night. Thank God for Mondays, and speaking of Monday...

Dinner tomorrow? she asked.

Sure, Eve replied.

Josie rolled onto her back, heart racing at the promise of seeing her again. *You pick this time. Just let me know when and where to meet you.*

Okay.

Can't wait. Josie added the emoji face blowing a kiss, hit Send, and climbed out of bed, feeling significantly more energized about the day ahead now that she had a date with Eve to look forward to tomorrow.

22

"Interesting choice," Josie said, eyebrows raised as she walked toward Eve outside O'Doul's Pub. She had on skinny jeans and a slinky black top, and Eve's pulse was already skyrocketing just looking at her. She drew her in for a quick kiss. Josie tasted sweet, like she'd eaten candy on the way here.

"How so?" Eve responded, hands sinking into Josie's back pockets as she drew them together, breasts meeting on each exhale.

"It seems more my style than yours," Josie said, leaning in to kiss her back.

"You think I can't do casual?" she murmured against Josie's lips.

"Based on the evidence in front of me, you can definitely do casual." Josie pulled back long enough to slide her gaze over Eve's sleeveless gray top and jeans before pressing their bodies back together. "Although I haven't seen a look yet that you couldn't pull off, including my pussy T-shirt."

"Never going to live that one down." Eve felt herself

smiling at the memory. "But I didn't choose this place because it's casual or for the cheap beer."

"No?" Josie asked, eyes locked on Eve's, clearly intrigued.

She tipped her head toward the club across the street. "You told me last Monday you wanted to go to a bar where you didn't work, let someone else mix the drinks, and go dancing."

Josie blinked. "Oh."

When she didn't say anything else, Eve felt a twinge of disappointment. She'd thought Josie would enjoy this, but maybe she'd read her wrong. Maybe it was too much, or maybe she was just too tired. "That's a lot for a Monday night, isn't it?" she said, backpedaling. "We can just—"

Josie pressed a finger against her lips. "Shut up. I want to go dancing. There is absolutely nothing I'd rather do tonight. You just caught me off guard, I mean...I can't remember the last time someone really listened to me like that. You're unexpectedly thoughtful, Eve Marlow."

And now Eve was caught off guard, because Josie had flat-out told her what she wanted on their last date, but suddenly, this felt like a much bigger deal than she'd ever meant it to be. "Who have you been dating that no one's ever paid attention to what you like?"

"Exactly," Josie said, bringing their mouths back together. "I told you I've been on a lot of shitty dates. Either I just have horrible luck, or the online dating pool is pretty shallow these days. You're the first person in years I really enjoy being with."

"Mm." Eve ignored that comment in favor of another kiss, because she felt the same way, not that she'd ever admit it. This thing between them was only casual, a few dates and some blisteringly hot sex when it suited them.

"Is dancing okay for your back?" Josie asked between kisses.

"Yes. In fact, it hasn't bothered me all week, but I wore these just in case." She gestured to her practical—albeit rhinestone-studded—flats.

"Perfect."

"Come on, I'm starving." She disentangled herself and led the way inside.

The pub was loud and crowded. Eve paused in the doorway as a heavy weight settled in the pit of her stomach, an instinctual reaction she thought she'd overcome after all her time at Swanson's. Her eyes flitted to the bar. But there was Josie, slipping her hand into Eve's with a reassuring squeeze. "Okay?"

Eve nodded, shaking off the moment before leading the way to an empty booth. To her surprise, Josie slid in beside her. She settled close, one hand on Eve's thigh as she reached for a menu. Sitting like this, with their backs to the rest of the bar, the clatter of glass and din of conversation became a cloak of background noise, sealing her and Josie in their booth.

At Josie's suggestion, they ordered whiskey instead of beer. She reminded Eve of the age-old advice against drinking beer before liquor, because they'd certainly want cocktails later at the club. They ordered burgers and sipped whiskey, leaned in close, hands clasped beneath the table.

"Why do you work at the *Do Over* office instead of having your own?" Josie asked.

"I lease it from them, mostly to save on office costs. When we're not filming the show, I keep to myself."

"So if you don't get renewed for season three, you'll have to find new office space, on top of everything else?" Josie's fingers trailed down her arm.

"Yes."

"When will you know?"

"Soon after your episode airs," Eve told her. "You're going to be our season two finale."

"Ooh." Josie gave her a playful smile. "Big pressure on me and Dragonfly. I hope we live up to expectations."

"If the episode doesn't perform well, it won't be because of you," Eve said. "Sometimes there's no predicting what will appeal to an audience, but you should feel good about what you've accomplished."

"I do," Josie told her, leaning in for a kiss. "Thanks to you."

They sat and drank whiskey until it was late, since the club didn't open until eleven. Truthfully, Eve was tired. She'd already had a long day, and all she really wanted was to take Josie home and fuck her senseless before falling asleep in her arms. But she'd committed to this, and she wanted Josie to have a good time tonight.

So she settled deeper into their booth, her back sinking into the cracked leather. She finished her whiskey and set the glass on the table as Josie pressed her face into Eve's neck, tongue skimming over her skin, leaving fire in its wake. She turned her head, bringing their lips together, kisses softened by the alcohol warming her veins, deep and languid and searching.

They kissed until Eve was drunk on the desire pulsing in her veins, her body humming with a need she knew Josie would satisfy spectacularly at the end of the night. But for now, she was content to wait. They strolled hand in hand across the street to the nightclub she'd chosen...a gay club, so they could be as hands-on as they wanted without attracting any unwanted attention.

Inside the club, music pumped, so loud she felt the beat

vibrating in her bones. A black light on the dance floor made her top glow bright white, but even more interestingly, it made Josie's hair glow like purple flames dancing around her face as she began to sway to the music.

Eve pulled her close, hips bumping as they moved to the beat. She pressed her lips against Josie's ear. "You're beautiful," she said, rewarded by one of those smiles that brought out her dimples, making her whole face seem to gleam with the same intensity as her hair.

It wasn't very crowded, being a Monday night, but there were enough bodies on the dance floor to set the mood. Eve couldn't remember the last time she'd been dancing. Certainly, it had been years. A lot of years. And to her surprise, she was having fun. She closed her eyes, hands in Josie's as she danced, letting the music guide her. The bass boomed, heavy and rhythmic, thrumming through her body.

They danced until they were breathless and sweaty before moving to the bar, where Josie perused the drink menu with the intensity of a woman who served them for a living. Eventually, she chose a raspberry mojito, and Eve—curious because she'd never had one—ordered the same. The drinks arrived, a fruity pink but smelling of mint and lime. Eve took a cautious sip. "It reminds me of your Midnight in Manhattan."

"It was loosely inspired by a mojito."

"I like yours better," Eve told her honestly. Something about the lemon and mint combo really worked for her. Or maybe it was the creator of the drink itself that worked for her. Either. Both. Who the hell knew at this point?

She leaned in and kissed her, tasting lime and mint on Josie's lips. They scooted their stools closer together, knees interlaced as they sipped their drinks and kissed. Eventually, the mojitos were gone, and she and Josie were just kissing, hands on each other's thighs, tongues tangling as they made out like a couple of teenagers.

Josie lifted her head, a giddy smile on her face. And then she was leading Eve back to the dance floor. With the added fuel of the mojitos driving them, they danced and danced, sometimes kissing, sometimes twirling and dipping each other, until Eve was smiling and laughing almost as much as Josie. Her heart felt light, which was mostly due to the flame-haired pixie in her arms, but also partly attributable to the alcohol swimming in her veins. Combined, she didn't stand a chance.

Josie checked the time on her phone. "About an hour until the kittens need to be fed," she said, loudly enough for Eve to hear her over the music.

Kittens. Right. Over the past week, Eve had finally gotten them out of her system, had quit thinking about feedings and schedules and weight gain. That was Josie's responsibility now, one she'd never shirk, no matter how much fun she was having.

"One more dance," Josie said, hands going to Eve's hips.

"Two if we take an Uber."

"You're on," she said happily, hips already moving to the beat.

They grooved together, bodies swaying in unison, mouths meeting in a never-ending kiss as one song became two and then three, before Josie finally pulled back, a kaleidoscope of disco lights dancing in her eyes. "Come back to my place?"

As if there had been any doubt. "Yes."

Josie smiled as she led the way outside. Eve pulled up the app on her phone and requested a car, which would be there in two minutes. Night air washed over her skin, refreshing and cool. The city felt strangely quiet after the noise of the club. She and Josie stood close, just enjoying each other's presence as they waited for the Uber to arrive. Eve's ears were ringing from the music, her head swimming slightly from too much to drink.

"Thank you for tonight," Josie said quietly. "I really needed that."

Eve nodded. She'd had fun tonight too. Their car arrived, and they slipped into the backseat together, mostly quiet on the ride home. Josie asked their driver to let them out behind her building. She unlocked the back door and ushered Eve in ahead of her.

It had been a full week since she'd been up these stairs, a week since she'd been inside Josie's apartment, and it felt as foreign as it did familiar, like a comforting habit she'd been denied in the interim.

Inside, Josie pressed her against the wall, kissing her with an intensity that put the rest of the evening to shame, tongue delving into Eve's mouth as the desire that had been simmering between them all evening went up in flames.

"They're still asleep," Josie whispered against her lips. "We've got at least fifteen minutes, could probably make it thirty if we don't wake them."

"I like a good challenge," Eve whispered back.

Then they were stumbling into the bedroom, fumbling with clothes, shoving down zippers and pushing up shirts. Finally, they were naked, bodies pressed together and hands groping as they kissed desperately. Eve could feel that she was already drenched in her own desire.

She pushed a hand between Josie's thighs, finding her just as wet, making her gasp at the contact. Her hips began to rock, meeting the movements of Eve's fingers, and then she was touching Eve back, completely scrambling her lust and alcohol-riddled brain. They moved together messily, hips rocking in a rhythm not unlike the one they'd shared on the dance floor as they drove each other toward release.

"Fuck," Josie gasped, head falling against Eve's neck, hips jerking as she sought more.

Eve moved her fingers harder and faster, giving Josie what she needed. She squeezed her eyes shut to keep the room from spinning, concentrating on keeping her shaky knees upright. Josie broke first, her cry muffled against Eve's shoulder as she came, her pussy fluttering around Eve's fingers. It was almost enough to send Eve over the edge with her...almost. She teetered on the precipice of release, her body coiled tight, every cell supercharged with energy, all centered in the throbbing need between her legs.

Josie lifted her head, a wicked smile dancing in her eyes as she moved her hands to Eve's hips. And she could hardly breathe as her body begged, *screamed* for Josie's touch. Josie dropped to her knees, still gripping Eve's hips firmly, holding her where she wanted her as she covered her with her mouth, and *oh God*, Eve couldn't contain the needy cry that escaped her lips. Josie's tongue swirled around her clit, so hot, so wet...

Eve saw stars behind her eyelids, her whole world distilled to the magic of Josie's perfect mouth. She felt herself swaying, and then she was flat on her back on Josie's bed, hips still moving, hands threaded deeply in Josie's hair.

Oh God. Yes.

She gasped, so exquisitely aroused, the world could have been ending, and she wouldn't have noticed. Her body ignited as Josie increased the suction of her mouth, pushing two fingers inside her. She curved them forward, hitting Eve's G-spot, and that did it. She tumbled headfirst into one of the most intense orgasms of her life, release rushing through her in sizzling waves.

Josie sat back, wiping her mouth against the back of her hand as she met Eve's gaze. *Wow.* Eve just lay there, panting as aftershocks of pleasure fizzed in her blood.

Josie slid in beside her as they caught their breath. Then she sat up, tugging at Eve's hand, dragging her toward the bathroom. She turned on the shower, drawing Eve's attention to the fact they were a sticky, sweaty mess. They stepped into a quick shower, rinsing the sweat and sex from their bodies.

Afterward, Eve accepted a T-shirt from Josie and followed her to the kitchen. She filled a much-needed glass of water as Josie began heating formula. Eve drained her glass and glanced into the living room, where four small faces stared back.

"Holy shit." She set her glass down so hard, it almost shattered against the counter.

Josie followed her gaze with a laugh. "They've grown since the last time you saw them, haven't they?"

These...did not look like the same kittens. They were alert in a way Eve had never seen. She walked into the living room as four pairs of eyes tracked her, tiny bodies jumping around inside the playpen. Crouching, she lifted Blanche, hardly able to believe how big she'd gotten in the week since Eve saw her last. She rubbed the kitten behind her ears, and Blanche nuzzled her face against the fabric of Eve's T-shirt, a tiny rumble vibrating out of her.

"Oh my God." Eve glanced over as Josie walked into the living room with bottles. "She's purring."

"Yes, she's a big girl who can purr now. And she likes you," Josie said with a satisfied smile.

"I smell like *you*," Eve said quietly, looking down at the T-shirt Blanche was kneading with her tiny paws.

"Give her some credit," Josie said, handing Eve a bottle. "And give *yourself* a little credit. You've been there for her since she was a newborn. She associates you with safety and comfort."

"She can't possibly remember that I'm the one who saved her," Eve said, positioning Blanche to accept her bottle.

"No, she doesn't, but she certainly remembers your voice and your scent from those early days."

"That's ridiculous." Eve refused to believe it. Blanche had been too little. They all had been. And they'd spent so much more time with Josie now. They probably didn't remember Eve at all. She was just another warm body... wearing a shirt that smelled like Josie.

Blanche finished her bottle—a much larger bottle than the last one Eve had given her—and looked up at Eve, meowing loudly. Eve reached for a paper towel to stimulate her to pee, at the same time noticing the litter box in the playpen. They couldn't have changed *that* much in a week, could they?

"You should still stimulate her," Josie said with a laugh, noticing her confusion, "but they're learning to use the litter box too."

"Wow."

"They grow fast."

"I guess so," Eve said as she finished up with Blanche, who was attempting to hop off her lap and run around the apartment.

"You can put her down if you want," Josie said. "They like to explore."

Eve set Blanche on the floor, where she proceeded to roll

belly up, wrestling with Eve's bare toes, gripping them with her front paws while her back paws kicked furiously. "Ouch," she said, prying the kitten off her foot.

Nigel strolled through the room, and Blanche launched herself at him, grabbing at his tail like it was a toy. He gave her an annoyed look before turning his amber eyes on Eve.

"Why does he always stare at me like that?"

Josie laughed. "Cats do that. He's just curious about you."

"I don't like it," she confessed.

"Aw," Josie said, nudging her with an elbow. "Pet him. Talk to him. Get to know him, and then he won't feel like you're a stranger in his home that he needs to keep an eye on."

"Hm." She slid a look in Nigel's direction, too tired—and tipsy—to sort it out tonight.

She and Josie fed the other two kittens and spent a few minutes playing with all of them before putting them in the playpen. They cleaned up their feeding supplies and returned to the bedroom, where they crawled between the sheets together, facing each other in the darkness, arms and legs entwined. Eve breathed in the comfort and closeness between them, feeling it fill something inside her that had been empty since the last time she slept in Josie's bed.

"You should adopt Blanche," Josie whispered, fingers trailing sleepily through Eve's hair.

"I don't want a cat," she responded automatically, but as she closed her eyes, she imagined having Blanche there when she got home at the end of a long day. Cats were pretty self-sufficient once they were grown. It wouldn't require her to change her schedule or shorten her work hours. Did her building even allow pets? She had no idea. She'd never asked, had never cared.

How long did cats live? Not very long, probably. In the end, it would be something else for her to outlive, something else for her to mourn, and while it didn't compare to burying her wife and daughter or being forced to walk away from her entire family, why should she set herself up to go through that kind of pain again?

She didn't need a cat. She was better off on her own.

23

"You look like you had a late night."

Josie glanced at Lauren, her weeknight bartender, not even trying to hide her smile. "I did."

"Girlfriend?" Lauren asked as she bent to unload the dishwasher, stacking clean glasses on the shelf behind the bar.

"More casual than that," Josie said, knowing instinctively that Eve would balk at the term. Josie hadn't been looking for a girlfriend either, not while she was so busy getting Dragonfly off the ground, but when she spent half her waking hours thinking and daydreaming about Eve, it was hard to imagine calling her anything else. This was certainly more than a casual hookup, no matter their original intention.

"Well, good for you," Lauren said. "If she's keeping you up late enough to cause those shadows under your eyes, it must be pretty hot."

"Yeah, it is," Josie admitted, feeling her cheeks heat at the admission.

"Okay, I'm jealous," Lauren said. "Do I know her?"

"No," Josie lied, because the whole staff had met Eve, and she'd been very clear that she didn't want that fact getting around.

"Well, if she comes in here, point her out to me," Lauren said with a conspiratorial grin. "I'd love to meet the woman who put such a smile on your face today."

Josie laughed. "Will do."

And then, because she couldn't help herself, she pulled out her phone and composed a text. *I can't wait until next Monday to see you again.*

Eve responded almost immediately. *No?*

No.

What do you propose we do about that? Eve asked.

By now, Josie was grinning like an idiot, and she didn't even care. *Come in for a drink?*

It would have to be just that...a drink. I can't hang around until the bar closes on a weeknight. My workday starts a lot earlier than yours.

I'm sorry, Josie replied. *I hate our opposite schedules. I wish I knew how to fix it. But please, at least come in for a drink.*

We'll see, Eve responded. *No promises.*

It would have to do...for now. At the moment, even seeing Eve for a few minutes while she drank a beer sounded like time well spent. Josie enjoyed seeing her, talking to her, sleeping beside her, going places with her. Hell, she enjoyed just being in the same room with her. Girlfriend indeed. *Shit.* She was falling for Eve, hard and fast.

But was Eve feeling the same way?

As it turned out, she didn't stop by for a drink after work. Josie didn't see or hear from her again until she arrived on Wednesday afternoon for their scheduled marketing meeting, the last consultation covered under her contract with

Do Over. They sat together in Josie's office, going over numbers while Eve offered advice and suggestions.

"You're ahead of my predicted profit margin for your second week in operation," Eve said, bringing up a graph on her laptop.

Josie leaned closer, as much to see the numbers as to catch a whiff of Eve's perfume. "That would be a first for me."

Eve glanced at her with a small smile. "Well, hopefully you're in for a lot of pleasant 'firsts' with Dragonfly. Our paid advertising will stop running on Friday, but your ads are performing well. And I expect you'll see another jump in business after your episode airs, which is only a little over a month away."

"Yeah. Wow." She was going to be on national television. Her bar was going to be on national television. "My dad would have been so stoked. I mean, he never would have let Swanson's become such a disaster that it qualified for your show, but he would have been absolutely beside himself to see his bar on TV. My whole family is going to freak out."

"Your family?" Eve asked, a curiosity in her eyes that had nothing to do with her job and everything to do with her relationship with Josie.

"Aunts, uncles, cousins. They don't live here in the city, so I don't see them as often. Holidays and birthdays, mostly. You know how it is." She glanced over at Eve and saw the stricken look on her face. *Shit.* "Don't you keep in touch with anyone in your family?"

She looked away. "No."

"Dammit, I'm sorry. Are they all just a bunch of homophobic assholes or what?"

"My parents are, anyway," Eve said with a shrug. "I thought I might hear from some of my other relatives after I left, that someone might reach out, or even that my parents might come to their senses once they realized what they'd done."

"What did they do, exactly?" Josie asked, one hand resting on Eve's thigh. To hell with this being a business meeting. The woman she cared about needed comfort right now, dammit.

"They said I was no longer welcome in their home."

"And how old were you?"

"Twenty-two," Eve said. "I'd just graduated from college."

Dear God, Eve's parents had missed out on her entire adult life? Josie missed her parents every single day. Mostly, she missed her dad. Her mom had been gone so long, she barely remembered her. If anything, she missed the idea of having a mother. But to know that her parents were out there, living their lives and pretending she didn't exist? She couldn't even begin to imagine what that was like. "I'm so sorry."

"It's been thirteen years," Eve said with a stiff-shouldered shrug. "At this point, I think it's safe to say they're not going to have a change of heart."

"Well, that's their loss, then," Josie said, pulling her in for a fierce hug. Eve hugged her back, just for a moment, before pulling free. "I hope someday they're filled with regret for losing the chance to have you in their lives."

"I'm not holding my breath." Eve gestured to her laptop. "Back on topic, this is ordinarily the point in our last consult where I'd offer my services so you could hire me through Marlow Marketing to continue working toward Dragonfly's success, but all things considered, I don't think that would be appropriate in this case."

Josie sat up straighter in her chair. "You're dumping me as a client because we're sleeping together?"

"No," Eve said quietly as she shut her laptop. "I'm just declining to let you hire me."

"Isn't that the same thing?"

"Not if I offer you unofficial marketing advice for free."

"Wait a damn minute." Josie stood, arms crossed over her chest. "I don't want your advice for free. That's not fair to you, and it makes me feel shitty."

"Taking your money while I'm sleeping with you would be even shittier," Eve countered. "I don't need the money." She raised her eyebrows for emphasis. "I have a full client list already."

Josie narrowed her eyes at her. "Well, I just..."

"Take my unofficial free advice, or don't. It's your choice," Eve said with an air of finality, indicating the matter was not up for debate as she packed her briefcase and turned to face Josie. "Or, I suppose, we could just go back to being business associates."

"Hell, no," Josie said automatically.

As she looked past her discomfort with taking Eve's advice for free, she saw that Eve was offering a way for them to keep seeing each other, a way around her rule about not mixing business with pleasure. And after learning that Eve's entire family had turned their backs on her, knowing she'd rebounded from that only to lose Lisa too...well, it put into perspective why Eve had built such a fortress around her heart. And if she was offering even a teeny, tiny part of it to Josie now, she was going to grab hold of it and treasure it with every fiber of her being.

She sucked in a deep breath. "I'll take your unofficial help, but don't put yourself out on my account. If you're too busy, or too tired, or too anything, focus on your paying clients, okay?"

"Fair enough," Eve said with a brisk nod.

Josie leaned in to kiss her, hoping that brief brush of her lips against Eve's conveyed the depth of emotion she felt. "Thank you."

"You're welcome."

"Since we're no longer working together in any sort of professional capacity, could I stop by and take you to lunch tomorrow? Or Friday?"

"I'm pretty busy these next few days, but I'll let you know." Eve picked up her briefcase, pausing in the doorway. "Just for the record, I still want to keep things low-key until after your episode airs. I'm not saying we can't be seen in public together, obviously, but we should be discreet here at Dragonfly and especially at my office."

"Okay," Josie said, trying not to read too much into Eve's words, because keeping things low-key until after her episode aired sounded an awful lot like Eve thought they would still be together next month and that she wouldn't mind kissing Josie in the middle of Dragonfly on a busy Saturday night after the *Do Over* segment was behind them.

And that felt...almost too good to be true.

"I'll text you," Eve said.

Josie nodded. "Or call me. Or, you know, just show up."

"Okay," Eve said with another small smile, and then she was gone.

AS IT TURNED OUT, Josie was too impatient to wait for Eve to make the next move and texted her on Thursday morning to ask again about lunch, but Eve replied that she was busy with clients. By Friday evening, Josie was feeling pretty glum about things. She missed Eve. Their work schedules made it almost impossible for them to see each other, and she hated it.

"Why the long face?" Adam asked, sidling up beside her as she unloaded the dishwasher behind the bar.

"Just wishing I didn't have to work all weekend, I guess. Eve works weekdays, and I work nights and weekends. It's... not ideal, to say the least."

"How are things going for you guys otherwise?" he asked.

"Good," she said, then sighed. "*Really* good. I mean, I can't stop thinking about her, and it's killing me that I hardly ever get to see her. I just want to be able to spend time together like regular couples do."

"Well, hey now, there are plenty of couples who have to work around challenging work schedules. I'm more interested in the fact that you're calling yourselves a couple, because the last time I checked, you guys were just casually hooking up."

"I'm probably getting ahead of myself, but we *feel* like a couple when we're together. Honestly, I've never felt this way about anyone before."

"You're falling for her," he said, looking delighted.

"I definitely could, if I let myself." She paused with a glass in each hand. "That's crazy, though, isn't it? I mean, we've only known each other a month, and we weren't even sleeping together most of that time."

"When you know, you know, right?" he said with a dramatic lift of his eyebrows. "That's what they say."

"Knock it off." She whacked him with a dish cloth. "You're supposed to discourage me here. Eve's very much a loner these days, and she's been through a lot. She's going to need to take things really slow, if she's ever ready for anything serious at all."

He rested a hand on her shoulder. "Then you take things slow, but keep that big heart of yours in check, Jo. I don't want to see you get hurt if she bails on you."

"I'll try," she told him.

"Are you guys gossiping without me?"

Josie turned to find Kaia standing at the bar, and her mood instantly lifted at the sight of her friend. "Adam was giving me relationship advice, if you can believe it."

"And I missed it?" Kaia leaned her elbows on the bar, listening with wide eyes as Josie and Adam caught her up to speed. "Wow. Things with Eve have gotten way more serious since the last time I talked to you."

"Well, they have and they haven't," Josie said. "We've only gone out a few times. I'm probably blowing it way out of proportion in my head."

"Hey, you can't help how you feel. I hope it all works out for you guys."

"So do I." Josie poured a beer for Kaia and set it on the bar in front of her. "How are you? Any news from that girl you went out with a few weeks ago?"

Kaia shook her head. "Never heard from her, but I've got a date with someone else tomorrow night."

"Fingers crossed," Josie said.

"Yeah." Kaia sighed, staring into her beer.

"What's that look for?" Josie hadn't talked to Kaia as much since Dragonfly opened, and suddenly, she was worried she'd missed something important, because her friend didn't seem quite like herself tonight.

"I just...I guess I miss you guys," Kaia said, her gaze flicking to Josie's.

Josie felt a pang in her chest, because she knew immediately what Kaia meant. Adam was working here with her now, which meant they were seeing more of each other... and less of Kaia. In fact, Josie had been so busy with work and Eve that she hadn't texted Kaia all week. "Shit. I've been a lousy friend, haven't I?"

"No, you haven't," Kaia said. "You've had a lot on your plate lately."

"I'm so sorry, Kai," Adam said, leaning over the bar to pull her in for a hug. "Working two jobs made me an asshole."

"No, it didn't," Kaia said with a laugh. "You guys have both been really busy getting Dragonfly up and running, and Josie's spending what little free time she has with Eve, which is amazing, but I just have no idea when we're going to all hang out together anymore."

Josie felt tears pushing behind her eyelids, and she pressed her palms against them. "My work schedule is killing me, you guys. I thought it might be different once Dragonfly opened, but so far, it's not."

"You'll get there," Kaia said with an understanding smile. "And I'll be here when you do."

"Brunch tomorrow?" Adam suggested. "Just the three of us."

"I'm in," Kaia said.

"Yeah." Josie blinked back her tears. "Me too."

They fist-bumped on their plans before Kaia finished her beer and headed out. The Friday-night crowd was starting to pick up, keeping Josie and Adam busy. He'd come a long way as a bartender, and she was so glad she'd taken the chance on hiring him. She enjoyed working with Lauren during the week, but nothing compared to having one of her best friends behind the bar with her on the weekends.

"Hey," he said as they bumped into each other while

filling beers. "I wanted to mention, since you're so worried about your schedule, I was chatting with Lauren the other night, and she mentioned she'd be interested in picking up an extra shift if I ever needed a night off. But what if you gave her an extra shift so *you* could take a night off? Or, if there's room in the budget, hire her to work Friday nights with me. Maybe you don't have to be here every night, you know?"

Josie stared at him, blinking slowly. "Yeah, you know what? I'll run some numbers and see if that's a possibility."

Maybe she could afford to give herself a night off, and surely Lauren and Adam could handle the bar on their own once a week. That had always been Josie's dream, after all, letting other people run the bar while she operated her kitten rescue upstairs. It had always felt frustratingly out of reach, but now, maybe...maybe it didn't.

She mixed drinks and chatted with customers, too busy even to check the clock until things finally started to slow down after midnight. By two, the crowd had thinned considerably. The front door opened, and she glanced at it automatically, inhaling sharply as Eve stepped through. She had on jeans and a black T-shirt, a very casual look for her.

She slid onto her usual stool at the end of the bar, watching quietly as Josie approached. There was something heavy in her expression.

"Hey," Josie said, reminding herself at the last moment not to lean across the bar and kiss her. Not for a few more weeks anyway...

"Hi." Eve's lips curved in a soft smile.

"You okay?"

She nodded. "Just tired."

"It's late for someone who worked all day. What brings you out at this hour?"

"You," she answered simply, resting her hands against the bar. "I couldn't sleep."

"Oh." The thought of Eve lying in bed, missing her... well, it was enough to make Josie weak at the knees. "You found me." She leaned in closer. "I've been missing you like crazy all week."

Adam came up behind Josie, resting an arm over her shoulders, drawing a thinly veiled look of annoyance from Eve at the intrusion.

Josie looked at him in surprise. "What's up?"

"Let me close tonight," he said. "I've watched you do it enough times, and I can totally handle this crowd on my own from now until then."

"Wait, what?" What in the world was he talking about?

He lifted his eyebrows meaningfully. "I'm saying, I've got this. You two should get out of here."

"Oh," she said as her brain finally clicked up to speed. "Really?"

"Yes," he assured her. "Go."

She looked at Eve, whose expression was unreadable, then back at Adam. "Okay, but text me if anything comes up, promise? I'll just be upstairs."

He laughed, shooing her away. "Get out of here already."

"Okay." She slid out from behind the bar, completely giddy at the freedom to do so. "Thank you."

Eve gave him a grateful look as she turned to follow Josie toward the back stairs. She'd barely closed the door to the stairwell behind them before Eve was in her arms, mouth pressed against Josie's, kissing her like she'd been as starved for Josie's touch as Josie had been for hers. They stumbled up the stairs and fell inside Josie's apartment, kicking the door closed behind them.

24

Josie hurried down Forty-ninth Street, her heart giving a little leap as she spotted Eve leaning against the building ahead. She had on a figure-hugging brown dress that shimmered in the sunlight, accenting the golden highlights in her hair. Mondays had become their unofficial weekly date night, and this one was starting early. Eve had taken the afternoon off work so they could attend an event at one of her favorite galleries together.

It had been Josie's idea, in a roundabout way. On Saturday morning, as they lay in bed together, she'd told Eve she wanted this date to be all about her. "Last Monday, you planned all the things I enjoy, and this Monday, I want to go to a gallery with you. I want to see the things you love, but I don't know enough about art to surprise you with it, so you may have to plan this one too."

Eve's satisfied smirk told Josie that she didn't mind a bit. She was good at planning things. And now they were at a fancy art gallery on a Monday afternoon, and Josie was positively giddy about it.

"Hi." She leaned in for a kiss as Eve slid her phone into her purse.

"Hey yourself." Eve looked so relaxed, so peaceful, so *happy*, Josie wanted to capture this moment and live in it forever.

"I'm excited," Josie said as she smoothed her fingers over the silky fabric of Eve's dress. "Are you going to buy anything?"

"Probably not," Eve told her. "No more room in my apartment, remember?"

"Hey, speaking of that, what do you say if we go to your place later? The kittens have shackled me to my apartment lately, but it's past time for me to see yours, don't you think?"

Eve looked down at her feet. "Maybe."

"I can't stay the whole night, but the kittens are getting a lot more self-sufficient. They're starting to wean onto solid food."

"Really?"

Josie nodded. "They're five weeks old now. Anyway, just think about it. I could probably bribe Adam or Kaia to check on them in a few hours, so I could stay out with you longer."

Something hesitant still lurked in Eve's eyes, and Josie internally slapped herself for dampening her carefree mood. She should have waited for Eve to invite her over instead of inviting herself.

"Anyway, no worries if you'd rather head back to my place," she said, nudging her shoulder against Eve's as she went for a joke. "Maybe you don't want me to find out you're secretly messy."

"I'm not messy."

Josie laughed, trying not to acknowledge the awkward reality that Eve just didn't want her to come over, which meant Josie was in way over her head here. She'd let herself build this relationship up in her head, and Eve had obviously not done the same. She stepped backward out of her arms, keeping her smile firmly in place. Hopefully it looked more natural than it felt.

She turned toward the door, but Eve stopped her, grasping her wrist. "Josie, you caught me off guard, that's all. We'll go to my place tonight."

"It's fine either way," Josie said, determined not to let it bother her.

Eve led the way, pausing just inside the door while Josie looked around the room. It was long and rectangular, with bright white walls covered in paintings. Half-walls crisscrossed the middle of the room to display more art as people milled between them, some of them with drinks in their hands.

"This is a new exhibit," Eve told her. "The artist is from Chile. He's known for his use of depth and color."

"Is he here?" Josie asked, sliding a hand into Eve's, a silent invitation for her to take the lead.

"Probably." Eve led them toward the back of the room, where they got wine from the bar and met not only the artist but the owner of the gallery as well, an older man who Eve seemed to know well. She was in her element here, mingling with the same confidence and ease she exuded in front of the camera. This was her professional smile. Eve Marlow, entrepreneur.

Josie was proud to know not only that Eve, but also the one who wore T-shirts and jeans, who pulled a bag of kittens out of the trash and refused to give up on them, who'd taken Josie on her dream date, given her some of the best sex of her life, and came to the bar at two a.m. on Friday night because she'd missed her.

She and Josie wandered through the gallery, sipping

wine and looking at paintings. This wasn't something Josie had ever done before. Sometimes she noticed paintings in people's homes or businesses and thought, *Wow, that's pretty*, but she'd never given it more thought than that.

She liked these, though. As Eve had said, the artist used vivid colors, and if there was one thing Josie gravitated toward, it was color. Eve lingered in front of a painting of a sunset, the rays of the sun streaking the sky bright orange and purple.

"It's pretty," Josie said.

"It is," Eve agreed.

"Thinking about getting it?"

She gave Josie an amused look. "I don't have a place for it, and anyway, it doesn't speak to me."

"It doesn't speak to you?" Josie felt her eyebrows creeping up her forehead, because that was about the most un-Eve-like thing she'd ever heard come from her mouth.

"I look for art that strikes a chord with me, something I just have to have," she explained. "This one is nice, but there's nothing special about it, at least not for me."

"Oh." Josie followed her down the aisle, fascinated by this peek into Eve's mind.

They looked at paintings of cities and landscapes, buildings and trees, and even a few animals. Josie was seriously enjoying herself, mostly because of the wine and Eve's company. She knew a lot about art, and Josie enjoyed hearing her thoughts on the paintings they'd seen. They reached the end of an aisle, and Josie turned to move on, but Eve stopped her with a firm hand to her wrist, much the way she'd done outside.

"Look," she said.

Josie turned to find Eve pointing to a painting in the corner. It was a brick-fronted rowhouse, sandwiched between several larger buildings, rather less colorful than some of the other paintings, except...*oh*. Now she saw why this one had caught Eve's eye. The street in front of the building was covered in pawprints, prints in every color of the rainbow, all leading up to the brick building's door.

"Okay, I get what you mean now," Josie said. "This one speaks to me."

"I thought it might," Eve said with a satisfied smile.

Somehow, Josie loved the painting even more because Eve had been the one to spot it. She'd known it would speak to Josie because she knew her that well. "I want it."

Now Eve looked surprised. "Really?"

"Yes. I want to put it on the wall behind the couch in my living room."

Eve pursed her lips, seemingly picturing this, and then she nodded. "Yes. It would go perfectly there. You should get it."

"Done. Wait, how much is it?"

Eve gestured to the plaque beneath the painting, describing its concept—which both Josie and Eve had already gotten on their own. It was called "The road home," and it cost two hundred dollars. That was more than Josie usually spent on, well, *anything*, and certainly more than she could afford at the moment. She flinched.

"Let me buy it for you," Eve said quietly.

"What? No." Josie crossed her arms over her chest, hating that Eve knew every sad detail about the current status of her bank account.

"What else am I supposed to do when I see a painting I love, now that my own walls are at capacity?" Eve asked with a twinkle in her eye.

"That's...very nice of you, but no."

"Josie." Eve turned to face her. "I brought you here to

show you something I love, and nothing would make me happier than to see this painting in your living room. Please."

Josie blinked, startled by the sincerity of Eve's words.

"If you say no, it's probably going to show up on your doorstep at some point as an anonymous gift, just so you know." Eve winked. She actually *winked*. And not only that, she was smiling wider than Josie had ever seen her smile.

"I..." Josie found herself completely flustered—and charmed—by this playful side of Eve. "Well, I don't see how I can say no to that."

"Excellent." Eve lifted her chin with a satisfied look.

"Thank you," Josie told her earnestly.

"It is absolutely my pleasure."

Eve bought the painting, and then they went to dinner to celebrate, where they drank more wine and she told Josie how she'd gotten interested in art after moving to the city. "It was something I could do alone. I could just stand there and lose myself in the art and not have to think about anything else."

That was a little bit sad, but also beautiful. "Well, now you can take me with you whenever you want to go look at art."

Eve gave her a sly look. "Art galleries are a surprisingly good place to pick up women."

"Really?" Josie laughed. "Well, don't do that anymore, okay?"

Eve's expression shuttered as they both realized the door Josie had inadvertently opened. Were they still casually hooking up, or was this something more serious? Josie had drawn her own conclusions, but they'd never had a conversation about it, and now, maybe it was time that they did.

"I know we agreed to keep things casual," she said. "But I

guess I just assumed...I mean, can we be an exclusive kind of casual?"

Eve softened. "I haven't been with anyone else since we've been together, and I wasn't planning on it. I wouldn't do that to you."

"Okay, then." Josie couldn't help her smile or the relief swelling inside her. "No picking up women in art galleries for either of us."

Eve laughed softly. "Fair enough."

They finished their meal and walked outside. Josie was quiet, letting Eve take the lead. She'd texted Kaia earlier and asked her to stop by and feed the kittens, so she was obligation-free if Eve wanted to take advantage of it. But maybe, especially after Josie had just pressed her on their relationship, she would want to maintain the status quo and head back to Josie's for the night.

Eve called an Uber for them, although Josie didn't see what address she'd entered into the app. They were quiet while they waited, but Eve threaded her fingers with Josie's as they stood together on the sidewalk.

Their car arrived, and they climbed in. It was almost immediately obvious that they were headed toward the East Village, not Brooklyn, which meant they were on their way to Eve's apartment, and suddenly, Josie's stomach was filled with butterflies. She wasn't sure why, but this felt like a big deal, one more step into Eve's private world.

Twenty minutes later, their Uber pulled up in front of a sleek high-rise apartment building that was almost exactly like what Josie had pictured in her head when she imagined where Eve lived. She smiled a little as she slid out of the car.

"Wait." She rested a hand on Eve's shoulder. "Before we go in, will you show me the trash can where you found them?"

Eve nodded, leading her around the corner. She gestured to one of the large city-managed bins. There were thousands like it all over Manhattan. "The police never made any progress finding out who dumped them in there."

"Not surprising, unfortunately," Josie said. "They're awfully lucky you found them."

She followed Eve to the front of her building, exchanging greetings with the doorman as they walked inside. The lobby was modern, with black marble floors and gray painted walls, a world apart from the decades-old brick and wood in Josie's building. They stepped into the elevator, which took them to the eighth floor.

Eve let them into an apartment on the front side of the building, standing back and gesturing Josie in ahead of her. She walked into a small but well-appointed living room. More gray-painted walls with hardwood floors stained so dark they looked almost black. That was where the similarity with the lobby ended, though.

Eve's living room was sleek and modern, yet comfortably lived in. Maybe because she hadn't expected to have company tonight, she'd left a throw blanket tossed over one side of the couch, a notebook and a mug on the coffee table. The walls, as expected, boasted an impressive selection of art, a mixture of black-and-white photography and colorful abstract paintings. Josie walked slowly around the room, taking it all in. The paintings added warmth and personality to the room that would have otherwise been lacking.

On the other side of the room, there was a small galley kitchen and a door that probably led to the bedroom. Josie peeked through, finding that Eve made her bed every morning whether she expected company or not, but the thin cotton gown she'd slept in last night was tossed over the end of the bed. Josie wandered to the dresser, having noticed photos there, while Eve lingered in the doorway.

But as Josie got a closer look at the photos, she saw that they were all of Eve with another woman. And not just any woman. These were pictures of Eve and her wife. With a horrible sinking feeling, Josie realized she'd overstepped. She shouldn't have just barged into Eve's bedroom without an invitation.

Was this why Eve had initially balked at the idea of coming to her place tonight? She'd known what Josie hadn't...that she would see these photos. And by bringing her here, she'd allowed it to happen.

Josie looked at her. "I'm sorry. I shouldn't have—"

"It's fine," Eve said quietly from the doorway. "Go on and look."

Josie blinked moisture from her eyes as she turned toward the photos. She saw Eve and Lisa at a Pride event with a rainbow flag wrapped around their shoulders, kissing for the camera. A wedding photo sat beside it. Eve wore a stunning white dress, with a snug lace bodice and a loose skirt that billowed behind her as she gazed adoringly at her wife. Lisa was a beautiful woman, with wildly curly brown hair and a radiant smile. She wore a white suit, one arm wrapped tightly around Eve's waist.

Josie's gaze fell on the next photo, and the bottom dropped out of her stomach. Eve's hands rested on Lisa's belly, which was obviously rounded. They'd been expecting a baby. Had Lisa been pregnant when she died? "Oh God," she whispered as she turned to look at Eve.

Eve kept her gaze on the floor, but Josie could feel the tension radiating from her all the way across the room.

"Eve..."

Eve shook her head, bracing a hand against the

doorframe.

Josie walked to her and rested a hand on her shoulder, unsure what to say. She felt Eve's breath hitch, saw her jaw clench before she turned her face resolutely away from Josie's gaze. She was trying not to cry in front of her, and that broke Josie in a way nothing else Eve had shared with her ever had.

"I'm so sorry," she whispered, wiping away a tear of her own.

When Eve finally faced her, her eyes were dry, but they gleamed suspiciously bright. "Well, now you know." Her voice was hoarse.

"You lost them both in the crash?"

Eve nodded, and Josie had a vivid image of her in that wrecked car, trying desperately to save Lisa and their unborn child as their lives drained away. Josie knew—on some level, at least—what that felt like. She'd held her father as his blood soaked her clothes, as his eyes went glassy and the last breath escaped his lips.

Eve had fractured her back in that crash. What must that pain have been like, on top of everything else?

Tears spilled over Josie's eyelids as she wrapped her arms around Eve, drawing her close. "You've lost so much... too much. I'm so fucking sorry."

"Don't cry for me," Eve whispered against her neck.

Josie swiped at her cheeks. "Someone should."

Eve didn't respond, but she hugged Josie back, holding on to her, and that meant more than any words she could have said. Maybe that was the moment Josie fell in love with her, or maybe it had already happened. Somewhere along the line, she'd fallen for this beautifully broken woman, and now she could only hope that at some point in the future, Eve would find the strength to love her back.

25

The first thing Eve registered was the scent of Josie's shampoo. She rolled toward her, recognizing the silky slip of her own sheets against her skin, not the soft cotton of Josie's. And something was buzzing. What was that? Her eyes sprang open as she remembered last night. Having Josie in her bed felt wrong, but at the same time...right.

She'd never shared this room with Lisa, but her memory seemed alive here anyway. This was where Eve kept her photos, where she lay awake at night missing her. On the rare occasion she'd brought a woman here, she put the photos away first and made the room as impersonal as the rest of her apartment.

Josie had seen every dark corner of Eve's mind now. She knew all her secrets, all her pain, and that was vaguely terrifying, because Eve had never meant to let herself get this close to anyone again. She couldn't give her heart to Josie, or anyone else. She'd already given away all her spare pieces. If she lost any more, she'd never survive it.

And yet, she couldn't bring herself to walk away. Not yet,

anyway. Last night, Josie had called their relationship "an exclusive kind of casual," and Eve could live with that. Surely in a few weeks, she and Josie would have tired of each other. Actually, she couldn't imagine ever tiring of Josie, but that was a problem for another day.

It was still dark outside, earlier than she usually woke. And now that she was fully awake, she realized the faint buzzing sound in her bedroom was the alarm on Josie's phone, the one she'd set to wake herself to go home and care for the kittens. The clock on the bedside table read four a.m.

Eve smiled into the darkness, marveling at Josie's never-ending dedication to those little cats. She nudged her, and Josie mumbled grumpily in her sleep. "Your alarm is going off," she whispered.

Josie groaned, squinting at her. She blinked groggily for a few seconds before sitting up and shutting off her alarm. "Sorry for waking you."

"It's okay. Sure they can't wait another hour?" Eve asked as she brushed Josie's hair back to place a kiss against the tender skin on her neck.

Josie pulled her in for a kiss that made Eve think she'd indeed changed her mind about leaving, but then she disentangled herself and climbed out of bed. "I wish they could, but I really have to go."

Eve nodded, tucking the sheet around herself.

"We'll figure out a way to see each other this week, though, okay?" Josie said as she pulled on her clothes. "I'm not sure what or how, but we'll think of something."

"Okay," Eve told her. "How are you getting home?"

"In an Uber?" Josie said, giving her a funny look. "I'm not very fond of the subway at this hour."

"And I'm not very fond of the idea of you riding off alone with a stranger in the middle of the night."

"I'll be fine," Josie told her. "I put people in cabs all the time at four a.m. when they leave my bar."

That was Josie, as trusting as Eve was cautious. "Send me a screenshot with the vehicle information, just in case." She rolled her eyes at Josie's amused look. "Humor me. And text me when you get home."

"All right," Josie said with a smile. "If it makes you feel better."

She leaned in for one more kiss, and then she was gone. Eve lay there, blinking up at the ceiling, determined not to fall asleep until she knew Josie was home safely. Although by then, it would be almost time for her to get up anyway, so she might as well just get up now.

Decision made, she slid out of bed, put on her robe, and went into the kitchen to start some coffee. Her phone buzzed with a text from Josie, a screenshot from the Uber app with the information about her driver.

Thank you, she texted back.

She poured herself a cup of coffee and sat on the couch, sipping it. When she'd finished, she did her morning yoga, and then, once Josie had texted to say she'd made it home, Eve hopped in the shower to get ready for her day.

She didn't see Josie again until Wednesday, when they had lunch together.

"Do you think I'm doing well enough to add an extra shift for one of my bartenders?" Josie asked as they ate sandwiches across from each other in a deli down the street from Eve's office.

"How do you mean?" she asked.

"Like, letting Lauren work an extra shift with Adam on

Friday night so I could take it off." She gave Eve a meaningful look.

"Oh. Well, I'd have to take another look at your numbers, but I think so, yes."

"Okay, I'm going to talk to her about it tonight," Josie said. "It might stretch me a little thin, but it's just one shift, and I need a break. I feel like I'm always working, and we hardly ever see each other, except in the middle of the night or on Mondays."

"It's fine, Josie." Eve wouldn't be the reason for Josie's stress. She shouldn't be the reason for Josie's *anything*. "I understand if you need a break, but we see each other plenty."

"I haven't had a night off that wasn't a Monday in close to a year, except for those few days when the bar was closed for renovations. I just want to be able to get at least a little bit of my old life back."

Eve sipped her water. That was an odd thing for Josie to say. "Your old life?"

"I never planned to own a bar, remember?" Josie picked at her sandwich. "I'm grateful every day that I was able to save it, but I miss being able to go out on a Friday night too."

"Fair enough. So hire Lauren to cover the shift for you, then."

"Planning to." She grinned at Eve. "On a related note, if you have plans on Friday, cancel them, because we're going out."

"All right."

Josie began to eat again with gusto, a sparkle in her eyes that hadn't been there before. Maybe she needed this night off more than Eve had realized. She did work a *lot* of hours at the bar. Many restaurant and bar owners did the same, but most of them had chosen that life for themselves. As Josie had just reminded her, she hadn't.

They finished their meal and walked outside.

"Text me about Friday?" Eve said.

Josie leaned in for a searing kiss. "Yep. See you then."

"YOU ARE my new favorite person right now," Josie told Lauren on Thursday evening as they worked together behind the bar.

Lauren laughed. "We can make this a regular thing if you want. I could use the hours."

"Yeah?" Josie glanced at her. Fridays off? Could it really be that easy? Maybe it could. And maybe, within the next year or so, she'd be able to afford another full-time bartender. She could run things behind the scenes and fill in as needed without spending every waking minute here in the bar.

She could get back to rescuing kittens, rebuild her YouTube following, go out with Eve whenever she wanted to. These were end-game goals, and they felt more tangible than they ever had before. She could really do this. She was doing it right now.

"I have to run some numbers," Josie told Lauren, "but you're on for tomorrow, and I'll let you know next week if we can make it a regular thing, okay?"

"Sounds good to me," Lauren told her.

They worked together for the next hour or so as the Thursday-night crowd began to thin. A little after midnight, Lauren said, "I could close up for you tonight, if you want to start your day off a little early."

"What?" Josie paused in the middle of mixing a drink.

"I can finish up by myself. There are only a handful of people left in here." Lauren gestured around the mostly empty bar.

It was true. Josie had tended bar alone with five times this many customers, not that it had been an ideal situation. Dragonfly closed in an hour and a half. It was basically the same as what she'd done with Adam last week, and that had been fine. Lauren was still new, but she'd been consistently competent and responsible.

Josie nodded. "Yeah, you know what? I think you're ready to close."

Lauren beamed at her.

Josie spent the next few minutes running her through the process, although Lauren seemed to already have it down, having watched and helped Josie close over the last two weeks. "Feel free to text me if you have any questions or need help with anything. I'll just be right upstairs."

"I'll be fine," Lauren told her. "I closed all the time at the last bar I worked at."

"I trust you," Josie told her with a smile. "Okay, I'm leaving. Thank you."

Lauren waved her off, and Josie headed for the stairs that led to her apartment. It was twelve thirty on a Thursday night, and she was off work until Saturday at five. The prospect was intoxicating. She almost texted Eve to see if she wanted to come over, but while this might not be late for Josie, it was for Eve, who had to be at the office in the morning. She was probably already asleep.

Josie let herself into her apartment and spent a while playing with the kittens. They were eating solid food almost exclusively now and using the litter box independently. Josie still had to prepare wet food for them every six hours, but it was worlds easier than bottle feeding.

She messed around with them for longer than she probably should have, but she was still in bed earlier than usual. When she woke the next morning, she took her time feeding and playing with the kittens and even recorded a new video for her YouTube channel, documenting their progress. She didn't earn nearly as much from it as she used to, but it still brought in a little bit of money.

She went out to run some errands, grabbing lunch while she was at it. When she got back to her building, she peeked into the bar to make sure all was well after Lauren closed last night. Chairs were neatly stacked, dishes run, the floor swept.

Good job, Lauren.

Josie went into her office and sat behind her desk, looking at the balance sheet for the last month. Realistically, adding one extra shift for Lauren didn't cost her that much. She could do this. She added Lauren's name to the schedule on Fridays.

Done.

Giddy, she texted Eve. *Consider me a free woman on Fridays, effective today.*

Congratulations, Eve replied. *I should be able to leave early this afternoon. Want me to meet you at your place?*

Yes. Can't wait to see you.

Josie jogged upstairs, feeling light as air. She re-dyed her hair to match her mood and took a long, hot shower, then spent a half an hour blow drying and curling it. Tonight, she wanted to look as good as she felt, and that was pretty damn good. She'd made reservations for herself and Eve at one of her favorite restaurants, and then they were going to visit a trendy rooftop bar in Midtown. She really did enjoy going to bars where she didn't work, where she could sit and sip a drink for fun.

After spending an obscene amount of time getting ready, she went into the living room to check on the kittens. She'd leave some extra wet food out for them, and they should be fine until she and Eve got back, whatever time that was.

Her phone rang, and she grabbed it, hoping it was Eve calling to say she was on her way, but Adam's name was on the screen. He must be downstairs getting ready to open. "Hey," she said. "Need my help before I leave?"

"Uh, you better get down here." His voice sounded strange, tense, completely unlike himself. "I think we've been robbed."

26

Eve entered Josie's building through the back door, intending to go straight up to her apartment, but something stopped her. A noise. Static, like a radio between stations. It scratched at her nerves, clawing under her skin. She closed her eyes. *Flashing red and blue lights. The crackle of static as a police officer rolls out yellow tape. Smothering pain as she's lifted onto a stretcher.*

Police radios.

She forced the image from her mind. Why was she hearing them now? Breathing hard, she strode down the hall toward the bar. A grim-faced policeman stood there, speaking to someone outside her line of vision. Eve's stomach went into freefall.

Josie.

Oh God. Something cold sliced through Eve's stomach, filling her body with an awful, paralyzing fear that she already knew too well. Her knees shook, and her chest seized. Not Josie. This wasn't happening. Not again. Eve's feet kept moving, propelling her toward the inevitable.

The police officer turned toward her.

"We're so sorry to inform you..."

A silent scream rose in her throat. The world around her was blurry and sluggish, silent except for the frantic whooshing of her heart inside her ears. She glanced toward the bar.

And there was Josie, seated on a barstool. Relief almost knocked Eve's knees out from under her. She pressed a hand to her heart, attempting to steady herself. It was all she could do not to fall into Josie's arms, hold her, kiss her, sob into the fluorescent depths of her hair until she'd found her balance again. Josie was safe and whole. Alive.

She'd changed her hair. That was the first thing Eve noticed. Pink stripes mixed with the lavender, and it was so fucking beautiful. But then the rest of the scene came into focus, Josie's red eyes, the devastated look on her face, the policemen on either side of her. Adam stood nearby, arms crossed over his chest, his expression pinched. Josie looked up and met Eve's eyes, chin quivering.

Eve's stomach bottomed out all over again. Two police officers had stood beside her hospital bed that night, just like they stood with Josie now. This time, it was happening to Josie, and Eve needed to be here for her. She forced herself to keep walking, the sound of her heels against the tile floor echoing way too loudly in the otherwise quiet room.

"What's happened?" she asked Josie gently.

"I was robbed," Josie said, blinking up at her.

Eve exhaled, squeezing her eyes shut. She'd jumped straight to thinking someone had died. *Robbed.* That was... way less horrible. "Oh."

"Who are you?" one of the police officers asked.

"Eve Marlow. I'm with—"

"She's my girlfriend," Josie interrupted, extending a hand toward Eve.

Girlfriend.

She'd been about to say she was with the team from *Do Over*, and now her head was spinning for an entirely different reason. She stepped closer, skin prickling uncomfortably as she took the hand Josie had offered.

"I let Lauren close for me last night, and it looks like she cleaned me out before she left." Josie stared at her with dazed eyes, as if she still couldn't believe it had happened. That made two of them. "She emptied the cash register and took a bunch of liquor and expensive wine from the cellar."

"How do you know it was Lauren?" Eve asked. Her whole body shook as the roller coaster of the last few minutes ricocheted through her system.

"There are no signs of forced entry," the officer said. "Everything points to an inside job."

"And Lauren's not answering her cell phone," Josie added. "Plus, she's cleared out of her apartment."

"Holy shit," Eve said, leaning against the bar.

"I trusted her," Josie said miserably. "I shouldn't have let her close. I just...I never thought...I never imagined..."

"Of course you didn't," Eve assured her, although the business part of her brain was already thinking how absurdly foolish it had been of Josie to let Lauren close for her last night. Adam was one thing. She'd known him for years. But Lauren had been a virtual stranger and, as it turned out, not a very honest one.

Eve stood quietly off to the side while Josie finished up with the police. Finally, she, Josie, and Adam were alone in the bar. She could see people outside the front door, peering in. It was past five. Dragonfly should be open. "Are you opening at all tonight?" she asked, pushing past the emotions still churning inside her to focus on the business at hand.

"I...I don't know." Josie looked around. "I don't have any cash, and..." she drifted off, swallowing hard.

"I'm going to print a sign for the door," Eve said, walking to Josie's office, where she printed out a piece of paper that said the bar was temporarily closed due to unforeseen circumstances. She took it outside and taped it to the door, locking it on her way back in.

"You can't afford to stay closed on a Friday night," she told Josie. "What do you need to open?"

"Cash for the register," Josie said. "And I'm short a bunch of liquor."

"You can make do without the liquor for the night," Eve said. "Adam, can you take her card and go to the bank? Josie, how much do you need?"

"A hundred in small bills to make change."

Eve looked at Adam, who nodded.

"I'm on it." He headed out the back.

And then she and Josie were alone. She pulled Josie in for a hug, holding on to her for a long moment as her throat constricted painfully. She couldn't seem to get past the initial shock of finding the police here at Dragonfly, that awful moment when she thought something had happened to Josie. Her body still shook uncontrollably. Could Josie feel it?

Eve pulled back, looking into her eyes. "Are you okay?"

"No," Josie whispered. "I mean, our date, and you look so pretty..." Her eyes welled with tears. "And now I'll have to work."

"Forget about our date," Eve told her. "We'll go out another night. I can hang out here with you tonight if you like."

"It's not the same." Josie slumped in her seat.

Eve stroked her fingers through one of Josie's newly pink curls. "Love your hair."

"Thanks," Josie said glumly. "I was in the mood to celebrate earlier."

"You'll still get the chance to celebrate. This is just a setback. Every business has them."

"I'm down a bartender," Josie said. "And a few thousand dollars in cash and inventory."

"Your insurance will likely cover at least some of that," Eve said.

"Right." She blew out a breath. "I'll give them a call in the morning."

"After tonight, Lauren wasn't scheduled to work again until Tuesday, right? We can probably find you someone new by then. We've still got that whole stack of applications from last month."

"Can I even afford it now?" Josie asked.

"It'll be tight," Eve admitted. "But you don't have a choice."

"Well, I could just work by myself like I used to." Josie propped her elbows on the bar, a faraway look in her eyes.

"You have more customers now. Could you even handle it alone?"

She shrugged, then sighed. "Maybe I should tough it out next week to recoup some of what Lauren took from me."

"That's an option, if you think you can manage it."

Josie stared dejectedly at the wall.

"You need to snap out of this," Eve told her. "Pick yourself up and get back to work. Tomorrow will be better."

"That's easy for you to say," Josie said before turning to Eve with a stricken look on her face. "I'm sorry. I don't know what...you of all people..."

And it was Eve's turn to sigh. "Come on. Get up."

Josie slid off the barstool, running her hands appreciatively over Eve's dress. "You got so dressed up for me."

"Yes." And it was a damn shame they wouldn't get to go out and have the night they'd planned, but such was life. Money was replaceable, as were employees and liquor. "Tell me what's going on here."

Josie's eyes flooded with tears, and she bit her lip before pressing her face into Eve's shoulder. "I never wanted this."

"Never wanted what?"

"This bar," she whispered.

"Oh." That wasn't what she'd expected her to say.

"I hate saying it. I hate even thinking it. I know it sounds awful. You know I'll do anything to save Swanson's—Dragonfly—but this isn't the life I wanted. I just want to rescue kittens and grow my YouTube presence, you know? Think of how many lives I could have saved these last two years if I hadn't been shackled to this bar."

"Shackled?" Eve repeated, arms tightening around Josie.

"That's how it feels sometimes. I'm always here. I never get to leave." Her voice was dull and monotone. "Every time I start to make progress toward getting my old life back, it gets taken away from me. I just want to have enough staff that I can start rescuing kittens again or take you out for a date on a Friday night. Is that so much to ask?"

"You will," Eve told her.

"I just...sometimes I hate this place," Josie whispered. "I hate it, and I wish I had let it go under."

Eve stared at her for a moment in shocked silence. "Hate is a strong word."

Josie stepped backward out of Eve's arms. She took a long look around the bar as her lips twisted into a frown.

"Right now, I hate absolutely everything about it. I wish I could walk out that door and never look back."

"Well, that's unfortunate considering I just spent the last month helping you save it." Eve's rampaging emotions had built to the point where she felt slightly hysterical. For a moment, she'd thought Josie had *died*, while Josie was ready to throw in the towel over some lost cash?

Josie gulped, nodding. "I know."

"You begged me for this." Eve's skin flushed hot, and that heavy feeling was back in her stomach. God, why couldn't she stop shaking? "I told you I didn't work in bars. You knew how hard it was for me to be here, and you begged and pleaded until I agreed to help, and now you're telling me it was a mistake?"

Josie opened and closed her mouth, blinking rapidly. "It wasn't a mistake."

"No?" Eve heard the ice in her voice. She was being unfair. She knew she was. But something deep inside her felt wounded and raw, and it was a feeling she'd never wanted to experience again. Her fingers clenched defensively.

"She's my girlfriend."

Josie's words echoed in her head, mixed with the static of police radios and the tangy scent of blood.

Lisa hooked her arm through Eve's. "Mom, Dad, I want you to meet my girlfriend."

Josie stepped forward, desperation morphing into defiance. "You're twisting my words. I just had the rug pulled out from under me, and I deserve a few minutes to feel sorry for myself."

Eve turned away, not trusting herself to speak.

"We're so sorry to inform you that your wife didn't make it. She and the baby died en route to the hospital."

"It wasn't a mistake," Josie repeated. "I'll keep working because I promised my dad at his funeral that I wouldn't let us lose this place. I'll save this bar, even if it's not what I want."

"That doesn't make any sense." Eve was hot and cold at the same time, lost between the past and the present.

"Family doesn't always make sense," Josie told her. "Sometimes you just have to do things because they're the right thing to do. This building is my home, and someday I'll be able to make it all work the way I want it to."

They faced each other, tempers sparking, and Eve's shoulders slumped as she realized with sudden, sinking clarity that the only person she was angry at was herself. She had an overwhelming, irrational urge to cry because she couldn't believe she'd let this happen, that she'd let them get to the point where Josie introduced her as her girlfriend, where just the thought of something happening to her could send Eve into an emotional tailspin.

"I never took it lightly that it was difficult for you to be here," Josie said quietly. "I still don't."

"I know." Eve swallowed roughly. "I'm sorry."

Adam walked in with a sleeve of cash, staring between them as he tried to read the tension in the room. Eve stayed out of the way as Josie stocked the cash register and Adam chopped lemons. By the time they were ready to open, it was past seven, and dusk had fallen across Manhattan.

"I should probably just go home," Eve said, feeling suddenly exhausted. She'd briefly entertained the idea of hanging out here at Dragonfly and keeping Josie company during her shift, but the thought of sitting on one of those barstools for another nine hours was too much. Tears pressed behind her eyes, and that sick feeling in her stomach just wouldn't go away.

Josie crooked a finger, indicating for Eve to follow her. She led the way into her office and closed the door, turning to face Eve. "Are we okay?"

Eve took a step back, feeling trapped in the confined space. "For tonight."

"Tell me what that means," Josie pressed.

Eve rubbed a hand over her brow. "It means, you've had a tough night, and we should regroup tomorrow."

Josie nodded. "Okay."

Eve blew out a slow breath. "Okay."

Josie stepped forward, wrapping her arms around Eve. They held on to each other for a long minute, and then they were kissing, and every cell in Eve's body was lit with the energy that seemed to charge them every time they touched. It was so intense that she felt herself splintering, because she knew this feeling. She'd felt it before, and she couldn't let herself feel it again. Her heart couldn't take it. She pulled back, breathing hard, tears stinging her eyes.

"Tomorrow," she whispered, already dreading the horrible inevitability of what she was going to have to do. She walked out of Josie's office without looking back.

27

Josie blinked over gritty eyes, tightening her grip on the bag of carry-out in her lap. As usual, it had been almost five by the time she made it upstairs last night—this morning—and then she hadn't been able to fall asleep. She'd been too wired, a swirling mass of emotions all warring for dominance inside her.

She was furious with Lauren for screwing her over, hurt by the betrayal, discouraged by the setback to her business, and utterly confused by whatever had happened between her and Eve afterward. While she felt a little guilty for dumping her deepest, darkest fears on Eve like that, she also didn't, because she'd had a profoundly shitty night, and she should have been able to vent about it for a few minutes before she moved on.

So now she was on the subway, holding a bag of Chinese food and hoping to set things right between them. She exited at Eve's stop and climbed the steps to the street, headed toward her building. Josie gave her name to Eve's doorman, who ushered her inside. She rode the elevator to the eighth floor and knocked on Eve's door.

She opened it wearing jeans and a sleeveless blue top, her hair in a messy ponytail. How did she manage to look even more beautiful every time Josie saw her? Maybe that was part of Eve's magic, this invisible force around her that drew Josie in deeper and deeper. At this point, there was no way back out, at least, not with her heart intact.

"Hi," she said, giving Eve a gentle kiss before following her into the living room.

"Any new developments in the case?" Eve asked.

Josie shook her head. "Lauren is long gone. The police don't seem super hopeful that they'll be able to track her down."

"People are profoundly shitty sometimes, aren't they?" Eve said with a frown.

Josie laughed, sitting next to her on the couch as they began opening cartons of food. "Yeah, they are." This felt right, like the balance between them had been restored. They'd both been upset yesterday, but now they'd had a chance to calm down and cool off.

Eve went into the kitchen, returning with plates and napkins, and they began to eat, not talking much. Eve looked as tired as Josie felt, and she figured she wasn't the only one who hadn't slept well last night. Once they'd finished their lunch and put the leftovers in the fridge, they went back into the living room.

"I'm sorry," Josie said earnestly. "Those things I told you about feeling shackled to the bar...they're all true. But it doesn't change the fact that I want to save it."

"And that still doesn't make any sense to me," Eve said, staring at the table in front of her.

"I guess a lot of things about me have never made sense," Josie said with a self-deprecating laugh.

Eve smiled, but it was a fake one, the kind she used on camera.

The wall between them was back up, and this time, Josie had no idea how to scale it. "What's happening to us?"

Eve shook her head. "I don't know."

"Yes, you do."

"I think, if we're really honest with ourselves, we both know," Eve said quietly.

Josie was about to retort that she didn't, but before she could get it out, she realized Eve was right. She did know. "We did what we said we weren't going to. We let it get serious."

Eve didn't move, didn't speak. She just stared at the table, her expression blank. "I said I'd do this thing with you until it didn't make sense anymore, and I think that time is now."

"What?" Josie looked at her, certain she'd heard her wrong, because that sounded like...

"You need to focus on your bar, and I need to focus on my career."

"No." Josie's chest tightened, like she might laugh...or cry. Because surely this wasn't happening.

"I can't get serious with you, Josie." Eve kept her gaze resolutely on the table in front of her. "I'm sorry."

"Don't do this." Josie grabbed Eve's hands, resisting—barely—the urge to shake her. "Please don't do this."

"You deserve someone who can give you all the things you want, but that person isn't me."

"You could be," Josie countered, as tears swam in her eyes and the world seemed to sway beneath her feet. "The only thing I want is *you*, Eve."

"And I can't give myself to you." Eve's bottom lip trembled, her palms damp against Josie's. "I'm sorry for letting us get to this point. I should have walked away weeks ago."

"But you didn't, because you feel it too." She let go of Eve's hands and flung her arms around her instead. "If you're going to dump me, you might as well know what you're walking away from, because I love you, Eve. I am so hopelessly in love with you."

Eve stiffened, tears shining in her eyes before she turned her face away. And Josie thought of the photos in her bedroom, the wife and baby she'd lost, the family who'd turned their backs on her, loss after loss etched into her heart.

Josie slid one of her hands to Eve's chest, feeling her heart thump wildly beneath her palm. "Please just let me love you," she whispered.

"I can't." Eve stood abruptly, sliding out of Josie's grasp. "And you shouldn't presume to know what I feel."

"Eve..."

"Stop it," Eve gasped as tears slid over her cheeks. "I can't do this. I'm sorry. I'm *so* sorry for putting you in this situation. But I just...can't."

Josie wrapped her arms around herself. In everything they'd been through together, she'd never seen Eve cry, and the sight of her tears now was almost more than she could take. She could keep fighting, keep pushing Eve, but to what end? Josie couldn't pretend to know what it felt like to be in a place where rejecting love felt less painful than allowing herself to love again.

"Please." Eve pressed a hand over her eyes, chest heaving with ragged breaths. "Just go."

Josie swiped at her own cheeks, wet with tears. Her throat burned, and her heart hurt. She wanted to scream at the unfairness of it all. Instead, she tugged Eve's hand from her face, meeting her tear-soaked eyes as she drew her in for a kiss. A last kiss. She poured all her love, her passion, and her heart into that kiss. When she pulled back, Eve's pupils were dilated, her cheeks flushed.

"I love you," Josie whispered. "You know where to find me if you change your mind."

And then, because there was nothing else to say, she walked out the door.

EVE RESTED her forehead against the door. She felt empty, hollow, drugged. Vaguely, she wondered if any of that had actually happened or if she was dreaming, caught in an endless nightmare. But the clatter of Josie's receding footsteps in the hall outside was very real. It echoed in Eve's heart as she remembered the press of Josie's fingers there.

She walked to the middle of the room and stood, breathing hard as the numbness began to wear off. Josie loved her. Eve had never expected to hear those words from her lips. She hadn't expected to hear those words ever again. She didn't want to hear them, didn't want to feel them, didn't want the pain that came with any of it.

Because it hurt. It hurt *so much*. She pressed her own hand in the shadow of Josie's, feeling her heart beat hard and fast, pumping pain through her veins. This hurt, but she'd recover, because it was nothing like the pain of losing Lisa, nothing like the pain of leaving her family behind. Better to nip it in the bud, before it had the chance to swallow her whole.

But as she blinked to clear her vision, she realized that letting go of Josie hurt a lot more than she'd expected it to. She walked into her bedroom, rubbing at her chest, which was bursting with the pressure of the emotions inside her, as if they'd vaporized into steam and she needed to scream until she'd let them all out.

But she wasn't going to scream. She sat on the bed, fists clenched into her blanket as she sucked in slow, deep breaths, waiting for it to pass. Tears streamed over her cheeks, and her throat grew too painful to swallow. She hiccupped, swiping at her tears, trying to hold them back, but it was no use. Finally, she curled on her side in the bed and sobbed.

She cried until her eyes swelled and her nose ran and her chest hitched. When her tears ran out, she just lay there, eyes closed, too tired to move. Eventually, she drifted into a restless sleep, waking sometime later with a dull headache. She sat up, rubbing her eyes, which were scratchy and tender.

She took a shower, changed into her pajamas, and climbed into bed with her Kindle. And that was more or less how she spent the rest of the weekend. Was she hiding from the outside world? Absolutely. But she didn't really care. This was the life she had chosen for herself, the life she needed.

When Monday rolled around, she blew out her hair, dressed, and went to work. At the end of the week, she'd have to return to Dragonfly to tape her follow-up segment, but until then, she would be focused on her Marlow Marketing clients, and she was going to do her best not to think about Josie—or her bar.

She kept the door to her office closed, working through lunch and often late into the evening. She'd fallen behind on some of her work this month, she'd been so caught up in...other things. And now it was time to get herself in order. It was a long, tiring week, but a necessary one.

By Friday, she was feeling almost like the woman she'd been before she pulled those kittens out of a trash can and set herself on a collision course into Josie's welcoming arms. Tonight would be hard. She'd have to see Josie, interview her, spend hours at Dragonfly. It had been a full week since the robbery. Hopefully, Josie had gotten herself back on track.

Later that afternoon, Eve went down the hall to hair and makeup—perks of working in a television studio—and changed into the dress she'd wear for the taping. She checked in with her camera crew and with Josie herself, making sure they were ready. Josie was polite on the phone, although distant.

And if the sound of her voice made Eve's chest ache and her eyes sting, no one needed to know about it. After tonight, she wouldn't see Josie again. This was the last time she would step foot inside Dragonfly. That whole chapter of her life would close.

Around five, she gathered her crew and headed out, riding over in the van as she usually did when she had the film crew with her. They laughed and joked all the way there, completely oblivious to Eve's internal turmoil. Because, after all, there was nothing unusual about her ignoring them in favor of answering emails on her phone.

When the van pulled up outside Dragonfly, she had to take an extra moment to compose herself before she stood. Emotion rolled over her in a smothering wave, constricting her lungs and leaving her in a sheen of cold sweat.

She squared her shoulders and pulled open the front door. Inside, music played, muffled beneath the buzz of conversation. The crowd was thick tonight, probably partly because of the notice on the front door about the taping, but also because Dragonfly was doing well. Josie and Adam were behind the bar, demonstrating some kind of synchronized dance move to a group of delighted women.

Josie looked up, and their eyes met. Eve steeled herself against the power of her gaze, the way it heated her from the inside out and made her whole body tingle. Would that ever go away? It didn't really matter if they never saw each other again, did it? She schooled her expression as she approached the bar.

"Hi," Josie said, her smile as bright as ever, although tonight it didn't quite reach her eyes or bring out the dimples that Eve loved so much.

"You changed your hair," she blurted, taking in Josie's turquoise locks, the color it had been the night they met. Full circle.

"I do that a lot," she said, tugging at a curl.

"I noticed." Eve cleared her throat. "Okay, then. We'll start setting up. My team will shoot footage while you work, and then I'll do a quick interview so you can tell me how everything's going."

"Okay," Josie said. "Hey, before you get started, you should go upstairs and see the kittens. You won't believe how much they've grown."

"I don't think—"

"Eve." Temper sparked in Josie's hazel eyes. "Will you for once not be stubborn about the damn kittens? Just go see them. Say goodbye to them. They're going to be adopted soon."

"Have you found homes for them?" she asked, trying to ignore the pinch in her chest at the thought of them going to live with people she didn't know. Somehow, it hadn't bothered her to think of them here with Josie.

"Remember that woman who came in on opening night? Jules Vega? She wants two of them. I had been putting her off, in case you wanted to keep Blanche, but I guess I should just go ahead and let her pick whichever two she wants." She held Eve's gaze as she lobbed the challenge at her.

"Yes," Eve said, looking away. "You should. But I'll go see them to say goodbye. Thank you."

She strode down the back hall, leaving the noise and chaos of the bar behind her. She punched in the code and let herself into the stairwell, making a mental note to tell Josie to change it. Jesus Christ, what did Eve have to do to lose her trust? How did Josie trust so easily? How did she love so endlessly when she got nothing but pain in return?

Eve walked into the apartment, steeling herself against the avalanche of memories waiting for her here. When she looked into the kitchen, she pictured Josie on the counter with a row of drinks in front of her and the kiss that had followed. In the living room, she saw herself sitting on the couch wearing Josie's oversized pink pussy T-shirt, bottle-feeding kittens after their first night together.

The painting she'd bought the night of their gallery date hung behind the couch now, jolting Eve out of her memories with its unfamiliar presence. It looked good there, though, a perfect fit. Holding in a sigh, she walked into the living room. She'd just peek at the kittens and go, because she needed to get the hell out of there as quickly as possible.

She could already see them, running and tumbling, wrestling with each other. As she approached the playpen, Blanche ran over to greet her, putting her front paws up on the plastic barrier between them and meowing loudly. Eve reached down and lifted her. "You're all grown up."

Blanche squirmed in her hands, purring.

"Maybe you'll go home with that theater actress," Eve told her. "I met her. She seems nice."

Blanche grabbed Eve's thumb between her front paws and bit down, hard.

"Well, you've turned into a handful, haven't you?" She sat on the couch, rubbing the kitten as she rolled across Eve's knees. White fur clung to her black dress. "Listen, I have to get back to work, but I know Josie will make sure you go to a great home. She's good at that."

She pressed a kiss against the kitten's fuzzy head, laughing at the lipstick stain left behind. As she rubbed it away, Blanche nuzzled her head against Eve's chin, still purring. Her whole body vibrated with the effort. Eve set her in the playpen, where she immediately pounced on Phantom, rolling him to his back. Hamilton joined the fray, while Pippin raced from side to side, chasing a ray of sunshine.

"You guys are cute," she said. "I'll miss you."

Nigel walked over and sat down in front of her, staring as usual. She reached out and rubbed him beneath his chin the way she'd seen Josie do, and he immediately began to purr, rubbing his head against her arm affectionately. Maybe it really had been that easy all along. She'd made him uncomfortable with her own discomfort.

And now, it didn't matter. After giving him one last pat, she stood and left the apartment, closing the door behind her. She went down the steps, attempting to brush cat fur off her dress, so distracted that she ran headlong into Adam in the hallway. "Sorry," she murmured, stepping back to let him pass.

But he stood his ground. "You have a lot of nerve coming here tonight, running around like nothing happened."

She blinked. "Excuse me?"

"You heard me," he said. "You broke her heart, and still,

she invites you into her bar, sends you up to her apartment..."

"I was going to tell her to change the combination."

"That's not the point. You weren't here this week to see the damage you caused."

She refused to flinch. "I'm sorry for that. I never wanted to hurt her."

"Then why did you do it, Eve?" He crossed his arms over his chest, filling the hallway, blocking her path to the bar.

She didn't feel threatened, though. There was nothing threatening about Adam. It was like being growled at by a puppy...or maybe a kitten, if kittens could growl. If anything, he deserved a hug for being a good friend to Josie. But she didn't know what to tell him. There was no way to make this right. She'd fucked up. "It was supposed to be casual."

"Bullshit."

"Look, I don't know what you want me to say."

"You didn't treat her like a casual hookup," he said. "I saw you guys together, remember? You looked at her like she was everything, told her all your deep, dark secrets—"

She recoiled involuntarily, her skin flushing hot. "Fuck you."

She was shaking now, furious with him for cornering her like this and with Josie for betraying her confidence. Her vision swam, and she refused to blink, refused to cry in front of him.

Adam held his hands out in front of himself, his expression suddenly apologetic. "Look, she didn't tell me your secrets, only that you'd been through a lot."

Oh. She looked at her shoes, searching desperately for her composure.

"My point is that you treated her like she meant something to you. You let her fall for you. And then you just kicked her to the curb because her feelings were inconvenient?"

"She did mean something to me," she said quietly, forcing herself to meet his eyes. "She does. But I can't be what she needs. I just can't. I'm sorry."

Adam shook his head, looking almost sad. "You'll regret this someday."

28

"Glad that's over," Josie said, pushing a strand of hair out of her face as the *Do Over* van pulled away from the curb outside.

"Me too." Adam leaned his elbows against the bar, looking as exhausted as she felt. And they still had five hours until they closed for the night.

This week had been never-ending. She'd decided to tough it out for a few weeks before she hired someone new, to make back as much as she could of what she'd lost before she added another salary to her budget. That meant she'd been on her own until tonight, and while she'd tended bar alone at Swanson's, it was different with Dragonfly. She'd been so busy, she barely had time to pee, let alone eat a meal.

In some ways, it had been good for her, because she'd been too busy to think about Eve, too busy to dwell on the pain of losing her, too busy to wonder if there was a chance she'd change her mind. Somewhere in the back of her mind, Josie had imagined that when Eve walked into the bar tonight, they'd fall back into each other's arms.

But it hadn't happened. Eve had been nothing but cool and professional the whole time she was here, and now she was officially gone. Josie would probably never see her again. And she really wanted to go upstairs and have a good, long cry about it, but of course, she couldn't.

"You okay?" Adam asked.

She managed a wry smile. "No, but I'll manage."

"That's the spirit." He tapped his knuckles against hers.

She bent to open the dishwasher. "You know what's weird?"

"What?"

"Eve didn't mention the robbery during our interview. I'd been worrying about it all afternoon because I knew the producers wanted her to play up any drama. And here's stupid, gullible me who let myself get robbed."

"You're not stupid or gullible, just too trusting sometimes."

"I let Lauren close for me, after knowing her for two weeks. That was stupid." She began stacking clean glasses on the drying rack.

"It was," Adam agreed. "But I love you for being such a trusting fool, and I think Eve does too."

"What?" She nearly dropped a glass. It slipped through her fingers, and she hugged it awkwardly between her arm and her stomach before setting it on the counter.

"I may have cornered her earlier," he admitted, looking sheepish. "I was angry with her, and I guess I wanted to pick a fight. But she didn't give me one. Instead, I almost made her cry, and now I feel like an ass."

"Oh, shit," Josie breathed. "What did you say?"

"A lot of nasty stuff about the way she treated you. I thought she'd give me shit for it, and then I could really hate her. But she didn't. She looked wrecked. She told me flat out that she had feelings for you, but that she could never be what you needed."

Josie's vision blurred.

"And if she hid the robbery from her producers so she wouldn't have to embarrass you with it on TV? Well, that sounds like love to me. I don't know what her emotional baggage is, but if it's any consolation, I think you can assume she's as miserable and heartbroken right now as you are."

She choked on a laugh, swiping tears from her cheeks. "That does make me feel a little better, actually."

"Love hurts, babe." He pulled her in for a hug. "I'm sorry."

"Thank you."

A large group entered the bar, disappointed that they'd missed the camera crew but still thirsty, and she and Adam stopped chatting to mix drinks for them. From there, things stayed busy until the crowd started to thin out around two.

"I have a proposition for you," Adam said as he expertly mixed three Midnight in Manhattans in a row.

"Oh yeah?"

"Hire me full-time, and I'll quit my job at the bank."

"What?" She stared at him like he'd just told her he had a date with a woman.

"This is more fun, and with tips, I could make more here than I'm making there. Doing both is wearing me out."

"You're already working three nights a week. How many more shifts do you want?"

"Give me two more to start. If five nights is too much, I'll drop back to four."

"Yeah, wow, okay." Having Adam here five nights a week was a million times better than hiring someone new, and it would only leave her one night a week on her own. It was doable. And it would get her by until she was back on her feet again.

If only she could find a similar patch for her heart.

EVE HAD THOUGHT everything about this was going to be easier. She'd thought that once she broke up with Josie, things would go back to normal. But here she was, over a week after she'd filmed her follow-up segment at Dragonfly, only a few days before the finished episode was set to air, and she was still miserable. She'd gotten back into all her old routines, but none of them brought her the same sense of joy and peace they once had.

She missed Josie. She even missed the damn kittens. She missed middle-of-the-night bottle feedings and waking to the fruity smell of Josie's shampoo. She missed holding her, kissing her, fucking her until they were breathless and sated.

On Thursday, when she still couldn't shake her melancholy, she wasn't entirely surprised to find herself boarding the commuter train to New Jersey after work, something she hadn't done in a long time. Too long. She got off near Freehold, Lisa's hometown, and called an Uber to take her to the cemetery. She almost smiled when she remembered the night she'd insisted Josie text her the vehicle information before she got into a car by herself.

Eve had ridden alone in plenty of Ubers, but there were certain situations—like when she was outside the city, about to travel on less populated roads—that made her more aware of her vulnerability as a woman. The irony of the situation was that she didn't have anyone to text her vehicle information to, not a single person in her life who cared enough to make sure she made it safely to her destination.

That wasn't entirely true. There wasn't a single person Eve had *allowed* to care. Because Josie had wanted to be that person for her. Hell, Josie would be here with her now, riding beside her while the annoyingly talkative but thankfully not creepy Uber driver took her to the cemetery on the other side of town.

Nostalgia rolled over her as the car passed a road that would have taken her to the apartment where she'd lived with Lisa. Eve had never wanted to live in the suburbs. She'd moved to New Jersey as a stepping-stone on her path to Manhattan. She'd never planned to fall in love and get married here, but she'd been happy.

If she hadn't lost Lisa, she would probably still be living in Freehold, commuting to work in the city, or maybe she'd be running Marlow Marketing out of her home office so she could spend more time with her family.

And maybe that was exactly what Josie meant when she said she'd never wanted to own her dad's bar but would still do anything to save it. She'd had to put her dreams on hold to take over the family business. Eve had put her dreams on hold to start a family. Both of their lives had taken unexpected turns, both altered by tragedy. As she watched her old neighborhood pass by outside the window, Eve finally understood Josie's motivations.

It was getting dark when she arrived at the cemetery, streetlamps flickering around her as they turned on, casting their yellowish glow over the setting sun. She'd bought flowers at a stand in the train station, although she hadn't been able to find sunflowers—Lisa's favorite—so she'd settled for a colorful mixed arrangement.

But as she crouched in front of the simple granite headstone that marked her wife and daughter's final resting place, she found an arrangement of white carnations already there. They were somewhat wilted, as if they were a few days old. Who were they from? Lisa's parents always brought roses or sunflowers. Eve moved them to the side and set down her own flowers. She touched Lisa's name, pressing her fingers against the cold stone.

"I miss you," she whispered, steadying her breathing until she could see through the tears clouding her vision. Then she stood, one heel sinking into the grass, throwing her off-balance. She shifted her weight, yanking it free. Rookie mistake, wearing heels to the cemetery. She was out of practice.

Eve had never known quite what to do with herself here. She wasn't going to curl up on Lisa's grave and cry, no matter how tempting that felt at the moment. Talking to her dead wife felt similarly uncomfortable. Instead, she walked to a nearby bench and sat. There was a heaviness inside her that seemed to press her into its harsh metal surface.

This was why she didn't come. The grief here was overwhelming. Her bottom lip shook, and her eyes ached with unshed tears. Her chest felt as if it had turned to lead. Casting a somewhat desperate glance around the cemetery, Eve's eyes caught on another arrangement of white carnations, identical to the one on Lisa's grave.

Curious, she stood. As she walked to the other grave, she was hit with a sense of déjà vu. Derek Felton. Why was that name familiar? But just as quickly, she remembered. She'd met Derek's widow, Regina, here at the cemetery just a few months after Lisa's death. Derek had been gone only a month. Eve and Regina had sat together for hours, laughing and crying, finding comfort in their shared grief. After that first afternoon, they'd met for coffee a few times before eventually losing touch.

Had Regina put flowers on Lisa's grave? Had she been bringing her flowers for six years?

Eve blew out a breath, wiping a stray tear from her cheek. She hadn't thought of Regina in years, had never brought flowers for her husband. Maybe she really did deserve her icy reputation. More tears fell, and she swiped at them angrily. This was her life now, alone and miserable, crying in front of a stranger's grave.

But he wasn't a stranger. She'd never met Derek, but Regina had told her so much about him, Eve felt like she knew him in some small way. He'd been a good man, and he'd left behind a widow every bit as heartbroken as Eve herself had been.

She should call Regina and thank her for the flowers. The thought crystallized in her mind, and before she could second-guess herself, she pulled out her phone and scrolled through her contacts, half-surprised to find Regina's number still stored in her address book. Eve pressed Send, resting one hand against Derek's headstone as the phone rang.

"Hello?" a woman answered.

"Regina?" Eve asked.

"Yes. Who's this?"

"I'm Eve Marlow. We met...well, we met at the cemetery about six years ago."

Regina gasped. "Eve. Wow, it's been a long time."

"It has," Eve agreed. "This might be an odd question, but I found carnations on my wife's grave, and the same flowers on your husband's. Did you bring them?"

"Yes, I did," Regina answered with a smile in her voice. "I've brought her flowers a few times over the years."

"Thank you." Eve's voice cracked, and she cleared her throat. "I really appreciate that."

"Of course," Regina said. "I'm so glad you called. I lost all my contacts a few years ago, but I've often wondered how you were doing."

"I'm...okay," Eve said, feeling anything *but* okay. Maybe this was why she'd really called Regina, because they had this in common. They both knew the pain of losing a spouse. Suddenly, Eve needed to commiserate with her on how fucking miserable it was, even now. "How are you?"

"I had a rough time after Derek passed," Regina said. "But I'm remarried now."

Eve inhaled sharply. "Oh, wow. Congratulations."

"Thank you. We have two little boys, Lucas and Braden. They keep me on my toes," Regina said as the sound of children's laughter carried over the line.

"I bet." Eve looked around herself at the deserted cemetery. She'd never felt more alone.

"Have you found someone new?" Regina asked.

"No." Eve shifted her feet as her heels again sank into the grass.

"It's a hard place to be," Regina said, her voice kind. "When you fall in love and walk down that aisle, you never imagine having to do it twice."

"I'm not sure I want to do it twice."

"Believe me, I understand that feeling. But we don't stop living when they die, so don't ever feel guilty about finding happiness again with someone else. Your wife would have wanted that for you."

Eve brushed at her eyes. "I couldn't go through it again, losing someone."

"Well, I hope you never have to. I hope neither of us do. But don't let your fear keep you from finding happiness."

Eve had a sinking feeling she already had. She wasn't sure she even remembered what it felt like to be happy. Maybe it felt like Josie's laugh, Josie's kiss, tiny kitten paws leaving fur all over her dress. She gasped, pressing a hand over her eyes to stanch the tears.

"Hey, are you okay?" Regina asked in her ear.

No. "Yeah," she said. "I should go. Thanks again for the flowers."

"It was my pleasure," Regina said. "Would you like to grab a coffee sometime and catch up?"

Eve blinked her composure back into place. "I wish I could, but I actually live in the city now. I don't get out here very often...hardly ever, to be honest. I just needed to be here today."

"I understand," Regina said. "Well, take care. I'll bring Lisa more carnations the next time I visit the cemetery."

"Are you free tonight?" Eve blurted, surprising herself. "I mean, if you wanted to get together while I'm in town."

"I'd love that," Regina said warmly. "I'd need to wait until my husband gets home to watch the boys, but I could meet you at the Starbucks on Main Street in about an hour, if that works for you?"

"I'll see you there." Eve ended the call, releasing a shaky breath. Since she had some time to kill, she sat on the bench closest to Lisa's grave—the same one she and Regina had sat on together all those years ago—as night fell around her. And there, alone in the cemetery, she let the tears fall. She cried for Lisa, for their daughter, for the long years she'd endured without them.

She'd broken up with Josie to protect herself from losing her too, but how was this better? She could either open her heart and risk getting hurt again, or she could live alone forever. And right here, right now, she couldn't bear to be alone another second.

Drying her eyes, she pulled out her compact and fixed her makeup. Then, feeling a sense of purpose she hadn't felt in weeks, she requested an Uber to take her to Starbucks.

29

"It's almost time." Adam turned up the volume on the TV they'd had installed in the bar just for the occasion. Dragonfly was bursting with people—friends, family, and customers. It seemed like everyone Josie had ever met was here tonight to watch her on *Do Over*...with one notable exception.

"This is so exciting," her Aunt Cecily said, perched on the barstool that used to be Eve's, looking very hip for her years with a beer in one hand, cell phone in the other. "I hope I made the final cut. That nice cameraman filmed me making a toast on opening night."

Even her Uncle Timothy had come tonight, although he wore a sour expression, nursing a beer at a table in back.

"Hush, you guys, here we go," Adam called out, practically bouncing with excitement.

Josie felt like bouncing herself, a combination of nerves and anticipation. This was the moment she'd been waiting for, the moment the world would meet her and watch her bar transform from Swanson's to Dragonfly, the moment that would hopefully give Eve a ratings bump and the third season she wanted.

Speaking of Eve, there she was on the screen, speaking earnestly to the camera as she walked through Swanson's, although Josie couldn't focus on what she was saying over the activity in the bar and the chaotic emotions churning inside her. She'd have to watch the episode again tomorrow in her apartment, when she could devote her full attention to it.

"Oh." Aunt Cecily pressed a hand against her chest. "Look at it. I can almost see Gerry behind the bar."

Josie blinked. Yeah, she could see her dad behind the bar too. She'd kept everything just the way he'd left it, until Eve came along. For a moment, she missed him—and Swanson's—so much, she had to bite her lip to force back the tears.

"There you are!" her cousin Bryce called out, raising his beer in appreciation.

"There I am," Josie repeated as she watched herself mixing drinks behind the old bar. She didn't mind seeing herself on camera. She had a YouTube channel, after all, but it was strange to see herself on national television, wearing all that makeup.

Kaia—sitting at a table in back with several of her friends—squealed when she and Adam appeared on screen, being interviewed by Eve about their friendship with Josie. She rushed over to the bar, and Adam joined them for a group hug.

The show cut to commercial, and the noise level in the bar exploded as everyone began to discuss what they'd seen so far. She and Adam mixed and poured drinks as quickly as they could, and before they knew it, *Do Over* was back.

Eve and Josie were seated across from each other in that

staged scene where Eve told her about her plans for the new bar, and Josie felt like the air had been knocked out of her lungs. Eve looked so impossibly beautiful, so confident, so poised. Josie looked away, stacking glasses to keep herself busy. Just a few weeks ago, she'd imagined this night going so differently. She'd thought Eve would be here with her, drinking and celebrating, sharing her bed later tonight.

It had been two weeks since they filmed the follow-up segment, and she hadn't heard a word from Eve, not even to remind her about the show tonight. At first, Josie had checked her phone obsessively, hoping against hope she might call or text. She'd spent weeks looking expectantly at Dragonfly's door every time it opened, hoping Eve might walk through it.

Now, she was just tired. And sad. But mostly tired. As the show continued, Josie found herself focusing more on her customers than the television, because seeing herself on screen with Eve was...hard.

And then, there was Eve in that zipper-front dress on opening night. God, she'd driven Josie mad in that dress. She could still hear the hiss of the metal as she'd unzipped it later that night. She'd probably never look at another zipper-front dress without thinking of her. There were a lot of things she'd never see without thinking of Eve.

Suppressing a sigh, she poured beer for her cousins as footage from opening night aired on *Do Over*. Aunt Cecily appeared on screen, drawing a round of cheers from the crowd in Dragonfly. She slid off her stool to bow dramatically, grinning from ear to ear.

"Bucket list item achieved!" she called out, pointing to herself on the television.

After another commercial break, the final scene began to air. This was the follow-up segment where Eve revisited the bar to see how Dragonfly was doing after its first month in business. There was Eve, as calm and collected as ever. The intensity that had shimmered between her and Josie during their earlier scenes was missing here. They barely looked at each other, keeping their interactions to a bare minimum. Josie didn't think anyone else would notice the difference, but it was all she could see.

When the show ended, the whole bar burst into applause. Uncle George bought everyone a round of drinks, and the party kept going for hours. Her relatives headed home around midnight, but she had a steady stream of regular customers until closing. Everyone congratulated her on the show, and she thanked them all for coming. She and Adam closed up together, exchanging a lengthy hug before he headed out.

"Congrats, lady. You really did it," he said, his hand rubbing up and down her back.

"We did it," she told him. "I couldn't have done it without you."

"It's been a good change for both of us."

She was exhausted as she climbed the stairs to her apartment, relieved that the episode had been well received —by her customers and family, at least—but overwhelmingly sad at the same time. Seeing herself on screen with Eve had stirred up so many emotions. She had a strong feeling she was going to burst into tears the moment she stepped into her apartment.

Halfway up the steps, she jolted to a stop. Someone was sitting at the top of the stairs, leaned against the door to her apartment. Adrenaline flooded her veins, but she'd barely registered alarm before she recognized the sleeping figure.

Eve.

Josie blinked hard, wondering if she was hallucinating.

Dreaming? Because there was no way the real-life Eve Marlow was slumped in the doorway to her apartment in the middle of the night, fast asleep. It was past five now. Morning, basically.

Josie crouched in front of her. Eve had on jeans and a pink sleeveless top, hair covering her face as her head rested against the doorframe. Josie reached out and touched her arm. "Eve?"

She tipped forward, almost toppling Josie down the stairs in her surprise. Josie braced one hand against the wall, the other on Eve's chest, steadying them. Her heart thumped beneath Josie's palm the way it had that day in her apartment, the day they broke up. Eve stared at her now, faces inches apart. Her eyes were wide and unfocused from sleep.

"What are you doing here?" Josie whispered.

Eve blinked several times, her gaze dropping to Josie's lips. "The show."

"Yeah, we watched it downstairs. My whole family was here." Josie smiled softly.

"Did they like it?" Eve asked in a hushed voice.

"Yes. Did you, um, want to come in?"

Eve nodded, still looking disoriented, but there was something else about her, something Josie couldn't quite put her finger on. Maybe it was just that she'd fallen asleep, but she seemed more subdued than she had the last time Josie saw her, like she'd left her armor at home.

Josie stood, opening the door and motioning Eve in ahead of her. "It wasn't locked, you know."

"I know." Eve's lips curved slightly. "I told you to change the code downstairs. You shouldn't let crazy ex-girlfriends have access to your apartment."

"Only one does, and while she may be a lot of things,

she isn't crazy," Josie told her. They stood facing each other just inside the door, awkward despite the lingering familiarity between them.

"You're too trusting," Eve said, eyes downcast.

"And you don't trust anyone."

"I trust you." Eve took a step closer. "Josie..."

"Yes?" She could hardly breathe, because surely Eve hadn't come here in the middle of the night to tell her they still couldn't be together.

Eve looked up, her expression open, earnest...vulnerable. "I made a mistake."

Josie's heart lurched inside her chest. "You did?"

"I thought I could protect myself if I let you go. I was afraid." She blinked, and a tear broke free, rolling down her cheek. "I couldn't bear to lose you, so I pushed you away. I thought I could go back to the way things were before."

Josie reached out and brushed the tear from her cheek before threading her fingers through Eve's. "I know."

"It was stupid." Eve shook her head. "Because I made the thing I feared happen. I made myself lose you, and it was awful."

"Oh, Eve." She tugged at her hands, drawing her close, pressing their lips together.

"I love you," Eve whispered against her lips as her arms came around Josie's waist. "I love you so much. Please tell me I haven't ruined my chance with you."

"Do I look like I'm pushing you away?" Josie tightened her arms around Eve for emphasis. Tears wet her cheeks as all the emotions she'd held in check during her shift downstairs came pouring out of her. Eve was here, and everything that had felt so dark and heavy inside her was now light.

"I wouldn't blame you if you did." Eve closed her eyes,

her bottom lip quivering. "I've been a total bitch to you these last few weeks."

Josie kissed her, drunk off the feel of her lips, the way their bodies fit together, so familiar, so *right*. "I didn't stop loving you just because you dumped me."

"No?" There was something heartbreakingly fragile in Eve's tone.

Josie shook her head. "Not even close. I have missed you every minute of every day."

Eve pressed her forehead against Josie's. "Me too. God, I missed you so much."

"I love you," Josie whispered, brushing the tears from Eve's cheeks.

Then they were kissing for real, hands pressing against skin, Eve's breath warming her cheeks as their bodies moved together. And it still wasn't enough. Somehow, she thought it would never be enough.

"I don't deserve your forgiveness this easily." Eve's voice was low and hoarse, fingers shaking as they cupped Josie's cheeks.

"Shh," Josie murmured. "Yes, you do."

Eve deserved the world, and Josie was going to give it to her, one kiss at a time.

"I—" Eve turned her face away from Josie, and a choking sound escaped her throat. Below Josie's arms, which were still wrapped tightly around Eve, her chest heaved violently. For a moment, Josie thought Eve was about to be sick.

"Hey. You okay?" Josie rubbed a hand down her back.

Eve exhaled roughly as more tears broke free. She pressed a hand over her eyes, and Josie realized she was trying to get control of her emotions.

"It's okay," she whispered, still rubbing Eve's back. "Just let it out."

Eve made a sound, almost like a moan, which became a sob. Her hands fisted in Josie's shirt, tears streaming over her cheeks as if Josie's words had given her the permission she needed to open the floodgates. She cried until her knees gave out, and Josie lowered them to the floor, murmuring words of comfort into Eve's hair.

"I'm sorry," Eve gasped through her tears, clinging to Josie so tightly it almost hurt. "I'm so sorry."

"Shh, it's okay. I've got you." Josie stroked her hair, her shoulders, her back as Eve released great soul-wrenching sobs, her face pressed against Josie's chest. She'd seen cracks in Eve's armor before but never like this. This was Eve with her heart laid bare, emotions spilling out of her like a dam had broken.

There was something so vulnerable about the way she clung to Josie, and she wondered how long it had been since anyone held Eve while she cried. Had anyone held her after her wife died? Josie hugged her even tighter. Eve's sobs gradually lessened, and she gasped and hiccupped against Josie's T-shirt.

"You can cry on my shoulder any time you need," Josie whispered.

Eve let out a shuddering laugh. "Thank you."

They sat there for long minutes as Eve's breathing calmed. She shifted to rest her head on Josie's shoulder, her chest hitching with the aftereffects of her tears. Their arms were still around each other, both of them holding on tight, and Josie's heart felt warm and full. Not only did she have Eve back, but there were no more barriers between them.

Eve lifted her head, looking at Josie through red, puffy eyes. "What happens now?"

"Well, we're still stuck with opposite work schedules," Josie told her.

"And I still don't care," Eve murmured as she leaned in to kiss Josie's cheek.

"I think we'll just make it work, don't you?"

Eve nodded, her gaze drifting to the living room, which was playpen-free. Her smile wilted. "Where are the kittens?"

"Jules adopted two of them."

Eve's eyes fell. "And the other two?"

"Are in my bedroom," Josie told her gently.

"Which two?"

"Come see." Josie grasped Eve's hands as she stood, pulling her up with her. She opened the door to her bedroom, and there were Blanche and Hamilton curled up in the middle of her bed, fast asleep.

"Oh." Fresh tears spilled over Eve's cheeks.

"Are you ready to adopt them now?" Josie bumped her shoulder against Eve's.

"Yes," she whispered, walking over to sit on the edge of the bed. The kittens woke, stretching and bounding toward Eve at the same time. "You didn't save these two for me, did you?"

"I wish I could say I had predicted this moment, but no, Jules actually picked Phantom and Pippin on her own." She sat next to Eve on the bed. "I did see the irony of it when it happened, though."

"Blanche was always my favorite," Eve said, as the white kitten scrambled into her lap.

"I know."

"I didn't necessarily want two, though. Don't you want one?"

Josie shook her head. "I've already got Nigel, and it's better to adopt two, anyway. Then they can take all their kitten energy out on each other, instead of on you or your apartment."

"Sold." Eve scooped Hamilton into her lap with Blanche.

Josie lifted both kittens and set them on the floor. She pushed Eve flat on her back, climbing on top of her. "I think we have some lost time to make up for."

"Yes, we do." She flipped them, pinning Josie to the bed, a wicked gleam in her eyes. "I want to make up for every night we missed."

"And then some."

EPILOGUE

SIX MONTHS LATER

The first thing Eve noticed, as always, was the scent of Josie's shampoo. Next, she registered the warm weight on her feet. Her eyes blinked open into the hot pink depths of Josie's hair. She brushed it aside to kiss her neck, resting her face against Josie's shoulder as she looked down, spotting Blanche curled over her feet.

The tiny kitten who had once fit in the palm of Eve's hand looked like a full-grown cat now, although she still acted like a kitten most of the time. She was becoming quite cuddly too. Eve woke to find Blanche on top of her most mornings, more often than she woke beside Josie. With their backward schedules, they still didn't see each other as often as they'd like, although Josie had Fridays off now, which meant they got to wake together every Saturday morning like this.

Hamilton strolled past the open bedroom door. He was more of a loner. He liked to be in the same room with her, but he wasn't a lap cat. Together, he and Blanche made the perfect pair.

"Morning," Josie mumbled, rolling to face her.

"Let's spend it right here in bed." Her hands slid over Josie's body beneath the sheet.

"Can't." Josie eyes looked almost green in the morning light, offset by her pink hair like some kind of magical fairy. "I have something to show you."

"Yeah?"

Josie nodded. "It's at my place."

"Okay."

"But first..." She rolled Eve onto her back, kissing her slow and deep. Eve nudged Blanche off the bed with her foot as she and Josie undressed each other, hands and mouths roaming as they made love in the soft morning light. It was gentle and unhurried, their movements slow and lingering, but Josie still managed to shatter her into a million blissful pieces with her talented fingers.

They showered and dressed, stopping at the café down the street for coffee and breakfast before they rode the subway to Brooklyn. The routine was as comforting as it was familiar. In the months since they'd been back together, they'd spent a lot of Saturday mornings like this. They didn't see each other every day, but they managed to spend at least one or two nights a week together, and often more.

Tonight, Eve would probably spend a few hours at Dragonfly. She and Kaia had become friends over the past months as they hung out at the bar, keeping Josie and Adam company. Eve had added quite a few people to her circle recently. She had gotten back into the habit of visiting Lisa's parents in New Jersey and had even met Regina for coffee a couple of times.

At Josie's urging, Eve had reconnected with several of her relatives. As it turned out, they'd had no idea what happened with her parents and thought Eve had left the family by her own choice. Last month, a couple of her cousins came to visit her here in the city, sharing thirteen years' worth of laughter and tears as they caught up on everything they'd missed in each other's lives.

Eve had begun a new chapter in her life on so many fronts, and it was all thanks to the woman beside her.

Josie let them in through the back of her building, checking her phone. "Right on time."

"The thing you want to show me has a time?"

"Yes. An appointment of sorts," Josie said with a mysterious smile.

Eve followed her up the stairs, intrigued. She honestly had no idea what Josie had up her sleeve. Her confusion only intensified when Josie passed her door and kept climbing to the third-floor apartment, the one she rented out. She stopped at the door and knocked, listening for a few seconds. When no response came, she pulled out her keys and unlocked the door.

Eve grabbed her elbow. "What are you doing? You can't just walk into their apartment."

"Actually, I can," Josie told her. "I'm their landlord. A few days ago, they gave their notice. They're moving out at the end of the month. So I told them I had a prospective tenant coming to see the place this morning at eleven."

"Me?" Eve felt her eyebrows rising. "I'm the prospective tenant?"

"No." Josie leaned in to kiss her. "We both are."

"What?"

"We could live here together. It's bigger than either of our current apartments. There are two bedrooms. I could use the second one for rescuing kittens."

"Hey, what about me?" Eve asked playfully, rapidly warming to the idea. "I could use space for an office, you know. Then I could move out of the *Life & Leisure* offices."

"I know. That's why I thought you could use my old apartment downstairs as your office space."

"Oh." Eve swallowed. "Really?"

"Yes. What do you think?"

"I think...it's perfect," she told Josie.

"Don't you want to see this place first?"

"Well, yeah, but my answer won't change."

"Okay," Josie said with a laugh.

Together, they walked around the living room. It was large and open, with high ceilings due to its location on the top floor. The back wall was exposed brick, with wood beams on the ceiling just like Josie's apartment. They went down the hall to see the two bedrooms and the bath. The space was warm and inviting, with more than enough room for Eve's artwork and all of Josie's kitten pictures.

"So?" Josie asked.

"I was wrong. My answer did change," Eve told her.

"Oh?" A wrinkle appeared between her brows.

"It's not just perfect, it's *ridiculously* perfect. Seriously, Josie. This place is amazing."

"Good," she said with a satisfied smile. "I can't afford to lose the income from this rental on my own, but if you give up your apartment, it should work."

"Definitely. Between the two of us, we make more than enough to afford this place. Then you'll own and occupy the whole building, just like you and your dad did before he died." She gave Josie's hands a squeeze.

"Yeah."

"We're going to need to go shopping," Eve told her. "New art for the walls, furniture, accessories..."

"I can't wait." Josie grinned, revealing the dimples that had always been Eve's undoing.

She pulled Josie in close as she looked around at the

apartment. Their apartment. No more commuting across town to visit each other. She'd wake beside Josie every morning, and maybe soon, she'd be able to cut her hours in the bar the way she'd been working toward. She could fill the smaller bedroom with rescue kittens while Eve ran Marlow Marketing out of the space downstairs.

The episode featuring Josie's bar had indeed given *Do Over* the ratings boost it needed, and soon, filming would begin for its third season. But production only lasted a few months out of the year. The rest of Eve's time would be spent here with Josie. It was everything she could have ever wanted. Sunlight filtered through the oversized window on the far wall, illuminating the pink tones of Josie's hair, and Eve saw her future reflected in those fuchsia depths.

"I love you," she whispered.

Josie's eyes seemed to shine with happiness. "Love you back."

"You know, that drink must really work."

"What?" Josie asked, giving her a quizzical look.

"The Midnight in Manhattan," Eve told her with a smile.

"Oh!" Josie's grin widened. "If you drink one at midnight, rumor has it you'll fall in love before the end of the year..."

"It sure worked for me."

Josie winked. "That confirms it. The rumors are true."

ACKNOWLEDGMENTS

First off, thank you to my family for your unending support. I couldn't do this without you! Thank you to my editor, Linda Ingmanson, for making this book shine. And as always, a huge thank you to my critique partner, Annie Rains. You make every single one of my books better and stronger, and I'm so grateful for it (and you!)

This time around, I asked my readers to help me name the bar in *Don't Cry for Me*, and you gave me so many great suggestions that I ended up using three of them. They became Josie's signature drinks, as well as the name of the bar and the series. So, a special shout-out to Kimberly Crockett for suggesting Dragonfly, Tina Buck for Midnight in Manhattan, and Sherry Presnall for Whiskey Kiss. I hope you enjoyed seeing them in the book!

Special thanks to Heather Siebert for naming Blanche the kitten and inspiring the rest of my "theater kittens." Also, thank you for being my Manhattan fact-checker. All mistakes are my own.

A huge thank you to all the readers, bloggers, and reviewers who've read my books and supported me along the way. Love you all!

xoxo

Rachel

KEEP READING

If you enjoyed *Don't Cry for Me*, turn the page to read the first chapter of *It's in Her Kiss*, the second book in the Midnight in Manhattan series.

IT'S IN HER KISS

CHAPTER ONE

Julia Vega closed her umbrella and ducked inside the brick building in front of her. She pulled the door shut behind herself, scuffing her wet boots against the mat as she glanced around to get her bearings. A directory on the wall showed that the production office she was looking for was on the second floor.

She entered the stairwell, grimacing as she caught a glimpse of her reflection in the window. The wet weather had really done a number on her hair. Luckily, she'd arrived early enough for today's audition that she should have time to polish her appearance before they called her back. A tingly feeling took hold in her stomach at the thought.

Jules had been working on Broadway for five years now, so the audition process was a familiar—albeit nerve-wracking—experience for her. Today's audition was more stressful than most for several reasons, most notably because she was auditioning for the lead.

This role, if she landed it, would be a dream come true, the culmination of a lifetime of training, the chance to step out of the chorus line and into the spotlight. She wanted it so badly she could taste it, a hint of something sweet on her tongue, teasing her with the flavor of success. Or maybe that was just the lozenge she'd finished on the walk over.

On the second floor, she approached the receptionist, a woman about her mother's age with gorgeous silver hair and a friendly smile. Jules returned it with one of her own. "Hi, I'm Julia Vega for the four forty-five audition."

The receptionist glanced at her computer as she tapped several keys. "Ah, there you are. You're all set, Julia. There's a restroom at the end of the hall if you need to freshen up."

"Thanks so much," Jules told her gratefully as she headed down the hall. Once she'd closed herself inside the restroom, she peeled off her damp jacket and tucked it into her bag before pulling out her toiletry case. She spritzed her hair with a polishing serum, smoothing away the frizz that had resulted from her fifteen-minute walk in the drizzling rain. Then, she reapplied her lipstick, painting her lips a shiny plum.

After repacking her bag, she surveyed herself in the mirror. She ran her hands over her blouse—almost a perfect match with her lipstick—making sure it was tucked neatly into her black slacks. Sucking in a deep breath, she made her way back to the waiting room. It was empty except for the receptionist and one other woman who was probably waiting to audition for the same role. Jules sat across from her. She set her bag on the chair beside her and pulled out her water bottle and the tin of Grether's pastilles she never auditioned without.

"Lozenge?" she asked the woman across from her, holding out the tin.

"Thanks, but I've got it covered," she answered, holding up an identical tin with a smile. She was about Jules's age—

late twenties or early thirties—with long, curly brown hair and a strikingly pretty face.

"Great minds," Jules joked as she popped a lozenge into her mouth. Nerves made her throat dry, and that was the kiss of death to an auditioning actress. "I'm Julia Vega...Jules."

"Sophie Rindell," the brunette answered.

"Are you reading for Bianca?" Jules asked. It was one of her more annoying habits, or so she'd been told. She felt compelled to make idle conversation in waiting rooms like this one. She couldn't help it. Apparently, nerves also made her chatty.

Sophie didn't seem to mind, though. "I am. You too?"

Jules nodded. "I don't know about you, but I'm really excited about this one. I don't get many chances to audition for a lead." *It's in Her Kiss* was an off-Broadway play, a brand-new production right here in Brooklyn, walking distance from her apartment.

"Same," Sophie said, leaning forward in her seat as her leg bounced with restless energy. "And a queer lead at that. It almost feels too good to be true."

"Yes, it's amazing," Jules agreed as her stomach gave a funny swoop. She embraced roles that stretched her as an actress, but playing a woman coming to terms with her sexuality hit uncomfortably close to home for Jules. She wasn't ready to think about that part yet, though. She had to get through the audition first.

"Sophie?" the receptionist called. "They're ready for you."

Sophie shot Jules a nervous smile.

"Good luck," Jules said as Sophie gathered her things and stepped through the door into the audition room.

Jules pressed a hand against her stomach to calm the

flutter of nerves there. Alone in the waiting room, she took the opportunity to run through the scene and the song they'd asked her to prepare. Her phone chimed with an incoming text message. She swiped it from her bag, revealing her mother's name on the screen.

Good luck! Can't wait to hear all about it.

Thanks, Mami, she replied. *I'll call you later and let you know how it went.*

Jules turned her phone to silent and sucked in another deep breath. No one else had entered the waiting room. She was probably the last audition of the day, which might work in her favor if she left the team with a positive impression, or the opposite if she didn't. Her agent had told her she should hear if she'd gotten a callback as early as tonight.

Jules ran through a few scales to warm up her vocal cords and crunched through what remained of her lozenge. The door opened, and Sophie reentered the waiting room.

"How did it go?" Jules asked.

"Really well, I think," Sophie said, a triumphant look in her eyes that Jules knew well, the look of an actress who had just nailed an audition.

"I'm so glad," Jules told her.

"Thanks." Sophie shrugged into her coat and headed for the exit. "Well...bye. And good luck."

"Thank you." Jules tapped her fingers against her thighs as the door closed, leaving her alone in the waiting room. It wasn't ideal, going in right after another actress had just wowed the casting team. Her stomach tightened uncomfortably, and her throat was dry again. She reached for another lozenge.

"Julia?" the receptionist called. "They're ready for you."

Jules grabbed her bag and lurched to her feet as the cold, tingly sensation spread from her stomach through her whole body. She went through the door beside the receptionist desk and found herself in a large, white walled room. A row of people sat facing her. Jules recognized the director, a petite woman named Kari Lang. She'd auditioned for her before. Kari's black hair was pulled back in a neat ponytail, glasses perched on her nose as she gave Jules a nod in greeting.

"Hello," Jules said, clasping her hands loosely in front of herself. "I'm Julia Vega. It's an honor to be here today."

After brief introductions, the casting director, a man named Frederick Beck, spoke. "You can start with the scene where Bianca speaks with her friend, Melissa. Liz will read for Melissa." He gestured to the assistant seated beside him.

Jules nodded, sucking in another breath as she got into character. "I'm ready."

"You look sad today, Bianca. Is something wrong?" Liz read.

"No, it's...well, I've had something on my mind," Jules said.

"It's Trevor, isn't it?" Liz said.

Jules gave a weak laugh, raking a hand through her hair as she let Bianca's discomfort become her own. "Yeah...Trevor."

"I knew it!" Liz said triumphantly. "You like him."

Jules let her eyes linger on Liz, giving her a veiled look of longing as Bianca wrestled with her secret feelings for her friend. "I like him, but I'm not sure I want to date him."

They finished the scene, and then Jules performed an upbeat song that would be part of a group musical number. She'd rehearsed it dozens of times, and yet, with the casting team watching, she flubbed the lyrics, beginning to repeat the first verse instead of moving into the second. Hopefully, it wasn't a fatal mistake, but it definitely wasn't the impression she'd wanted to make.

"One last thing," Kari said after Jules had finished singing. "As you know, *It's in Her Kiss* is a coming out story. Are you comfortable kissing a woman onstage?"

What? "Yes, of course," she blurted, hoping they hadn't seen her momentary panic. She'd never kissed anyone onstage before, and she'd never kissed a woman, period. She'd thought about it, though. Lately, she'd thought about it kind of a *lot*, and *oh God*, she wasn't sure how she felt about her first time being onstage. But that was something to sort out if she got the role, not while the casting team was watching, scrutinizing her response.

"Thank you," the casting director said. "We'll be in touch."

Jules thanked everyone for their time, gathered her things, and left. She didn't feel nearly as confident as Sophie had looked as she made her way back through the waiting room. Jules jogged down the stairs, bursting with restless energy. Maybe she should change and go to the gym. Anything but sitting around her apartment waiting for the phone to ring.

The first thing she noticed as she stepped outside was that the rain had stopped, and thank goodness for that. The second thing was Sophie Rindell walking out of the coffee shop next door.

"Post audition caffeination?" Jules called with a wave.

Sophie glanced over her shoulder, pausing so Jules could catch up to her. "Something like that. How did your audition go?"

Jules put on her jacket, sweeping her hair out from beneath the collar. "Good, I think."

"I'm glad," Sophie said.

They stared at each other for a few seconds of awkward silence. Making idle conversation in the waiting room was one thing, but Jules didn't make a habit of hanging out with her competition after the audition. Something told her Sophie didn't either.

"Which way are you headed?" Jules asked, halfway hoping they were going in different directions, an easy way to say goodbye.

Sophie gestured to the left. "I don't live too far from here, near Prospect Park."

"Oh yeah? We're practically neighbors." Jules fell into step beside her.

"You audition a lot?" Sophie asked.

"Everything I can get," Jules told her with a laugh.

"Same." Sophie gave her a thoughtful look. "You look vaguely familiar to me. Maybe we've crossed paths before."

"It's possible," Jules agreed. They fell into an easy conversation as they walked, discovering that they'd auditioned for several of the same productions, although maybe not at the same time, and Jules found herself glad for Sophie's company after all. It was always fun to chat with someone else who understood the crazy whirlwind of the theater life.

"Hey, I'm actually meeting a few friends for a drink on my way home," Sophie said. "Want to join us? There's a new gay bar on Seventh that we wanted to check out, if that's your scene."

"Dragonfly?" Jules asked hesitantly. She didn't know much about gay bars, but she did know this one.

"That's the place," Sophie confirmed with a nod. "Have you been?"

"I have, although maybe not for the same reason as you. I adopted two kittens from the owner."

"Oh yeah?"

"Yes. Josie runs a kitten rescue, in addition to owning the bar. And sure, I'll join you guys for a drink," Jules said, making a snap decision. She enjoyed hanging out with other theater types, and she liked Sophie. Plus, it would be nice to see Josie and update her about the kittens.

"Cool," Sophie said.

They made a left onto Seventh and walked several blocks to Dragonfly, its lavender logo reflected on the wet sidewalk. Jules hadn't been here in a few months. Hopefully, Josie was working tonight. She followed Sophie through the door, pausing just inside while Sophie looked for her friends. Soft jazz music played inside the bar, and the white fairy lights that usually spanned the ceiling had been accented tonight with purple and orange, in honor of Halloween, which was just a few days away.

A pair of women waved from a table along the back wall, and Jules and Sophie made their way over to them.

"Hey, ladies," Sophie said warmly, giving each of her friends a quick hug before turning toward Jules. "This is Jules. We met at the audition, and she stopped by for a drink. Jules, this is Gia and Kit." She gestured across the table at her friends as she introduced them. They waved at Jules, their expressions open and friendly.

Jules dragged an empty stool over to their table and sat beside Sophie. "Nice to meet you guys. Are you theater actors as well?"

"Nope," Gia told her. "I'm a financial analyst, but I love to live vicariously through Sophie."

As it turned out, neither of Sophie's friends were actors, which was somewhat unexpected. Not that *all* of Jules's friends were part of the theater world, but certainly most of them were. They both seemed nice, though, and Jules was glad she'd decided to come. The four of them chatted through a round of drinks, the alcohol helping to keep the conversation flowing.

"So, you guys auditioned for the same role today?" Kit asked, eyebrows lifted as she sipped from her drink.

"Yep," Sophie told her.

"And, according to my agent, we should hear about callbacks tonight," Jules added.

Sophie straightened on her stool. "Really?"

She nodded. "Yes."

"Ooh," Gia said, looking delighted. "This could get interesting."

Jules glanced at Sophie. "Yes, it could."

"Jules?"

She turned to see Josie, the bar's owner, standing beside their table. Tonight, Josie's ever-changing hair was streaked with pink and purple, a perfect match for her personality. Jules beamed at her. "I was hoping to see you tonight." She turned toward Sophie and her friends, remembering that this was their first time visiting Dragonfly. "This is Josie Swanson. She owns the bar and runs a kitten rescue in her spare time. I adopted two kittens from her this spring."

"My theater kittens," Josie said.

"Yes," Jules confirmed. "I named them Phantom and Pippin."

"The other two are Blanche and Hamilton," Josie told them. "My girlfriend adopted them."

"That's freaking adorable," Sophie said as awwws went around the table.

Jules pulled out her phone, scrolling through her photo roll until she found pictures of her cats.

"I assume Phantom is the black one?" Sophie asked, leaning in for a closer look.

"How did you guess?" Jules turned her head, and their eyes met. Sophie's were warm and brown, crinkled with laughter. She smelled nice too, like spiced vanilla.

"They've gotten so big," Josie said, looking over Jules's shoulder at a photo of Pippin and Phantom curled up together in her bed.

"They sure have," Jules agreed, returning her attention to her phone. "They look like cats now but still act like kittens. Thank goodness they take most of it out on each other instead of me."

"The reason I always recommend that people adopt two," Josie agreed.

"If I ever get my own place, I'd love to have cats," Sophie said, sounding a bit wistful.

"You should follow Josie's YouTube channel," Jules told her. "She posts super cute videos of all her foster kittens. That's how I got my kitten fix until I was ready to adopt."

"And generally, all of my kittens are adoptable," Josie added.

"I'll check it out." Sophie reached into the back pocket of her jeans, pulling out her cell phone, which was ringing. And if the wide-eyed look on her face was any indication, her agent was calling. "I need to take this. I'll be right back."

Phone in hand, she rushed out the front door. Jules sipped her drink, swallowing her disappointment that Sophie might have gotten a callback instead of her. Of course, it was possible for them both to be called back for the second round, but it wasn't very likely.

"I'm so glad you came in tonight," Josie said, drawing Jules out of her thoughts. "I had been meaning to catch up with you and see how the kittens were doing. It's so good to see them. And you, of course."

"Would you like to come see them sometime?" Jules

asked. "I mean, you and Eve could totally stop by and visit them if you'd like."

"Please." Josie clasped her hands in front of herself dramatically. "We would love that."

"Yeah, totally. You've got my number. Just give me a call and we'll figure something out."

"Oh, we are totally going to take you up on that," Josie said before heading back to the bar with a wave.

Jules was halfway through her drink and a lively conversation with Gia and Kit when Sophie came back inside. Her cheeks were pink from the night air...or her mood. Jules couldn't be sure which, but Sophie was rushing toward their table with a visible excitement that seemed to hint at the latter.

She hopped onto her stool and lifted her glass, casting Jules a slightly apologetic glance. "You guys, I did it. I got a callback for *It's in Her Kiss*."

The table erupted in cheers and whoops, glasses being clinked in celebration. Jules joined in, tapping her glass against Sophie's, happy for her despite the sting of disappointment in her belly. Her phone, poised on the edge of the table, remained silent. "Congratulations," she told Sophie earnestly.

"Thank you," Sophie said. "You may still get a call too, you know."

"Aw, aren't you guys being good sports," Kit teased. "No catfights at our table!"

"This is part of the job," Jules told her with a shrug. "I've auditioned with friends before...not that Sophie and I are friends, exactly, but you know what I mean."

"Yep," Sophie agreed. "And it's not like this means I've got the part either. But, hot *damn*, it feels good to still be in the game. I want this one so bad, you guys."

Jules studied her for a moment in silence. Yes, she got that feeling about Sophie. There was a hunger about her when it came to this role, or maybe that hunger reflected her attitude toward her career in general. Jules didn't know her well enough to say. As much as Sophie wanted this role, as much as *Jules* wanted this role, there were probably a dozen other women across the Manhattan area tonight just as eager, just as sure they were the perfect Bianca.

Jules exhaled slowly. She felt it in her bones, the feeling that this was *the one*. If only her phone would ring...

Sophie lifted her drink and took a hearty sip in an attempt to ground herself, because she had the crazy urge to dance on the bar, and she wasn't even drunk. Not on alcohol anyway. She was pumped up on adrenaline, almost giddy with it. She'd actually gotten a callback for *It's in Her Kiss*.

Not only was this a lead role, it was a *queer* lead role. The role of a lifetime.

She'd been at this for ten years now, a decade of never-ending auditions that had netted her a decent resume of supporting roles on and off Broadway, as well as a handful of walk-on roles in television and commercials. But she didn't want to be Dancer #3 this time. She wanted to be the star.

Maybe even more importantly, she needed the paycheck this role would provide. It had been over a year since Sophie had landed an acting role, and she was sick to death of waitressing and picking up various behind-the-scenes jobs in local theaters to make ends meet. If you could consider sleeping on her friends' sofa making ends meet. Her parents sure didn't. Once upon a time, they'd been fully supportive of her Broadway dreams, but lately they thought it was time for her to accept that it hadn't worked out and get a real job. Her bank account seemed to agree with them.

But Sophie wasn't ready to admit defeat. She just needed her big break. And maybe it had come with *It's in Her Kiss*.

"What's that?" Gia asked, pointing to Jules's drink. "It's pretty."

"It's called a Midnight in Manhattan," Jules told her, tucking a strand of honey brown hair behind her ear. "It's similar to a mojito, but with lemon instead of lime juice. It's one of the house drinks. Josie convinced me to try one, and now I'm hooked."

"Oh, that's the one with the myth attached," Kit said. "I'm too superstitious to risk it."

"A myth?" Sophie leaned closer to Jules, peering into her glass.

"If you drink one at midnight, supposedly you'll fall in love before the end of the year," Jules told her with a smile. "But I've been drinking them for months now, and no such luck."

"You want to fall in love?" Kit gave her a skeptical look. "Girl, I've been there and done that, and it sucks. Trust me."

"I'm in no hurry, but I'm certainly not opposed to the idea," Jules said, taking another sip.

"Any prospects?" Sophie asked. Yeah, she was fishing. Now that she wasn't preoccupied with waiting for a callback, she wouldn't mind asking Jules out, if she could just figure out whether or not Jules was straight.

"Not at the moment." Jules shrugged. "I dated a guy for a few months over the summer, but things fizzled pretty quickly after that. So, like I said, I'm not in any hurry. You should try the drink, though. It's good."

Kit threw her hands out in front of her. "No way. Not taking any chances."

"Me either," Sophie confirmed as she lifted her whiskey sour.

Jules pressed a hand against her heart, drawing Sophie's attention to the plunging neckline on her blouse and the cross pendant glinting there. "So many skeptics at this table."

"I haven't sworn off love forever," Sophie told her. "I'm just not at a place in my life right now where I have much room for it."

"Fair enough," Jules said, glancing at Sophie. Her eyes were a deep brown, highlighted by thick eyeliner and a shimmery eyeshadow that sparkled under the bar's track lighting. And her hair...well, she looked like she'd walked out of a shampoo commercial. It was long and wavy, with golden highlights in her natural brown. Combined with her charismatic personality, it was no wonder she was an actress. If Sophie ever got the chance to see her on stage, she was certain she wouldn't be able to take her eyes off her.

Right now, she'd settle for Jules's number. She'd mentioned a boyfriend, but that didn't mean she wasn't bi or pan. Usually, Sophie had excellent gaydar, but she couldn't quite make up her mind about Jules.

On the table between them, Jules's phone began to ring. The name Pierce showed on the screen, and she let out a little gasp. "My agent," she said breathlessly, grabbing her phone and rushing for the door as Sophie had done earlier.

"What are the chances?" Sophie muttered, reaching for her drink.

"Does this mean you've both made it to round two?" Gia asked, looking delighted at the prospect.

"Maybe. We'll see," Sophie said as she drained her glass.

She walked to the bar for a refill. By the time she'd made it back to their table, Jules had reentered Dragonfly with an unmistakable bounce in her step.

Sophie caught her eye with an inquiring lift of her eyebrow. "Good news for you too?"

"Yes," Jules confirmed. "And my agent says that unofficially, there are only two of us in contention for the role."

"Oh wow." Sophie gulped. "So, it's between you and me?"

"Sounds that way."

They stared at each other for a beat of loaded silence before Sophie lifted her chin with a smile. "Better bring your A game on Friday, Vega."

Jules met her gaze, amusement sparkling in her eyes. "I'm not worried."

"You should be." Sophie lifted her glass, tapping it against Jules's. "May the best woman win."

ALSO BY RACHEL LACEY

Love in the City

Read Between the Lines

Vino and Veritas

Hideaway

Midnight in Manhattan Series

Don't Cry for Me

It's in Her Kiss

Come Away with Me

Almost Royal Series

If the Shoe Fits

Once Upon a Cowboy

Let Your Hair Down

Rock Star Duet

Unwritten

Encore

The Stranded Series

Crash and Burn

Lost in Paradise

The Risking It All Series

Rock with You

Run to You

Crazy for You

Can't Forget You

My Gift is You

The Love to the Rescue Series

Unleashed

For Keeps

Ever After

Only You

ABOUT THE AUTHOR

Rachel Lacey is a contemporary romance author and semi-reformed travel junkie. She's been climbed by a monkey on a mountain in Japan, gone scuba diving on the Great Barrier Reef, and camped out overnight in New York City for a chance to be an extra in a movie. These days, the majority of her adventures take place on the pages of the books she writes. She lives in warm and sunny North Carolina with her family and a variety of rescue pets.

facebook.com/RachelLaceyAuthor
twitter.com/rachelslacey
instagram.com/rachelslacey
amazon.com/author/rachellacey
bookbub.com/authors/rachel-lacey

Printed in Great Britain
by Amazon